THE LAST DAYS OF HONG KONG

G.D. PENMAN

Meerkat Press
Asheville

ACKNOWLEDGMENTS

A very special thank you to Tricia at Meerkat Press for being the first one to fall for Sully's dubious charms. Without your tireless efforts, these books wouldn't exist.

Additional thanks go out to Cassandra Khaw and Gareth Powell for the kind words about the series that gave me the energy and impetus to keep pushing on, to Dashiell Hammett for hard-boiling some private eyes, and of course to Robert the Doll, for lending his likeness and story to Eugene.

Finally, thank you, dear readers, for coming along for the ride. Here is hoping you like where you end up when the tracks run out.

AUGUST 3, 2013

Hong Kong was a city the way that a well was a bath; your odds of coming up again when you took a dip were very different. It rose up out of the sea fog like a great glowing lantern, every part of it alive and moving within the gentle embrace of its towering walls. Every building glowed with neon, flickering and stuttering as the galvanic supply struggled to keep up with the demand. Dazzling, but inherently flawed.

Sully had been here before, in another life. She could feel the memory of it tickling at the back of her mind, like a grain of sand in the oyster of her brain, but she couldn't find the details. Just a little case of déjà vu, except she'd read through her military records while she was pulling herself back together again after the war, and she knew for a fact that she'd sailed out of this port.

Every time she butted up against those lost years it was like she was standing on a precipice. She knew that who she had been was down there somewhere, but each and every time, she had to make the decision whether what she might find out was worth the dive and the pain. Very little was.

Outside of those weary walls, war was waiting. The Khanate had Hong Kong under siege today just as surely as they had for the past three decades. Their various armies had been camped out there for so long that the untrained eye might have mistaken the mass of buildings and bodies as an extension of the city proper. Only the odd glint of gunmetal reflecting a campfire gave them away by night, and only the uniforms gave them away in the light of day.

There was another tickle at the back of Sully's memory: this view had changed. The last time she'd been in Hong Kong there had been demons on the doorstep. The Khanate wasn't above cutting deals with the hells, when they were still open for business, and they'd secured plenty of recruits with no greater promise than the freedom to serve out the centuries up here instead of back home. It wasn't much more than Sully had been promised in her own recruitment office, if she was being honest.

She'd come around the world the long way, slow and steady on a steamer out of New Amsterdam, a big lumbering ship that would have been the laughingstock of her old Royal Navy buddies, if any of them had still been alive. Slow and steady, the flame-runes in the boilers pulsed. Slow and steady the inches of the map moved behind them.

Pratt had been in a hurry. He wanted her there yesterday and he'd been willing to throw his not-inconsiderable weight around to get her bounced through a half-dozen portals by the American Empire's allies. It would have been fast, yes, but it would have been loud, too. The whole world would have heard that Sully was coming to Hong Kong, and that was a recipe for trouble.

At the last count, Sully judged that approximately half of the people in the world wanted her dead for one reason or another. She didn't feel any particular need to advertise her travel arrangements to those people; particularly when portal travel was a precarious proposition at the best of times where one "accidental" miscalculation could leave her spleen strewn across four different dimensions.

She had other reasons not to travel by magic, but they were none of Pratt's business. A private eye without secrets was like a vampire without fangs.

Those snoozing Mongol Hordes slipped out of sight as the steamer puffed its way into the harbor, the only safe water in a thousand miles, cradled by the sea wall and the fortress islands at their back. When she first went off to sea, Sully hadn't been fearful. She'd been sure of herself, certain of her talents, and she'd trusted in her ship to keep her out of the water. Now she knew just how fragile a ship was compared to the other forces at work in the world and she trusted absolutely nothing.

The ship's crew had been the hardest part of the whole trip to navigate. Sully knew from personal experience that nobody gossiped harder than sailors, so she had to walk a tight rope to keep herself nice and boring for the duration of the trip, feeding out enough information to avoid becoming mysterious, spending just enough time in the common spaces of the ship to make her presence normal.

It was the same deal with her quarters on the ship. The whole trip was on Pratt's dime, so Sully could have had something palatial if she'd asked for it, but she was sticking to a story that was as close to the truth as possible. She was a private investigator heading to Hong Kong to find a missing person, and no PI could afford anything outside of steerage. Given the choice, she probably would have wanted that tiny cabin for herself anyway; the warm throbbing of the engine on the other side of the wall felt like home.

Disguises were thankfully unnecessary. Her appearance was one of the easiest things to manage in this whole deception. Her mug might have been plastered over the papers often enough in the years before the war, but after her injuries, that face was gone forever. The crisscross scars and even the little hump from her broken nose had been burned away. Her hair was still red now that it had grown back, but she kept it conservative and slicked back with a pomade that took the brightness right out of it. She was still unmistakably Sully, but all the distinguishing characteristics that a stranger trying to spot her might have used were gone.

As an added bonus of traveling by boat, the sea air was cold enough to justify a pair of gloves, so any awkward questions about her prosthetic hand could be avoided too; not that stories about that particular injury had spread far in the aftermath of the war. Having a hand chewed off by a gryphon wasn't nearly salacious enough to compete with all the other rumors about her. Was it any surprise she tried to stay incognito nowadays?

On this trip she'd forgone a suitcase in favor of a messenger bag to keep her one good hand free, but even that didn't have much in it. A change of clothes, a phrase book, a pistol, some cash, and absolutely no official papers whatsoever. Real cloak and dagger, plausible-deniability luggage. Needless to say, packing up her cabin as the steamer scraped into dock wasn't exactly time consuming.

Pulling on her trilby for one extra bit of camouflage, she gave the crew some curt goodbyes then strolled down the gangplank into the mass of bodies milling around the docks. The trick was never to flinch. Sully might have been short, but she was solid and she walked like she would keep on going through anybody that stepped in her way. It wasn't pretty, but it worked.

The early evening crowd in Hong Kong went beyond busy and over the edge into chaotic. Any other city would quieten a little toward the end of the day, but here it seemed like there were more bodies on the streets than before. It didn't take Sully long to realize why. It seemed like every third face that passed her by was pale. Not just the regular pasty white of Europeans like her, but the special pallor normally seen only in creatures living in the darkness of a cave deep underground. Vampires. More of them than Sully had ever seen in one place, even when she was bludgeoned into working prostitution stings during her policing days.

For a moment she assumed that she had failed to notice that she had wandered into the red-light district, thanks to the abundance of neon, but these vamps weren't out selling themselves for blood—they were just living. One was selling newspapers on the corner. Another was haggling with a street vendor over the price of an embroidered sweatshirt with a big pink cat on the front. More importantly, the humans were just letting them live. Sully couldn't understand a word of half the languages being spoken but the tone was clear. Business as usual.

Sully looked around surreptitiously to see if anyone else was surprised by the sheer volume of cold bodies but only one other person in the whole street seemed to notice them—a doomsday preacher up on an orange crate on the street corner. Stringy gray hair framed a face that wouldn't have looked out of place on a Halloween mask. Sunken eyes. Yellowed teeth. Lines cut in so deep they could have been scars instead of wrinkles. Sully leaned away from the spray of spittle as she moved past him. "The Holy Fool said unto us that the dead should lay down in the ground until such day as our reckoning comes. Each one of you walks in sin. Sin! Abandon this charade. God still has love in his heart for you. You can still be forgiven for even this most immoral of acts. If you will just do penance by laying down as you are meant to. Lay down as all men must and your spirits can rise again!"

Catholic school was another cluster of memories that Sully hadn't put too much effort into retrieving. What was the point of rebuilding yourself if you used the same crumbling bricks? Still, there was enough left echoing in her head for his words to make her skin crawl. Abomination. That was the word he was dancing around. Wrong for just existing. Subhuman. Sully had heard enough of that through the years to know that she was on Team Abomination every time.

She sank further and further into Hong Kong without a backward glance toward the water. There was a logic under the surface, nothing as formal as the different boroughs of New Amsterdam but a clustering of purposes. She'd passed through streets full of bars closer to the sea, and now there were shopfronts competing with the omnipresent street vendors. The flow of traffic from this area, branching off through alleys and odd-angled crossing streets, gave clues about the adjoining parts of the city. Feather boas and eveningwear to the east hinted at nightclubs or the theater. Strays with soot-stained hands and flat caps to the west suggested industrial work. Sully was riding on the crest of a wave of sailors heading inland, but the better part of that tide had already broken on the bars, so uniforms and salt-stained jackets were getting less and less frequent.

Strict instructions had been issued by Pratt's agents before she boarded the ship—she was to head directly to the American Embassy on arrival. The diplomats and their support staff were to be her eyes on the ground, furnishing her with everything that she needed to complete her mission. It was just a shame that nobody had told her where the embassy actually was.

To begin with she'd assumed it was an oversight, that one of the well-meaning aides would give her an address at some point in the many rambling lectures, but now that she was here it made sense. Presumably all of these streets had names—and it was even possible that under the posters, graffiti, and banners plastered over every wall those names were written on these streets somewhere—but Sully was damned if she could find any hint of where she was or where she was heading.

Despite all of that, she was surprised to discover that she was enjoying herself. She had never been a tourist before, but if she had, this was probably how she would have explored, wandering free and absorbing the culture of the place directly through her skin. Going with the flow of bodies and learning the patterns of the living creature known as Hong Kong.

When the crowd around her suddenly changed direction, she went with them like she was a part of the same school of fish. When a gleeful cry went up from ahead of them and it echoed back along the road, she felt the same buzz and the same draw. It wasn't magic, just people being people. The shopfronts gave away to solid, surprisingly western looking buildings, a residential district, or the closest thing that any city that had built on top of itself over and over could muster. The neon hadn't died out entirely—it had just crawled up the sides a little higher—but down here on the street level it was dim enough that the roaring red glow up ahead seemed abnormal.

There was a six-foot wall abutting the pavement, built in the local style, but beyond that stood the brickwork of a thoroughly modern and western building. The expanses of sleek glass gave the street a fantastic view inside as the whole thing burned. Sully's suspicions were already prickling before the enterprising souls at the front of the crowd started setting off fireworks. It was a simple bit of enchantment, crude but effective, and it twisted the colored explosions above them into the shape of a bald eagle on a rich blue backdrop. It wasn't a perfect representation of the American flag, but it was close enough that there couldn't be any doubt at their intentions. The lack of street signs persisted, so Sully moved on through the crowd to eavesdrop as more fireworks started popping off. A veritable festival of lights filled up the smog-shrouded sky. There had to be somebody speaking English somewhere.

Near the wall, where sanity might have dictated you would find fire-fighters, she came across an enterprising firework vendor instead, setting up shop. He looked like a local, so she was surprised to hear him barking his wares in English, but a win was a win. "Hey, what's all this about?"

"This is our tradition. Fireworks! They drive the evil spirits out, and what spirits could be more evil than the Americans? You want some firecrackers? Best price in Hong Kong."

"So what, that was their embassy?" Sully already knew the answer, but playing dumb always got you more than a smart mouth.

"Of course! They kill our protectors, abandon us to the Jaeseumin Sog, Gangshi and the Khan, then they try to build this monument to themselves. In our city? No. It will not stand."

Sully faked a laugh. "Sounds like you're the one who lit it up."

"I wish I had. But someone got here first. Anyway, firecrackers?"

Sully was already pressing her way back through the crowd, but she called back over her shoulder, "Maybe next time."

That took care of one bit of business. She wondered for a moment how the diplomats would have talked around the fact that everybody in Hong Kong hated America, then followed that thought up with a brief spike of concern that those same mealy-mouthed diplomats had still been in the building when the arsonists swung by. There was nothing she could do about it now.

"LIES."

Sully stood very still until the echoes of the word on the back of her skull had died away. It wasn't a lie. If she kicked up a fuss now, she'd blow any chance she had of getting what she'd actually come to Hong Kong for. The mission was what mattered.

A tactical retreat seemed expedient, if only because the firecracker salesman was still staring after her while bellowing about his wares. She needed to find somewhere to regroup, somewhere that people would be talking freely. She needed a pub. Someplace far enough inland that the local news wouldn't be drowned out by the influx of new arrivals. Her studies of the Mongolian languages had been focused entirely on phonetics—since she had planned on talking to people rather than writing to them—so the signage above the darkened doorways could have said anything.

Trusting to luck, Sully pushed through a beaded curtain into what sounded from the outside like a bar, and was rewarded with the deathly silence of a private function interrupted. It was a bar, just not the kind that Sully was used to. Cloth draped all of the walls, there were big bubbling contraptions along the bar and more arrayed around the room on low slung tables that were surrounded by cushions. The room was shrouded in sickly sweet smoke, constantly refreshed by the puffing customers where they lounged about the place. The stools by the bar were mostly unattended compared to the rest of the establishment, but the vampy girl behind the counter had a smile that said she might have something to talk about, and even if she didn't Sully needed a moment to collect her thoughts.

Playing the besotted tourist, Sully struggled through a few words of pidgin Mongolian before the hostess graciously switched over to English and hooked her up with some kind of pineapple tobacco. Sully was surprised to discover that it wasn't altogether unpleasant when she took the first tentative draw on the pipe. It wasn't like the cigars she used to smoke; drawn out through the water, it was cool, almost refreshing. She wasn't going to have to fake her way through that part at least. By the time Sully looked back at her, the hostess had already sidled off to refresh some of the other patron's pipes. Five minutes to think this all through wouldn't hurt anything. She slowly spun the band of dull metal on her ring finger with her thumb and let her mind wander through the fragments that she had welded back together into a history.

APRIL 15, 2019

The gold leaf on the door was scratched half to death, but Leonard Pratt could still make it out: M. K. Sullivan. Private Investigator. The sly bitch had already set up shop in New Amsterdam and applied for her license under that alias before the first hint of news got back to him. For all that he had oversight of every port and portal in the country, it never ceased to amaze him just how much could slip past. He could have kept track of her through her war pension if she had ever claimed it, but as he should have predicted, Sullivan had chosen privacy over security. Her mother had been happy to take his money during the long period of convalescence following the incident in London, but Sullivan herself was less pragmatic.

The old woman had understood their arrangement quite clearly: she was to care for Sullivan to the best of her abilities, keep her out of the limelight until all of the furor over the destruction had died down and warn Pratt if it seemed that any memories of her past life had returned. At the last check, she had recovered skills and a general understanding of the world, but specific memories from her personal history still eluded her. To his mind, this was the perfect state of affairs. She would become a viable and valuable tool once again, without any of the baggage that had previously been attached. Sullivan had always made a better friend than an enemy. It had been almost six months since the postmark of that last letter, and it was only after making extensive diplomatic and private enquiries that he established that Sullivan's mother had expired. Presumably of old age, since she had been quite possibly the contemporary of wooly mammoths in her youth.

Sullivan's activities during those six months were unaccounted for, and that was a source of considerable concern for him. He had not parted on the best terms with the version of Sullivan that was in full command of her faculties. Indeed, he was pricing some competitive bids from international assassination firms when news of her injury and its consequences reached him.

His own fortunes seemed to have followed a trajectory similar to Sullivan's following the war, in that his political career had also gone up in flames. The flames that consumed her may have been more literal, but Leonard Pratt felt that his had a greater sting. He had been at the heart of the new-born government that had tacitly sanctioned the annihilation of London through the use of magic. He was not so much of a fool as to believe that the fact that he had nothing to do with the explosion that wiped half of the British Isles clean would be relevant to the conversations that followed, so he adopted Sullivan's moment of madness as his own act of realpolitik brilliance.

The war had been won in a single stroke, and the United American Alliance had proven to the other imperial powers that it wasn't just a force to be reckoned with, it was capable of ending them. What a position of power to forge trade pacts and alliances from.

Alas, it was not only his nation's enemies that he had to contend with but also its allies, and they had ejected him from his seat of power promptly after hearing that particular explanation. Simpering moralists, the lot of them. He had been the one that forged the alliance, he had been the one that had driven the British out of America, and if he had been callous on occasion, it was only because the cost otherwise would have been unfathomable.

So it was that his stature within the halls of power was greatly reduced, his startling intellect quietly shuffled off into a dead-end department, and his precious fame stripped and chipped away from him day by day. If those cretins in power had their way, he would be forgotten entirely, a note in the margins of history. It would not stand.

He still had allies enough to reclaim his position; all that it would take was finding the correct lever to pivot the current state of affairs. Which was of course, why he was here.

He rapped tentatively on the glass with a leather-gloved knuckle, then stepped inside briskly before he could lose his nerve. This was the moment of truth, when he found out just how much Sullivan truly remembered. He tried not to flinch when she looked up at him and asked, "Can I help you?"

He had an entire speech planned, but all of his calculations seemed too cold for the moment. She had been his friend once, before he had used her. It wasn't so hard to remember that, and to feel happy that she was well. "Sully?"

She looked so young without the scars. It was easy to forget the life that she'd lived and the fury that had driven her. Her eyes seemed to lose focus for an instant, then she smiled. "Prime Minister Pratt? To what do I owe the pleasure?"

"Oh ho, I regret to inform you that my position as Prime Minister has long since passed me by. These days I am enjoying a quiet retirement in the customs department. Tangentially related to my persistent interests in law enforcement and arcane transportation without any of the stress of managing the entirety of either one."

"So is this visit business or pleasure?" Sully cocked an eyebrow, and it was so familiar Leonard had to bite back a little gasp.

"Hah, very good. I would love to say that this was merely a social call, and indeed, I would likely have made a visit for that purpose earlier if you had informed me of your return to the Americas, but alas, my purpose here is to offer you something of a business opportunity. Or rather an opportunity to settle some old business that I am sure must have been preying upon your conscience through these last few years."

Her smile had gotten a little strained. She was trying to being polite even though he was being deliberately loquacious to jibe her. It really was just like old times. "So you've got a job for me, and it's one you think I'm actually going to want to do?"

"Very much so." He drew the file out of his briefcase and cast it onto her desk. "You were something of a crusader in the years before the war, pursuing all threats to this great nation and her people with a zeal that I wish the agents who are now under my command could match. I believe that this case offers you the opportunity to return to form, while still maintaining the low profile that I understand you wish to pursue."

Sully was reading the file and ignoring him completely; it was one of her most admirable talents. After almost a full minute had passed, she looked up. "A demon."

"Not just any demon. The last demon on earth. A ravenous murderous force for evil that has plagued the world for centuries, and one that was unleashed upon it once more by none other than—"

Sully cut him off with a glare that was, now, entirely familiar. "Me."

"Indeed." Leonard resisted the urge to flinch. This was dangerous territory. "Do you happen to recall the circumstances of the demon's release?"

"It is bound in a doll. We were questioning it. Then—my case-notes get a bit fuzzy. Piecing it together now, I think that we used him to break the taboo on Manhattan?"

"I believe it was something to that effect." Leonard tried to keep the edge of glee out of his voice. She didn't remember anything, she was working from notes, and she would never have been so foolish to put her enmity toward him down on paper. He was free and clear. "Regardless of the exact reasoning behind your decision to release the demon from captivity, the consequences must still be faced. Four dead in New Amsterdam, then the entire crew of the UNS Barham, twelve hands in all. The trail grows cold after that. It is known that the creature escaped to Old Europe ahead of the first round of settlers but our tracking from that point forward was guesswork at best."

"Until now." She leaned back in her seat, eyes still darting over the pages in her hands.

"A few weeks ago, information was passed to me through a

network of interested parties who wondered if the American government might be interested in acquiring a certain antiquity of interest to scholars of the arcane."

Sully sighed. "Okay, so somebody found Eugene. Skip to the good bit."

"There are few places in this world that are not under some form of imperial provenance, few dark corners where an artifact of such value would not instantly be seized by the local authorities. In the wake of the dissolution of the British Empire, there are considerably more dark corners than one might previously have expected, but there is only one with such a burgeoning criminal underworld that it would dare to fence goods of this sort."

She flicked to the last page. "Hong Kong?"

"The very same. Now it is certain to have occurred to you that a man of my stature cannot be seen associating with the criminal elements. Nor can America risk the embarrassment of becoming embroiled in a bidding war for possession of this demon." He paused for breath. "We require an agent to operate on our behalf, to secure the object and return it to confinement safely. An agent who can pass into Hong Kong undiscovered, yet possesses the necessary training to extract the artifact by guile—or force if it should become necessary."

Sully dropped the file and gave him a smile. "Sounds like you need to hire a PI."

"The very best in the business." Leonard hooked his thumbs into the pockets of his waistcoat and rocked back on his heels. "Would you consider—?"

Her smile turned predatory. "Let's talk rates."

AUGUST 3, 2013

"So what is a sweetheart like you doing in a place like this?" It was hard to flirt around the gurgling noises of the hookah pipe, but Sully was always up for a challenge. The hostess had obviously been well trained in dealing with flirtatious customers and Sully's usual attempts to bypass those defenses by being a woman had run into a feigned language barrier. It wasn't the first time Sully had played this particular game, although her end goal now was probably a bit more honorable. "I mean you've got the looks to be a model or something, why are you waiting tables?"

A single-shouldered shrug that suggested she might be convincible. "Maybe I like it here?"

Sully looked around incredulously. "What's so great about Hong Kong anyway?"

That statement, innocuous enough anywhere else in the world, was enough to make three separate pairs of ears prick up around the room. Sully noted their positions before they could slouch back from that moment of stiff restraint. Who had ever heard of a crime hive filling its people up with patriotic fervor? She had been seriously misinformed about the situation over here.

The hostess leaned over the bar, giving Sully an eyeful of carefully calculated cleavage. "Haven't you heard? Anything that you desire can be bought in Hong Kong." Her delicately painted lips split, revealing the fangs beneath. "And of course, some of us are not free to live as ourselves anywhere else."

They might have been playing a game, but the hostess looked a little pleased when Sully didn't flinch away from those fangs. Sully leaned in closer, so her warm breath could tickle over the girl's cold skin. "Freedom, that sounds pretty tempting."

That was when somebody tapped her on the shoulder. The vamp was a local, cheap suit, shaved head, looked Mongol, but Sully really couldn't tell the difference yet. Wherever he was from originally, the accent was pure imperial finishing school. "Madam, I have to ask you to stop monopolizing the time of our staff."

In that suit he wasn't the owner, and with that attitude he wasn't the manager. He had the universal mannerisms of a bouncer, but he'd clearly just gotten up from one of the lounging tables. This must have been the criminal element that Pratt was so worked up about. Time to make some introductions. "Piss off, chuckles. Me and the dame are talking."

Sully had been punched many times in her life, normally for a good reason, but this was the first time that she had been hit so fast that she didn't see it coming. One minute she was smirking at the vamp, the next she was looking up at the dreary drapes on the ceiling. The pain creaked through her jaw like slow spreading fire, but she'd had worse. That was the nice thing about living through hell, she'd always had worse.

When she straightened up, he was still standing there in a weird boxer's pose, smart enough not to overestimate the power of a blitz attack. She was pleased to find that she still remembered enough of basic training to get her hands up before his next kick connected with the side of her head. It wasn't enough to keep her from getting flung along the length of the bar, but it kept her conscious.

She came back up with her fists hovering in front of her and the gray around the edges of her vision already fading. She spat blood at him, heard it spatter across the floorboards and watched as his pupils dilated to fill his eyes. "You fight like a girl."

Whether it was anger or bloodlust, all of his nuance and fighting form vanished as he charged Sully. It was almost too easy to duck under his grasping arm and hammer an elbow into his ribs.

He bounced back off the bar and came at Sully with both fists swinging. She caught one on her forearm and the other with her prosthetic, which snapped clean off.

While he was gawking at the rubber hand flipping through the air, Sully hammered her forehead into his nose. That crunch was still satisfying after all these years.

It wasn't enough to put him down, but it was enough to stagger him long enough for her to get a couple of good licks in with the one fist she still had. Vamps didn't bruise like humans—they didn't have the blood to spare—but his face was getting nice and puffy, even if it wasn't changing color.

Sully had never seen somebody knock a vampire out—she wasn't even sure it was possible—but she had enough personal experience with pulled hair and scratches to know that they felt pain. You'd be amazed how many people just roll over and give up so that they don't have to hurt any more.

Her next punch was deflected with a clever slap on the wrist that left her fist numb and ringing. Then he was hitting back, so fast that his movements were a blur. She blocked a punch or two, but the rest hit. Her ribs, her gut, her thigh. An open-handed whack to the side of her neck that made the whole world go black for an instant.

"YOU ARE LOSING."

Through bloody teeth Sully hissed, "Shut up."

She ducked under the next kick and hammered her fist up into the vamp's crotch. That was enough to slow his momentum. He said something in a language Sully didn't know, but she was confident it wasn't complimentary.

Now was the time to press her advantage, but she found that she was too punch drunk to even connect with her next swing. She overbalanced and had to grab onto one of the stools to stay on her feet. She tried to pick it up to smack the vamp with it, but was distressed to find that it was bolted to the ground, surely for situations just like this.

A kick found her spine before she could straighten up. A fist found her ear. After that, the individual punches and kicks started to blend together into a fog of pain. She was still moving. Still swinging. But if her feeble punches connected, she was no longer aware of it.

"YOU CAN END THIS."

She was curled up on the floor. The vamp's patent leather sole was coming down at her, a dark shape in a world of dark shapes. "I can take it."

November 5, 2018

Ceejay had a bounce in his step as he moved among the shipping containers at the Jersey Docklands. There were few occasions when the Director of the IBI could walk around freely without an armed guard trailing after him, and he was enjoying every minute. Sure, he had to create an entirely illegal and unstable portal inside his own home and throw himself through it bodily before it could collapse, but that was a small price to pay for a little bit of freedom.

He wasn't sure when the change had come about, when he went from being a man capable of protecting himself to being a coddled pen pusher. Perhaps it had been when he stopped staying later than the janitors in the office, or the first time that he ate a meal in a restaurant at lunchtime instead of grabbing takeaway to bring back to his desk. He was fairly confident that he could still blast apart any problem that crossed his path if it came to it. It wasn't like he had forgotten the spells, or that his instincts had completely faded. That said, his three immediate predecessors in the job had exploded, been turned into a parrot, and been turned into another parrot, respectively, so perhaps some degree of caution was warranted.

The one thing that he still refused to surrender to was the glasses. His new wife told him that they made him look dignified and academic, not old, but he had more than enough reason to suspect that her opinions were biased. He had taken to casting a very minor enhancement spell on himself when he had to read things at work, but the constant drain on his reserves was too exhausting to carry it over outside of office hours. As he passed each container, he slowed, squinted and eventually leaned closer, his lips moving almost imperceptibly as he read the serial numbers stenciled onto the sides. He should have just worn the damn glasses.

When he was sure he had the right one, he took one last look around out of habit, then rapped his knuckles on the side. A moment later, something knocked back. He grinned. Snapping the locks was the work of a few quick spells, yet opening the doors was surprisingly difficult. Maybe he was out of shape. It was worth all of the effort when Sully came lunging out of the darkened interior of the container to wrap him in a one-armed hug. "Took you long enough, you lazy old bastard."

"Lazy? I risk my life and freedom to come help you on this fool's errand and this is the thanks that I get? Lazy?" He half-heartedly tried to shove her back into the box.

With a laugh she shoved him back. "You spend a week in one of these things, pissing in a chemical toilet and tell me I'm crazy for wanting out faster."

"A chemical toilet? Your tastes have become so refined since you spent time in Europe." He threw an arm around her shoulders and started walking her up toward the lights of the city. "Why, I remember when just a bucket was good enough for young Agent Sullivan, fresh off the boat."

Sully cocked an eyebrow. "I have no idea if that is true, so I'm just going to assume you're a filthy liar."

His serious expression held for all of a moment before it collapsed and he let out a guffaw so loud it echoed all the way out of the stockyard. "That—that is always a good assumption. I've missed having you around, Sully."

Her smile faltered. "Well, don't get used to it. I'm just passing through."

"I know." Ceejay's own perpetual good cheer had recovered much faster than hers. "I know! Off on your next grand adventure. No time for the little people like me."

She squeezed him a bit tighter around the ribs. "I'll always have time for you. You ever need me, you know you just have to say the word and I'll come running. After everything that you've done for me . . ."

"Ah, this is when you segue into asking me about all the chores you left me before you vanished for years? Very smooth, Sully. Very subtle."

She thumped him in the gut with her prosthetic hand. "I was saying thanks, you dick."

"How many years did I watch you pulling this shit on suspects? You don't get to talk circles around me, Sully. I know all your tricks."

She laughed again, and it was enough to bring him to a halt. He'd never heard Sully laughing like this. He'd drawn more than a few chuckles out of her through the years, but she had never managed to laugh like there was nobody judging her for it. She continued, "All right, all right! Where is she?"

He untangled himself from her shoulders and moved off, forcing her to jog to keep up with his longer stride. "Where is who? I don't know what you're talking about. You left me so many jobs to do, Sully. Head of the IBI. Protector of the whole American Empire. It's a nightmare. Before, I was just running out my years until I could retire, then you blew up the whole bloody thing and left me to clean it up. Zombies. Manhattan. Fairies. Wars. I just wanted to catch criminals."

She caught him by the hood of his camouflage sweatshirt and jerked him to a halt. "You know who I'm talking about."

"My charming new wife that you have not asked about yet?"

"Ceejay . . ." She carefully ungritted her teeth. "How's the wife?"

"She is driving me insane." Ceejay warmed to his subject. "She wants me to have babies and live in a big house and work regular office hours. She wants me to wear gray and be respectable. She wants me to eat family meals. I can't do any of those things. I must be making her oh so miserable. Why do people get married Sully?"

She was trying very hard not to laugh. "Love?"

"Idiots."

That was enough to draw out a snort before Sully got it under control. "Come on, you're saying you didn't love Christina before you married her?"

"How am I supposed to remember a thing like that? It's been years." They plodded along in silence for a long moment before he added. "I do love her now. If I did not, after she threw out all of my good suits she would have woken up inside a shark. She knows I love her; she's banking on it. Me loving her is how she gets away with tormenting me!"

"Sounds like the two of you were made for each other."

He grinned. "She is a very handsome woman. It's a good match."

When they got to the gates of the yard, Sully politely stood aside and let him melt the locks away with a spray of acid. "Ah, it feels good to be doing things again instead of just reading reports about other people doing things."

"You could always quit." Sully tried to shrug while pushing herself through the bars of the gate and nearly got stuck. "Go back to being just a regular agent."

Ceejay scoffed. "And let one of those other idiots run the place? Let one of them be *my* boss? Can you imagine?"

They headed deeper into the city on the hunt for a taxi, and it was like Sully had never left. "I did some of my best work when I had to report to idiots."

He nudged her with his shoulder. "Don't think I don't know you're talking about me."

"Don't think I don't know that you know I'm talking about you." She nudged right back.

They came to a halt by a street just busy enough that they had some hope of catching a taxi sometime this week. He looked down at her with almost the same broad smile he'd been comforting her with for decades and she finally realized that something was wrong. "What happened?"

"I lost her, Sully." His fake smile crumbled. "You asked me to move her out of the country, to hide her where Pratt and his spies couldn't find her, but they are my spies, too. I couldn't hide her from one and not the other. For a year she was collecting mail and wire transfers from the stockpile you'd left for her. For a year she stayed where I hid her in Morocco and waited patiently for your return, but then . . . I don't know what happened to her after that. The more that I do to find her, the more suspicions that I raise. I was going to end up bringing the danger to her if I persisted, so . . . I gave up."

Sully had her eyes closed. When she opened them, Ceejay was fairly certain that he was going to be vaporized, so he very briefly wished that he had spent more time at home with his wife and then readied a defensive shield. Her mouth opened before her eyes and he braced himself for the curse she was about to unleash. "You did the right thing. Thank you."

When she looked at him, there was neither sadness nor betrayal on her face, only the first inkling of the determination that had always defined her. "There are people I can talk to. Resources that you can't tap. Favors I can call in. If she's out there, I'll find her."

"You seem very certain."

She grinned. "I didn't come all this way to turn back now."

AUGUST 1, 2019

Only one of Sully's eyes would open, and she wished that it hadn't. Somehow the preceding acts of violence had turned her eye into some sort of prism that converted light into pain. There was a lot of light. More than you would have expected to filter down from the tiny bit of blue sky she could see between the buildings around this reeking alleyway. Sully sincerely hoped that she had thrown up, because the possibility that some passer-by had thrown up right next to her face and then strolled off was infinitely worse.

Moving was painful, because everything was painful right now, but she was pleased to find that she didn't have the tell-tale dizziness that she associated with a concussion. She spat out half a molar. Everything was coming up Sully. The buckle on her satchel was digging into her back, her ring finger was so swollen—probably broken—that any attempt to steal her only piece of jewelry was doomed to failure. She forced her way through the full body ache and to her feet. Drawing in the next ragged breath was hard, but not too hard. Nothing inside was damaged. More good news.

The alleyway was clear of litter, in stark contrast to every other part of Hong Kong so far, but it only took Sully a moment to realize why. Somebody had built a barricade at each end of it, one with what looked like a heap of shopping trolleys and the other with scrap wood, vaguely resembling a fence. There was a little shack built out of the same stuff leaning drunkenly against the opposite wall, providing no shelter to the makeshift bedroll she had been dumped on, but plenty of protection to mounds upon mounds of shakily photocopied pamphlets proclaiming vampirism and magic to be sins worthy of eternal damnation. Sully groaned. "Oh, shit."

"Have no fear, for even in this lawless den of iniquity the faithful can find sanctuary in the arms of the Lord." The preacher lurched out from behind the far end of the shack. His eyes were still bulging, despite the lack of volume and audience. Great.

"Thanks for the assist back there." Sully said, playing nice.

"No thanks are required, child." It was like his eyes were focused on some distant horizon. He didn't even seem to be looking at her. "It is my divinely ordained purpose to give succor to those that the vampire preys upon."

Sully's jaw ached when it clenched, so she tried to ignore what he was actually saying. "Well, it is appreciated all the same. Did they just dump me here?"

He was getting closer than she would have liked, but since she really didn't want him on the same continent as herself, that was a hard line to judge. "You were laid without grace in the alley behind their establishment. They did not drink of your blood, if that is what you fear. It is bad for business when tourists are made into the feast of their unholy communion, and their lust for money exceeds even their thirst for blood."

"But a solid beating is fine?"

He was flushed, drunk on his own righteousness. "There is no order or dominion laid over this city. Only the cold grasp of the undead holds the peace. They suffer no disrespect. They set themselves above the living, their betters, and those who will not bow down before their corpse throne, they must strike down mercilessly as an example to others."

Sully had reached the limit of her patience in record time. "So what is this you're doing, some sort of elaborate suicide attempt? You go into a city that's full of vamps, run by vamps, and yell that vamps are the worst pieces of shit to ever exist? How do you see that ending?"

"We are all called to serve. And no missionary has ever converted among the already faithful."

Sully rolled her eyes and headed for the more passable-looking wooden barricade. The preacher called after her, "And what of you, child? Was it an elaborate suicide attempt when you stormed into a bar owned by the Jasmine Society to pick a fight?"

So the vamp gangsters had a name. Sully filed it away for later. "I'm just here on holiday. I don't want any part of your holy war. Where's the theater?"

The sudden change of tack flustered him so much that he answered like a normal person. "Kowloon."

There was a makeshift gate, where the chicken-wire could be peeled back enough for her to squeeze through. "Where's that? North?"

"Far to the northeast. But I should warn you that it is a den of profound sin surpassing even this evil place."

Sully let the fence snap shut behind her and gave him a dismissive wave. "Yeah, I've met actors before. Thanks."

Moving on briskly, she could feel the steadying weight of the pistol in her satchel bouncing off a bruise on her hip every time she took a step. Her ring was digging into her swelling finger. The only things that she'd lost in the fight were the plastic hand—which she hated anyway—and her damned hat; even her money clip was somehow still intact.

There were cars moving through the crowds at a crawl, but nothing identifiable as a taxi. The only vehicles getting any sort of traction at all in the face of the population seemed to be little wagons pulled by bikes, although Sully suspected that you'd have to be shameless to ride in one. She caught a glimpse of her reflection in some aluminum sheeting nailed to a doorway. It wasn't like anyone was going to recognize her looking like this anyway. She raised her hand.

"Kowloon." It felt odd in her mouth, but the driver seemed to understand and before she knew it, they were zipping in and out of the ceaseless parade of bodies at a speed Sully just knew was going to end in tears. She tried not to look for the gaps in the crowd that the bike was going to turn into, just as she'd squared her shoulders and marched through them all earlier. Trusting other people to keep her alive did not come easily to Sully. Even the first spark of her anger at the bigot in a dog-collar had come from resentment that he'd dragged her from one alley to another and saved—if not her life—then at least her stuff.

The deeper into the city that they went, the thinner the crowds grew and the faster they moved. From downtown, Sully hadn't realized just how big Hong Kong was. It didn't sprawl out as far as New Amsterdam by any stretch of the imagination, but what it lacked in breadth it made up for in height. By now, you would have hit a suburb back home, but here there didn't seem to be a single building under four stories. She had only known it as a military base, a stronghold of British might out in the far eastern seas, but inland there were new worlds waiting to be explored.

Pedestrians started to coagulate as they drew closer to Kowloon. Sully managed to communicate to the driver through some pidgin Mongolian, and some more-universal shouting, that she wanted to stop before they hit the theater district proper. Her target would be in there somewhere, there was no doubt in her mind, but she might not be found in one of the big gold leaf coated institutions that Sully could make out up ahead. She tipped the driver heavily, and clambered out onto the street amidst a storm of complaints from her knees, hips and elbows. She really needed a quiet corner somewhere to fix herself up.

The street vendors had been cleared from these streets, and the restaurants and shops catering to the theater clientele weren't open yet. It was as close to quiet as Sully had seen in the whole damned place, and yet she still couldn't breathe too deeply without bumping somebody. Yesterday that had just been a nuisance but now it set her bruises ringing and her temper boiling.

Getting into the theater district was like swimming against the flow of a river, and the tide wouldn't reverse again until just before the curtains went up, but the slow pace she was managing gave Sully plenty of time to eyeball the signage. She knew who she was looking for, and there was no shortage of faces on the posters plastered all over the place. A crawl worked out nicely. Sully was amazed at how many of the plays, musicals, and movies on display were exactly the same as the ones back home. She'd always known in the abstract that American studios exported a lot of entertainment, but she hadn't realized just how thoroughly they had the world saturated. This was the other side of the globe, and she could see the same blonde hair and blue eyes on every other poster. Small wonder everyone here was so angry at America—familiarity breeds contempt.

Halfway along the main street, just before she hit the biggest buildings, Sully paused and contemplated a noodle bar. She knew noodles from home. There wasn't likely to be any spicy, glutinous or amphibian surprise hidden in any of their dishes, and she hadn't eaten a damn thing since the steamer. She actually took a step toward the awning before a hand on her shoulder dragged her to a halt.

"IoNa sULliVAn."

There was a wrinkled-up little Mongol woman in a luminous pink tracksuit hanging on to Sully's sleeve, but the voice was pure nightmare, a cacophony of dozens of people all trying to croak through one dead throat.

"Oh, shit."

In a circle ten feet around her, every living person dropped dead.

Sully went for her gun but the old woman's cooling hands tightened on the satchel strap and ripped it away from her. "hOW mUch SWEEteR our reVENGE will BE For tHE WAIting. Who COULd haVe GUEssed THAt afTEr ALL thEse YEars, we wOULd FINd yOu heRE."

Somebody started screaming, and the rest of the crowd picked it up. The dead bodies were on the move. Sully counted twelve in all, a decent mix of British ex-pats, Hong Kong locals, and tourists. None of them armed, but she was surrounded. "What's Manhattan's interest in Hong Kong anyway?"

The answer came from every one of the corpses' mouths. "LeT US NoT PLAy gaMES in YOUr FINal momENts, sULLivan. WE COME foR the sAMe PrizE AS you. The LASt wiSH on EARth. TO REStore whAt you deSTroYed."

Manhattan had not fared well in the war. Pratt had been eager to commit them first to every offensive. Any magi who had survived that slog had been on the front lines in London when it went up in smoke. Sully couldn't even muster an argument against the accusation. She had almost certainly killed most of them, and *Sorry* wasn't going to cut it. "All right, let's skip to the end."

She slugged the old lady as hard as she could, then she was enveloped in a maelstrom of flailing limbs. The flesh-puppets didn't have much in the way of skill, but they did have an uncanny coordination on their side. They moved together as one fluid entity, attacking Sully from all sides, all at once. The blows rained down on her like hail, driving her to her knees. There were just too many of them. What could one person do against all of that?

"YOU CAN END THIS, NOW."

"No." As Sully tried to push herself back up onto her feet, her hand pressed against pink velour. The old woman, dead again before she hit the ground. So much had changed since the war, but Sully's jagged grin was the same as always.

She rose with an uppercut, punching the life out of another of the puppets and scattering the rest.

"wHaT IS THIs?!"

Every time her fist made contact, another body hit the concrete. Adrenaline had given her strength enough for this one last wild melee, but she was faltering as she started to sink into shock from the latest round of injuries.

Scrabbling hands tried to close on her, thought rather than fury finally guiding the puppets' movements. The Magi didn't know how she was killing their vessels, but they knew it had something to do with her punch. She bit into one dead hand as it closed on her wrist, her teeth digging into tendons beneath the surface of the skin, breaking the hold mechanically. Enhanced strength meant nothing without muscles to empower.

She spat out a mouthful of lukewarm blood with a grunt as the next wave tackled her, driving her back off the street and through the front window of the noodle bar. There was more screaming, but Sully didn't have time to process it. Every punch made the press of bodies lighter.

Only two were left now. One hugging her around the waist and the other trying to pin down her foreshortened arm. A European tourist in a little black dress and a local guy with a pencil mustache and a garish suit. She freed her arm with one cross, then kicked the feet out from under the tourist. "wE WILL be BaCK for YOu."

Sully hammered her fist down into the corpse's slack face so hard that she nearly broke her own wrist. "Take a number!"

The patrons of the noodle bar had fled sometime between the window breaking and the bodies hitting the floor but the three chefs behind the counter were staring out at her, cleavers and woks held up in front of them like protective talismans. Sully made it almost to the door before one of them gathered his wits enough to call out after her. "Bianpao?"

She had scraped together something resembling conversational Mongolian on the trip over, and that definitely wasn't one of the words she'd picked up, but still it sounded familiar. She mouthed it to herself. "Bianpao?"

"It is her. It is Agent Sullivan! And I am me. Monkhbat!" The chef was tumbling over the counter with his arms outstretched. While the other two had gone for weapons or armor from behind the counter, he was holding a leek, completely forgotten in the chaos.

Monkhbat stood a head shorter than she, and while she'd met a lot of fat men in her life, he was the first to be almost spherical under his chef's whites. He wrapped her in a joyful bear hug before she was able to reply, so her answer came out in a squeak. "Have we met?"

"Sully! You must remember. I was head chef in New Amsterdam. There were werebeasts! Gin! Surely Monkhbat is not so forgettable."

He'd called her agent, so he knew her from her time in the Imperial Bureau of Investigations. She had worked so many cases in her years with them that recovering each painful memory would have been arduous even if she hadn't suffered a complete burnout. The aforementioned gin probably didn't help her powers of recall either. She pushed against his weirdly firm torso and he released her. "Monkhbat, right. What brings you to Hong Kong?"

"I have friends here. It is a good place to start over. America, she wasn't ready for my noodles, but here, they are beloved by all."

"Glad to hear you found your feet." She was surprised to find that her words were genuine. He seemed like a nice guy, and New Amsterdam had never been kind to nice guys. "I'm, uh, sorry about your window."

Monkhbat barked out a little laugh. "What is a window between friends? It had cracks already. Long past time for replacement. Do not worry about it."

Sully took in the rest of the destruction. "I'd better get these bodies out of here, too. I don't want to cause you any more trouble."

"This is Hong Kong, Sully. There are no police, there is no law until sunset. You do not have to worry. Even if the neighborhood boss comes in, I will tell him they started it. There are no crimes here. Only criminals." His jolly rambling stopped abruptly as a thought crossed his mind. "But not very good hygiene. We should probably move them. Arms or feet?"

By the time they had dumped the third body in the alley around the back, Sully was fairly confident that Monkhbat had been a friend. Folks didn't typically help you hide a body if you were just acquaintances. The bodies from out in the street had begun to vanish over the course of that half hour of hard labor, too, and Sully was doing her best not to wonder where they were going. This wasn't her town, these weren't her people, and it wasn't her job to lay down any sort of law. Hadn't been for a long time. Regardless, she still wouldn't be eating at any of the Mongolian Barbecue joints around here.

After the last body, Monkhbat had smuggled her into his storage space "office" at the back of the restaurant, harangued her into sitting on the camp bed he had folded out there, and forced a bowl of soupy noodles into her lap. They were the most British tasting noodles she'd ever had in her life, beef and onion and just a hint of mustard lurking under the oily surface of the water. She could have kissed him. "Thanks."

"After all that you have done for me?" He looked aghast. "It is only a fraction of the rewards that you deserve!"

Against her better judgment, Sully decided to trust him. "If you're really looking to settle the score, maybe you can help me out. I'm looking for somebody, probably works in the theater, or around it; a blonde American dame, a vamp with a decent set of pipes on her, freckles for days. That ringing any bells?"

"You know me, Sully." He gestured sadly to the bed beneath her. "I work, I sleep, I work again. If she isn't in catering and she isn't a customer, I haven't seen her. And you know Xi Xue Gui, they don't love noodles."

She sighed into the dregs of her noodles. "Any chance you could ask around?"

"You want me to betray the trust of my brothers in white and use the secret cabal of caterers, wait staff, and restaurateurs to find your missing girl?" He managed to maintain a serious expression for almost a whole minute. "Of course! I shall ask."

His voice changed to a throaty growl as he switched to Mongolian and started rattling off orders to the other cooks. The other men looked like they were on the verge of panic, inexplicably serving a full house, despite the absence of a window out front. Monkhbat looked her up and down and sighed. "You stay here. Sleep. Let me serve customers, ask questions. Tonight I will have answers."

Sleep was sorely tempting, sleep with free answers attached was even better. Lying unconscious on cold concrete wasn't the same as a proper nap. "I can't take your bed."

"You can, and you must. I will be busy making the food that keeps the people happy. You will be here, dreaming the dreams that keep you happy."

"Hey man, thank you." Sully shifted uncomfortably, then handed him back his bowl. "Seriously, it means a lot."

That was more than enough awkwardness, but Sully still had to ask for more. "Listen, while you're talking to all your cooking buddies, could you check if there is some sort of auction going on in town? Something black market. Big ticket items?"

"The Peninsula Auction?"

Sully stared at him blankly. "Seriously. Does everybody in town know about this thing?"

"It is world famous! Whatever you want, you can buy in Hong Kong. Nobody told you this?"

She put her face in her hands. "Any chance you can find out what's up on the block?"

"I shall bribe one of their waiters with my special meatballs to bring the list to us before dinner."

"Why before dinner?"

He shrugged. "First Sunday of the month is auction night."

The deal was going down tonight. If Sully had spent one more day settling things up in New Amsterdam, it would have all been over before she got here. If there had been one storm, one delay at any of the ports they had passed through, the demon would be gone, the world would have been changed, and none of them would have even known it. She let out a little breath she hadn't realized she was holding and gave him a weak smile. "Thanks again."

"You want to go? I can get you in? I mean, I can't get you in, but there is a cook in the Peninsula kitchen who is always willing to leave the loading bay jammed. It would cost nothing. Maybe my burger recipe."

She stared at him blankly again. "Burger recipe?"

"You think people here don't like foreign food? You think gwailou like you come here and say, oh yes give me twelve pidan?"

Sully raised an eyebrow. "Gwhat? I'm Irish?"

"I am from Wei. Those two out there are from Shu and Tatarstan. We have customers from Samhan, Khangai, Gobi, Gansu, Burma,

Bhutan, Kiev, Manchuria. You call us all orientals, we call you all gwailou. Get used to being a minority." It was the first time that his pleasant demeanor had slipped, but even now it had fallen only to brief irritation.

Sully bit back her own irritable reply. He had done her plenty of favors already, and this seemed to have touched a nerve. "Fair enough."

He waved it away. "Anyway, Hong Kong was Britain longer than it was Mongolia. Many British are still here. They love my genuine-tasting American food. Very popular with young people, also."

This seemed like safer ground. "It is delicious."

His face lit up. "You see! Good food makes people happy. Now go to sleep. I will throw onions at you before dinnertime."

There was another beaded curtain drawn over the doorway, and while it did nothing to keep out the light or the noise of the front shop, it gave the illusion of privacy, for which Sully was grateful. She spun the ring on her finger drawing out a little hiss of pain on every rotation. Turn by turn, she worked it up past the swelling, even though it felt like the smoothed edges were cutting right into her flesh. She closed her eyes and kept turning until it slipped past her knuckle, then with an adrenaline tremor, she laid it down on the blanket beside her.

All the magpies in the city took flight at the same time, the sound of that first simultaneous wingbeat sweeping through the streets, audible over the endless bustle for just an instant before it was drowned out again.

Sully slipped the ring back up her finger smoothly and let her eyes open again. After that, all it took was one good stretch and she was able to settle into sleep like a rock being dropped into a pond. It was one of the great dichotomies of being a soldier, the two essential abilities of, first, never letting your guard down and, second, being able to sleep anywhere in any circumstances. Logically, the second one only made sense if you had your army around to watch over you, but here in a city of vampires, strangers, and enemies Sully went out like a light.

DECEMBER 7, 2018

The radio crackled in the morgue. The signal was always terrible down here, and the channels that Raavi liked were off the beaten track of wavelengths at the best of times. In theory, Raavi should have fiddled with the dial until he got a better signal, but currently all four of his hands were occupied with the body on the slab. Throughout the war, the Fae had been switching their abductees with magical replicas that were nearly impossible to detect without the application of fire. There had been extensive screening for just about every citizen, but a few of these dummies had still managed to slip through the cracks to start causing problems.

The biggest problem was that the vast majority of the substitutes were absolutely convinced that they were the person that they were impersonating. With the annihilation of the Fae, there was nobody left to pull on these puppets' strings, and they very quickly became the masks that they were wearing. They tried to inhabit the lives of their counterparts, trying to maintain the illusion of normality for their friends and family. If anything, Raavi considered it a kindness that they were doing—keeping the memory of the missing ones alive—but in practical terms it meant that there were potentially hundreds of sleeper agents for an alien power lurking among the citizenry. That was something that the IBI was really concerned with. Since shit rolled downhill and Raavi lived in the basement, that meant that detecting the imposters that had managed to escape screening had been added to his list of jobs.

Which was why he was faced with the rather peculiar thing on his table at present. On the outside it appeared to be a perfectly average middle-aged Caucasian woman, and even when he made his first incisions that illusion was maintained. There was blood, fat, muscle, bones. It was only when he dug down into the organs that he began to find evidence that this was not a completely normal human being. The intestines, while soft and pliable, had an unmistakable wood-grain pattern stretched across them. The lungs were bright green with chlorophyll. The heart itself was a gnarled knot of wood. All easily identifiable as plant rather than animal and connected by a series of vine-like tendrils to all of the other systems. The brain was what Raavi was really excited about. The mechanics of the pulmonary system were fascinating—no doubt—but they were still almost purely mechanical and replicable with alternate materials. The brain though, that was a fascinating and delicately balanced mash-up of chemistry and biology. Working out how the Fae had made a fully functional brain out of tree bits, that could advance medical science by a decade. Which went some way to explaining why he was so absorbed in his work—trying to carefully remove the part-bone, part-wood skull cap with a handsaw—that he did not notice someone strolling right into his workspace.

He was vaguely aware of a physical presence, certainly. He heard footsteps and he could sense somebody standing just a little out of arm's reach. His body didn't stop reporting these things to him just because his mind was otherwise occupied. His mouth did exactly the same. Mumbling requests for specific implements to the convenient new assistant that had just shown up at two in the morning. It was only when a cold can of ginger beer was placed in one of his outstretched hands and he nearly inserted it into the pulsating mass of folded petals within the subject's open skull cavity that he realized consciously that there was someone else in the room. He spun on the spot, then froze in place, all four arms splayed. "What? *You?* What?"

"'Welcome home, Sully. How are you doing, Sully?' Did they forget to socialize you while I was away?" There was a wry grin on her face.

He almost tried to grab her—to prove that she was actually here and not some sleep-deprived hallucination playing a cruel trick—before he remembered his hands were covered in blood and other more viscous fluids. "Sully!? You're here. Like, actually here and talking. Talking to me."

"Beats talking to myself," she quipped, helping herself to a soda next to one of the corpses in the fridge.

"But, how? The last time I saw you, you were practically a vegetable."

She shrugged. "I got better."

Raavi peeled off his gloves so that he could start pulling out his own hair. "You got better?! You . . . you just got better from acute arcane dementia? Making you the only person to ever make an even partial recovery of your faculties in all of history?"

She slurped her drink. "Yup."

"I think I might need a little bit more than a *yup*." Frustrated tears were brimming in his eyes unexpectedly. "I thought you were—I thought— It was worse than if you'd just died. You know that?"

Sully's shrug was a bit stiffer this time. "Imagine living through it."

He was actually vibrating with irritation. "So that's it? You aren't going to tell me *anything*?"

"I'm not going to tell you anything that might compromise your viewpoint."

That brought his building fury abruptly to a cold plateau. "So this isn't just a social call? My god, Sully, how long have you been back without even letting me know you were all right? How long have you been back in New Amsterdam? You can tell me that at least."

"All right, all right!" She held up her clunky prosthetic hand to calm him but it was molded into a fist, so it looked more like a threat.

"I've been back in town a few weeks. I would have come sooner, but I'm trying to stay out of sight, and you basically live inside the IBI."

He crossed both pairs of his arms, inadvertently smearing his concave chest with sticky fluids. "And how long have you been yourself again?"

"I'm still not sure if I am myself now. It took a long time before I could even remember little things, and even today I don't know how much of what I remember is me remembering things and how much is what I've been told happened. It's been months, maybe a whole year."

His lip was trembling, setting the sparse mustache he had been trying to grow flopping all over the place. "Let's say it was a year. Just for the sake of argument. What stopped you from picking up the phone for a year? What stopped you writing for a year?"

Sully rubbed her eyes. "Pratt."

"Asshole," he snapped back at her.

It was enough to draw a little breath of laughter out of her. "No. Pratt. Leonard Pratt. I didn't know if he was keeping tabs on you. I didn't want to drag you into any more trouble than I already had."

"Sully, I know you've been out of the loop for a while, but Pratt isn't Prime Minister anymore. He isn't anybody anymore. Nobody who was in charge during that cluster-fluff of a war is still running things. You could have come back any time you wanted."

She slumped. "And you think they would have just left me alone?"

"If they had any bloody sense, they'd throw you a parade. But failing that, yep, I'm pretty sure they'd leave you alone."

She finally met his gaze. She looked so very tired. "What about the Inferno? Do you think they'd leave that alone?"

That drew him up short. "That's what all this cloak and dagger stuff is about? You think they want the spell?"

"The spell that wiped out a whole plane of existence and scorched the British Empire off the map as an afterthought?" She raised an eyebrow. "Yeah, I'm pretty sure they want it."

He flung all his hands up in the air. "Well then give it to them, this isn't cosmic geometry! Hand it over to the government, bugger off, and have a good life."

She avoided his eyes. "It isn't that simple."

He ducked to try and get back into her line of sight, inadvertently crowding her. "Why can't it be, though? Why can't it be that simple?"

"Because I don't trust anyone with that kind of power. Especially the kind of people that are already making moves to establish their little empire as the toughest kid on the playground."

"So, what? It dies with you? The spell that couldn't be solved? The formula you spent three decades cracking?"

Her voice went flat. "It's already gone. It burned away with all my other memories, and I'm in no rush to try to get it back. I've had enough of being a soldier, Raavi. I'm done with being a weapon."

"But that's perfect. If the spell is already gone then—"

She cut him off with a shake of her head. "As long as they think I have the spell, I don't have assassins crawling up my ass day and night. As long as they think I could wipe out a whole city without breaking a sweat, all the people who want revenge can't come right at me. I'm screwed either way."

Raavi slumped down onto a stool and nearly slipped off the mound of paperwork that was resting there before finding his balance. "It's funny, I should probably be happy that you're alive and yourself again, and that you're doing what you need to do to stay that way. But the truth is, this new sensible Sully freaks me out. I never knew you to run away from a fight before. No matter how pointless it was."

"People change." It was almost a sigh.

Raavi couldn't believe his ears. "People don't change, they just learn to lie better. That's what you always told me."

"Then I guess I've learned to lie." She was so hunched over, so sad looking that Raavi finally took pity on her.

"So, what is this medical mystery that needed the best mind in the colonies to solve? You always did bring me the most interesting corpses."

"Well, this puzzle is still alive, and I'd prefer if you kept her that way." Sully managed a smile.

Raavi went to rinse off the worst of the gunk while she got onto an unoccupied slab. By the time that he got back she'd stripped off her jacket and was kicking her dangling legs. As an afterthought she detached her rubbery prosthesis and dropped it onto a metal tray with a clatter. "All right, solve the mystery."

"You aren't going to give me a hint? What am I looking for here?"

"How forthcoming are your usual patients?" She smirked.

"Hilarious. Right. Fine." He cleared his throat. "Subject is a Caucasian female, mid-fifties, terrible attitude."

"No wonder they've got you working the graveyard shift if this is your bedside manner."

He grinned. "Oh dear, some gasses are escaping the corpse and making a dreadful whining noise. Best just to ignore those."

Sully pointedly closed her mouth.

"The body seems to be in good physical condition. No visible scars except for the missing hand." He actually examined that scarred stump properly. "Any pain?"

Sully shook her head.

"Good stuff. So with no obvious physical injuries we move on to more complex diagnostics." He wheeled over a Schrödinger probe to start the usual hunt for curses, but when he looked at the read-out he frowned. "Oh, blast it all. I keep telling them I need new equipment. Stay put a minute, I've got a hand-held one somewhere."

He went digging through some drawers, and by the time he got back Sully was lying back, pretending to snooze. He turned on the little beeping probe and turned it toward her only to get the same puzzling absence of readings. He turned the calibration all the way down, then all the way to its most sensitive, so that even the flows of magic in the other tools around the room were setting it screaming and all that he could find was a baseline of magical energy coiling around Sully. "They can't both be broken."

"I'd guess that neither is."

He carefully set the Schrödinger back on the table beside her before he lost his grip. "You've lost your magic?"

"Is that your professional diagnosis?"

"Is this how you recovered from the dementia? Removing your magic? How is that even possible?"

Very carefully, she answered, "No, that isn't how I recovered."

"You expect me to believe that these two completely impossible things are unrelated?"

"I'm not saying they aren't related, I'm just saying that your theory is wrong."

Raavi scooped up the probe again. "I do love a challenge."

Over the next half hour, he ran through a battery of tests and diagnostic spells, each one slightly more desperate than the last. He came up with nine different theories as to what had happened to Sully's magic and she shot down every one of them promptly.

"All right, you win. I give up. You are to all intents and purposes a perfectly normal, healthy, totally magic-free human being."

"And none of your tests show anything different?"

He bit back his frustration. "Not one."

"Good."

"I can see why you aren't running around trying to duel every assassin in the world now. Very sensible."

Sully's grin persisted. "I could still take them."

He was practically bouncing up and down on the spot. "Will you just tell me how the trick is done, please?"

"You're going to kick yourself."

"Just tell me!"

She held up her hand and he stared at it blankly for a long moment before he spotted the ring. Raavi's head cocked to one side. "You got married?"

"Didn't you used to be smarter?"

He leaned in closer and then groaned. "Oh my god, I really did used to be smarter. They've had me down here too long with nothing to engage my beautiful brain. The ring. It's Cold Iron. That's what's blocking your magic. How on earth did you get your hands on that much Cold Iron?"

"Scraps and spent bullets left behind in Ireland after the war." She toyed with the ring, turning it slowly around her finger.

"Well, that solves the mystery, at least. But what's the point? Do you think somebody is tracking you by your magical signature? Do you need to pass for normal to fit in with some anti-magic organization?"

"My little secret."

Raavi's excitement came to an abrupt end. "Everything you do is a bloody secret, but if you're going to use me to test your camouflage, you could at least have the decency to tell me what you're hiding for."

"You know what. That's fair." She sighed. "I know I haven't been the best friend. I'm still trying to put myself back together most days, but if there is anyone in the world I can trust with this, I guess it's you. But Raavi, I'm really going to need you to keep this quiet. Not like the time you caught me with your intern and half the building knew about it by lunchtime. Not like when the details of that polymorph case went out to the press so you could get new bowling shirts. This is life and death. You get me?"

He nodded eagerly. So, with a sigh, Sully took off her ring.

AUGUST 1, 2013

True to his promise, Monkhbat's onion bombardment began a little after four in the afternoon. The first one bounced off Sully's knee, but she caught the second and lobbed it back at him. "I'm up." Another onion set the bedframe ringing. "I'm up!"

Monkhbat stood there, grinning at her, never realizing how close to death he had come. "You are looking much better. Swelling's gone down. Will you eat before you start your new job as a bartender in the Peninsula Hotel? We still have time before the sun is down."

Noodles for breakfast was too much for Sully, so she nestled herself on the last barstool with a sludge-thick coffee and a glower. Monkhbat laughed each time he passed her. "There is the Sully I remember. Angry little firecracker."

Grumbling, "I will stamp on your throat," just made him laugh louder.

Eventually she was awake enough to do more than just function. "I'm a bartender now?"

"My friend, he mentioned that they were looking for somebody. Seemed easier than sneaking you in, and I don't have to give up my burger!"

"Seems like I'm going to be owing you a hundred favors by the time I leave town."

He clapped her on the back. "Nonsense, tonight all debts are finally paid!"

The listings from the auction were innocuous enough at first glance, elegantly presented on fresh cream paper, but otherwise not ostentatious. There were no pictures, just a simple list that those in the know could understand perfectly and that those in law enforcement would struggle to connect to anything illegal. Good to know that the local crime bosses hadn't gotten sloppy just because the police had gone the way of the dinosaur.

There were some ship deeds on the docket first, probably privateered from their rightful owners somewhere in the ocean to the south. A few very specifically worded lines describing jewelry, which almost certainly meant something to the people looking for equally specific stolen goods. She was halfway down the list before things took a turn to the arcane.

Eclipsim Ferrum Ore Sample. That one was self-explanatory, a hunk of Cold Iron. Incredibly valuable, capable of negating magic on contact, and almost certainly a stolen heirloom that had been melted into its currently unrecognizable shape.

Aetherially Saturated Biological Specimen. One of the surviving Fae. Sully had heard rumors that a few of them had escaped London ahead of the explosion, but she'd assumed that they would have withered away to nothing by now without the ambient magic levels that they were accustomed to.

Historically Significant Doll. Sully felt a little thrill run through her. *Sold as seen with original cloth English Navy Uniform.* That was Eugene, no doubt about it. How he had made it around the whole world on a pair of legs with no articulation wasn't entirely clear, but that was definitely him and she definitely couldn't let any of the Empires lay their hands on him.

After the war, the wish-trade had ended. It had always been about supply and demand, with demons escaping the hells in exchange for a communal effort on their part to rewrite reality as the wisher requested. They had offered some extremely fair deals through the years, trusting in the human race to uphold the spirit of those deals and not just the letter of them. That had been a mistake. Even once they realized that they were being exterminated on arrival in about ninety percent of their arrangements, enough demons were still so desperate to make their escape that the wishes just kept on coming, with the only restriction being the demons' refusal to directly countermand a previous wish, because they were fundamentally honorable creatures, and because unplucking the kind of threads that they used to rewrite history came with the risk of unraveling the whole grand embroidery of existence.

After the war, the demons were in no rush to escape any more. Hell had become hospitable again now that the Fae were gone. Demons would come when they were summoned, because it was polite, but they had no particular desire to linger. For the imperial powers, this was a crisis. Rewriting history to make themselves the victor in every conflict had been their go-to solution in any situation. Now they were having to work for it.

When wishing had been business as usual, nobody could dominate the world, because they'd all been constantly wishing over each other; but now with just one wish left, any given empire could claim the whole planet, permanently.

"This is a robbery?"

Monkhbat said it so softly that Sully almost didn't hear him, but when she looked up from the list, his round face was grimacing into what she supposed was his best attempt at a serious expression. She shrugged. "Well, I don't have the cash to put a bid in."

"The Peninsula has very good security. Magi on staff. Cold room vaults built into the foundations where the auction goods live. Unless you have a very good plan, robbery might end badly."

"The goods won't be in the vaults during the auction." Sully didn't have to give it a second thought. "I know what I'm doing."

"There she is." Monkhbat rocked back on his heels with an amused huff. "Every time I think you are different, the Old Sully is there, under the surface, scowling out."

"People don't change, they just become more themselves." Sully said with just a tinge of sadness.

She lurked behind the scenes while the pre-theater crowd hammered the noodle bar out front, feeling awkward with nothing to do while the cooks performed the intricate dance of large professionals in a confined kitchen. It felt like it went on for much longer than the hours it actually took. She was drifting on the verge of sleep when Monkhbat knocked on the doorframe of his office. "Ready to go?" He gave her a terse nod and they were off, shuffling out through the back alley and straight into a car. She couldn't show her face on the streets, not when Manhattan could have their "agents" anywhere at a moment's notice. She didn't think that they would squeal on her to security at the hotel—not when they could make off with the doll under cover of the chaos she was going to create—but she had no doubt that they'd take another shot at her if they were given the chance.

In her mind, Sully started to compose a theory that every taxi in the universe was interconnected on some fundamental spiritual level and that was why they all shared the same smell. She was pulled out of her reverie by Monkhbat. He had been staring at her when he thought she wasn't looking all through the day. She figured that he must have heard at least part of the story about what went down during the war and was trying to be tactful, and now that he was running out of time to ask his invasive questions he was going to blurt them all out. She was surprised when he asked, "You really don't remember, do you?"

She met his gaze, then decided to be honest. He had done a lot for her today; he'd earned it. "I really don't. I don't remember a lot of things from before the war. At the end . . . you've heard of burnout? When you cast spells beyond your limits and wipe your brain? I got hit real bad with it. Didn't even know my own name for a while. Whoever I was before, whoever helped you back in New Amsterdam, she's gone now. I'm . . . I'm all that's left."

His eyebrows drew down over the vast expanse of his forehead. "Then I am very sorry."

There was something just a little off in his inflection. Not enough to make Sully leap out of the moving car, but enough to make her eyes narrow and her hand drift toward her satchel. "What are you sorry about, Monkhbat?"

His hands were shaking. Just a little tremor, barely noticeable in the moving car, but still there. "You do not seem like a bad person now. But in New Amsterdam, you were a terror. America was my dream, a fresh start away from all of this, a whole new world of people to love my food, and you took it away from me."

The tell-tale weight of the gun was missing from her satchel. Out on the street she'd give herself even odds in a fight with a guy the size of Monkhbat, but in a cab he could just crush her. She had to stall. "You want to tell me what happened?"

"You were chasing love potions, thought they were smuggled through my restaurant. They weren't but you could smell secrets and you kept digging. Everyone found out I was Yaoguai. Nobody would eat my food. My restaurant was shut down by health inspectors. They said I could contaminate food. I just wanted to cook. I just wanted to make people happy." Tears were pooling on his cheekbones. "I lost everything. Everything."

She should have been angry, but this wasn't the first story like this that she'd heard. "I could say I was just doing my job, or that I never meant for it to go down like that, but I really don't know what happened, so all I can say is that I'm sorry."

The tears were flowing freely now. Monkhbat wailed. "I know you are! How could you not be? Sully is gone and this new Sully is here."

The taxi driver was diligently paying no attention to them, or maybe he didn't speak English. The engine was rumbling and coughing away, the radio was on—murmuring out some Ophiran rock band that Sully didn't get the appeal of—it wasn't silent by any stretch of the imagination, but she still felt like she was puncturing something when she finally asked. "What did you do?"

"All the money I lost, I had to take on so much debt to open a place up here, and the bloodsuckers, they take every drop from you, one way or the other. I didn't know you were someone else. I thought you . . . I sold you."

Sully's jaw set. "To who?"

"The Peninsula. The auction. You are . . ."

"I'm a hot property. Yeah, nothing new there. Do you want me to knock you out before jumping out of the car, or can you talk your way out of this?" Dread was starting to settle in her stomach. It had always been there, lurking in the sea of rage that had kept her afloat through all these years. Fear like bedrock.

"You misunderstand me, Sully. This was just an apology. There can be no escape."

"And why's that?"

Monkhbat dragged his eyes away from her to look out of the window. Face still wet. "Because we are already here."

There were men with guns, because in situations like this they were a requirement even when they were useless, like decorative ferns. They had the taxi surrounded by the time that she stepped out of the car but she paid them no more attention than she would the bollards. There was another man in the midst of them, wearing a suit so expensive it looked like it had grown on him organically. He didn't have a gun or anything more threatening than the slightly crooked smile on his face, but the many men with guns deferred to him, which presumably meant he was in charge. Sully let her eyes pass him over and kept on looking.

The hotel was an impressive, imposing tower of gray stone and golden windows, the kind of place where folks with more money than sense would have tripped over themselves to stay. Lighter on the classical columns than you would have seen in New Amsterdam but still recognizable. They were at some sort of service entrance, so Sully didn't get the full effect of the place.

Back by the door, tucked unobtrusively out of sight and dressed like a waiter, was the Magus that she had been looking for. At a glance Sully could tell she used to belong to one of the imperial powers—she had that glazed expression that all of them did. The people running things did not appreciate anyone having more power than they did, so a burnout like the one that had taken Sully's mind in an accident was applied deliberately to them throughout their training, over and over, year on year, until they could weave spells like nobody else, and couldn't function like anybody else.

Monkhbat had decided to stay in the car. He couldn't meet her eye, and if she'd been her old self, Sully was pretty sure he would have been a corpse by now. But at some point between passing through the fire and remembering her own name, Sully had decided that life was too short to hold grudges.

That was the lay of the land, and while Sully would have taken those odds any day in her old life, now she raised her hands slowly and laced her fingers on top of her head. "Monkhbat needs paying before the car takes him home."

Pricey suit slithered forward. "Of course, of course. I am glad that we are being civilized about this."

Sully tried to shrug, then realized it wasn't possible with her hands in their current position. "It's just business. No point crying over spilled milk."

Up close, the guy had a pencil mustache and enough oil in his hair that Sully was surprised the British hadn't invaded it. "It is good that you feel that way. It will make this process much more pleasant for all of us. And of course, in turn, we will endeavor to keep you comfortable until the auction is complete. Just like any of our other guests."

She couldn't keep an edge of sarcasm out of her voice as two of the men with guns hustled her inside. "Dandy."

Even in these back corridors that only deliverymen and staff would see, the hotel was sleek and opulent in a way that spoke to taste as well as wealth. Sully didn't know if the Peninsula was owned by the local vamp gangs, some international consortium, or a single abstract party, but whoever was behind it was doing pretty well out of the deal. Their cut from the auctions probably paid the bills, so all the guests and the rest were pure profit.

"Your timing was absolutely impeccable, Ms. Sullivan. The other items are just now being arrayed in the display room. It is unfortunate that you are forced to share attention with an item of considerable import; given the opportunity, I would have preferred to list you separately." Oily had fallen into step beside her, chatting as if they were friends. "Still, many of our guests tonight would have made the trip especially for you if your listing had been announced ahead of time. Perhaps you shall serve as a consolation prize to our second highest bidder?"

Sully rolled her eyes. "Lucky me."

Their journey through the bowels of the hotel was short and dull, with any staff catching sight of the guns scampering out of the way with little more than a squeak. The auction items were laid out in a long line across the back of a space that was unmistakably a stage. A lectern stood out front for the auctioneer and beyond that there was a dark expanse, like a theater, where all the bastards in the world were going to line up to take a shot at her.

She was led along the back of the row. The smaller items sat on little tables, the bigger ones on the hardwood floor, but each and every one of them was encircled by an inlaid band of silver, inscribed with spells of binding and barriers. Any creature of magic, from a lowly hedge witch all the way up to a reality warping Fae would be trapped by that circle until the Magus who cast it chose to intervene.

Sully hadn't seen one of the Fae since the end of the war, and as it turned out, lingering in a world with only a fraction of the magic that they were used to subsisting off of had taken a dire toll on the creature in front of her. The pallid skin had turned gray, sagging. The huge almond eyes were clouded with cataracts, but they still contracted as she approached. "Jesus, I thought you were ugly before."

"A curse on you, flame-bringer. May your spirit wither and rot. May your—"

Whatever it was going to say next was cut off abruptly by a punch from one of the armed guards. The monster collapsed against the side of its cage. Spongy flesh spread across the invisible wall that encircled it.

The next few circles boasted the Cold Iron, something that looked suspiciously like a dragon's egg, some crystalline sculptures that probably should have meant more to Sully, and finally, second from last, Eugene.

He was doing his inanimate object act, but he wasn't fooling anyone. "We've really got to stop meeting like this."

The doll's head turned, ever so slowly, to follow her movement in such tiny increments that if you had glanced away, you would never have guessed that he had moved at all. "YOU."

Oily interrupted their reunion. "Please, step inside the circle, Ms. Sullivan."

The last circle lay empty, just waiting for her. On a stand beside it there was a little card, hastily printed on the same cream stock as all the rest. "Iona Sullivan, The Genocide."

She was about to argue about the accuracy of this title, then remembered the Fae at the end of the row. The title was painfully accurate. She stepped into the circle before she could give it another thought, and the Magus on staff shuffled forward to lay a hand on the invisible barrier around her, ensuring that it would hold her. Oily pulled the Magus aside and she could make out some fierce murmuring, including the word *Inferno* repeated several times. Whatever the argument was, the Magus seemed satisfied with her work, drifting off to pet a fluffy white rabbit that she'd just conjured out of thin air. Well, at least somebody was having a good time.

This close, Eugene's voice was almost deafening. "OH HOW THE MIGHTY HAVE FALLEN. WHEN LAST WE MET I WAS YOUR PRISONER, AND NOW YOU ARE BOUND AS SURELY AS ME."

Sully scowled over at the doll as his head moved through a slow three-hundred-and-sixty-degree spin. "I actually came here to rescue you, you plush asshole."

For a face that was painted on, Eugene's little scowl could be fairly expressive. "HAD I SUCH AN ORIFICE, I WOULD INSTRUCT YOU TO KISS IT."

"Come on now, I cut you a fair deal last time around. You helped me out, I set you free. Hell, I didn't even chase you."

"AND NOW YOU COME AS YOUR MASTERS' FAITHFUL

HOUND TO FETCH ME BACK TO SOME FRESH IMPRISON-MENT ONCE AGAIN." Eugene rocked to his feet on the pedestal. "DO YOU THINK I KNOW NOTHING OF THE TREACHERY OF MAN?"

Sully knew that for the longest time, she had been defined by her temper—by her rage—and she was finding more and more frequently that her newfound and hard-won calm was taken as weakness by those that had known her before. "You know what? I was doing this because I felt bad for you, but now I am going to enjoy slam dunking you right back into hell."

"BETTER MINDS THAN YOURS HAVE BEEN TURNED TO THE TASK OF BANISHING ME AND THEY HAVE ALL BEEN FOUND LACKING." Eugene was practically hissing now.

"Because you're bound to the doll, dumbass." Sully scoffed. "They were scared you could use it as an anchor to this plane. Now nobody is trying to invade. I'm just going to throw you in whole and let your own people sort it out."

There was a long pause as one of the guards strolled by, then Eugene snapped back to it. "WHAT PURPOSE DOES THIS DECEP-TION SERVE?"

"Why don't you think about that yourself? Why would I lie to you when I've got nothing to gain from it?" She slumped down to sit on the floor, careful not to touch the edges of the circle. She would have been just out of his line of sight if he'd had functional eyes.

"YOU TRY TO TRAP ME IN SNARLS OF LOGIC, BUT I REMEMBER YOU WELL IONA SULLIVAN," he raged. "I REMEM-BER THE PRICE YOU EXTORTED FOR MY FREEDOM. MY VERY BEING WAS RENT. MY STUFFING POPPED OUT."

Sully let out a snort of laughter. "I'm sorry, but your stuffing?!"

"THE VERY FABRIC OF MY BEING WAS—"

He was interrupted by Sully's cackling.

The pedestal rocked from side to side. "DID MY AGONY AMUSE YOU THEN, AS IT DOES NOW?"

Sully actually had to wipe a tear from the corner of her eye. "Oh, will you lighten up? You're an all-powerful demon trapped in a cuddly toy. It's funny."

"I FAIL TO SEE THE HUMOR IN THE SITUATION."

"I know." Sully snorted. "That's half of what makes it funny."

"THE AGONIES THAT YOU SHALL SUFFER AT MY HANDS WHEN I AM FREED FROM THIS CIRCLE WILL BE THE HORRORS OF LEGEND. YOUR STILL-LIVING SKIN SHALL BE A TAPESTRY UPON THESE WALLS. YOUR STILL-BEATING HEART SHALL BE—"

"Will you give it a rest?" Sully snapped. "This is as bad as it gets for you. They are going to sell you to the highest bidder, then that highest bidder is going to trade you your freedom for a wish. Then you are going to go home and neither one of us will see the other ever again. If you give in fast, it will be painless."

There was a positively chirpy edge to Eugene's voice when he replied. "EVEN WITHOUT MY INTERVENTION YOU SHALL SUFFER. OH, HOW YOU SHALL SUFFER. IT MATTERS NOT THAT I AM GONE. WHOEVER PURCHASES YOU WILL PUNISH YOU IN WAYS THAT EVEN I COULD NOT IMAGINE. EVERY MOMENT OF YOUR BRIEF FUTURE SHALL BE PAIN. THERE COULD BE NO MORE FITTING END FOR YOU."

"Or I can bust us both out of here, send you home, and neither of us needs to get tortured to death."

There was another long pause as the guard passed by again, nodding politely to Sully. "IT WOULD IRK ME TO WIELD MY POWER IN THE SERVICE OF MEN ONCE MORE. PARTICULARLY THOSE TINY MEN WHO THINK THAT THEIR SCRABBLING ACCUMULATION OF SHINY THINGS ENTITLES THEM TO RULE."

Sully had to bite her lip to hold in the laughter this time. "So what, you consent to my rescuing you?"

"I DO." Eugene intoned. "IF YOU SOMEHOW UNCOVER A MEANS TO RESCUE YOURSELF FROM CONFINEMENT FIRST."

Sully grinned. "Why don't you let me worry about that?"

When there was no further provocation, she settled herself more comfortably on the floor and dug out her phrase book to help pass the time. There didn't seem to be a section for vicious threats, so she went over "business language" again, on the premise that it was probably the closest.

JUNE 6, 1911

Beyond the great barrier there was a living darkness. Not the simple absence of light, but a roiling desperate absence of everything that pressed and writhed constantly against the transparent dome of the ancient spell. There were tides to oblivion. The nothingness swept over Atlantis in waves, still trying after all of these years to blink it out of existence. It was like living at the bottom of the ocean, having that great pressure above you, always grinding down, desperate to get in but never quite succeeding.

At a glance, the Atlanteans looked little different from the human vermin that had overrun the world in their absence. Their skin came in a wider variety of tones perhaps, and the additional eyes on both their forehead and the nape of their neck certainly helped to differentiate them, but unlike their vile eternal enemies, they were almost entirely corporeal and fixed in form. Up close, the differences grew more conspicuous. Their skin had a rubbery, cetacean quality to it and the colors beneath that surface flickered and changed with their moods and whims. The superfluous eyes had always been the easiest way to spot them when they traveled the mainland, impossible to hide no matter how many intricate glamours were laid upon them. These eyes were crystals set in their flesh where the humans and the enemy had gelatinous orbs, and light ever emanated from within, a hint of the immense power contained within these simple forms.

Theirs was the language of magic, the language of creation that all other mortal tongues were bastardized corruptions of. They could speak their will into being just as readily as they could carve it into the raw core of reality with spellfire. When voices were raised in Atlantis, it was cause for concern.

Every family in Atlantis was of blood so royal it set them far above the common rabble beyond their shores, but even among their most excellent lineages, some rose above, scions of ancient lines that had ruled over the earth since driving the dragons and the demons out. They were the wellspring from which all magic on earth had been drawn, the deepest root of Atlantis's wide-spanning family trees. Those scions stood now, looking out upon the barrier that maintained their existence, not with awe and respect for the craftsmanship, but with contempt.

"If only someone competent had been in charge," Estria of House Pheonides proclaimed. It was a sly jab at the antecedents of House Aorta, who had ruled over Atlantis in the days preceding their attempted annihilation.

Aeserius of House Callutian interceded before any of the Aortans could start sniping back. "The study of the High Art was not so far advanced in those days, so we must not judge those who came before on the standards of our mastery."

A particularly fierce wave of oblivion broke above them, setting the sky of their world vibrating for one awful moment among a million others. The song of their sky had been a lullaby to each of the Atlanteans in their youth, but now that they were old enough to understand the meaning of each whine, it kept them awake instead. How could anyone sleep knowing what hung above them?

At last Vasarian of House Aorta spoke. "The Art is advanced now, far beyond what anyone might have ever dreamed. All credit to House Callutian for their endless studies. All credit to House Pheonides for the maintenance of our barrier, so that those turned inward had the time required to reach this point in their progression."

That was a gentle rebuff wearing the robes of a compliment, a reminder to Estria that their family's place as caretakers of the barrier made them little higher than the servitor street sweepers that were called up from the sandstone on demand. The hierarchy of the noble families of Atlantis had complexities that would have taken several human lifetimes to fully comprehend. Fortunately, longevity was one of their many natural gifts.

Vasarian pressed on, carefully allowing a flicker of pink pleasure to run the length of their exposed skin. "The Ancient and Noble House of Callutian has long guided our efforts to reverse the cataclysm that left us stranded on these shores of infinity, and it is with great pleasure that I can now repeat to all of you the joyous information that was passed into my care only a short time ago. Our troubles with the geometry of our situation has ever been rooted in the lack of any solid metaphysical ground upon which to balance the levering forces that would return us to the world. So it is that Callutian proposes that we reach out instead to the prime plane from which we were cast, and finding some influence there, apply force from that direction."

"Ally ourselves to the humans? This idea is beneath contempt." With charm and finesse like that, it was little surprise that House Balora was the least respected among the gathered company.

"It may have escaped the notice of House Balora, but the situation on this island of ours is tenuous. Unless a more permanent solution is devised, the barrier will one day fall and all the ancient and noble houses of Atlantis will fall along with it."

Before there could be any more sniping comment, Estria cut in, clearly intrigued. "What plan has been devised to secure us this foothold?"

"Through no small loss of life and sanity, our void-watchers have succeeded in peering beyond the curse laid upon us to the world beyond. It has been changed and rechanged more times than can be counted since our own fall from grace, but the one constant that remains is that the humans who have learned some scraps of magic from our leavings maintain their dominance over the unenlightened." Aeserius rambled on. "Among their number are some sensitive enough to receive our aetheric communications. Our proposal is to reach out to the most sensitive of these, ply them with knowledge beyond the limitations of their simple understanding of magic's periphery and win them over to our service."

Estria sighed. "Loathe as I am to align my House with Balora for even an instant, they make a valid point about the quality of mankind. Is it not more likely that the apes will simply take all that is offered to them and provide nothing in recompense?"

"With respect to your concerns, what exactly is our alternative? Wait even longer?" Vasarian shuddered, the deep purple of sadness rippling out from around their eyes. "How many millennia must roll by with our entire existence forgotten before we take action?"

"You would give away all that we have earned, all that makes us special in the hope that creatures without empathy or culture will reciprocate with kindness!?" Estria almost hissed the words, but the volume of their conversation was continuing to grow, the ancient words echoing back and forth, trapped beneath the dome of the barrier, creating unforeseen harmonics that spawned sparks and ripples in the air.

When Vasarian next spoke, it was so softly that humans would have had to strain to hear. "If you believe that the new tricks that House Callutian have crafted are the only things that make Atlantis and its people special, then you prove yourself even more of a fool than I took you for."

Silence fell then, and rightly so, for it was never the nature of those who ruled the High Houses to speak so bluntly. It seemed enough to shock even the ever-ready Estria into silence. All the color left them, gradually replaced by the dull gray shades of shame that were seen so rarely among this caste. "You speak truly."

Vasarian did not flush with pleasure. They were not so crass. "I am pleased that you see the truth in my words. Now, what say you all to the plan?"

It was actually the honorable representative of House Balora that spoke first, startling them all. "What have we got to lose?"

JUNE 8, 1911

Madame Blavatski was not young. She had buried three husbands by the time the Great War heated up. The Roman Legions were marching out into Europe with impunity and not a single one of the so-called Great Powers was doing a thing to halt their spread. Blavatski's beloved Prussia had been the latest to fall under the jackboots, and it would not be the last.

She knew all of this, despite being nestled safely in the underbelly of Paris, because each one of those three husbands of hers still came creeping into her chambers at night, whispering their secrets in her ears. She knew all of this because for every soldier that died, another whisper was added to the chorus that dogged her every waking moment, the chorus that burst out screaming in her dreams. She had always been a woman of great sensitivity and unique gifts. Not the showy kind of gifts that would see her co-opted into one of the imperial armies, but a more subtle and lasting kind. Secrets came to her that she had no right to know, and even in a world when words could conjure fire, secrets held their own unique powers.

She had the ear of many generals, and the heads of many states came to call on her when evening fell and she held her salons. Ostensibly, each of them came to play at cards, but they were far more interested in what she could read in those cards than they were in any sort of game. Those thin slips of cardboard held all the secrets of the universe and her head was an empty vessel. Every general left with secrets, of course, some that they could use personally, some that they could share among their comrades to bring even more knocking and nervous champions of freedom to the door of her apartment. Most of all, though, they left with their minds clouded by the wonders that she had shown them, wonders unseen among even the most educated wielders of magic. The conjurations and specters with knowledge that no mere illusion could concoct. It was not much, but it was a living.

The tirade of voices seemed to quiet after one of her salon nights, as though she had released some of the pressure that built up behind her eyes when she let the dead sap her vital fluids and blossom out from her lips. The gatherings were worthwhile for that peace alone, yet it was in that peace that she was now troubled by a singularly clear voice calling out to her as she sat supping on the very fine brandy that a young descendent of Merovech had pressed into her hands in thanks for fair warning about some weak fortifications in Belgium.

Usually, compared to those with news to impart, the dead with questions came through softly. They were the lost and the confused of the afterlife, often drowned out amidst the flood of sound, but this voice wielded its words like a blade, as incisive as a knife set right upon the very edge of Blavatski's mind. "What do you remember of Atlantis?"

AUGUST 5, 2013

It would have been nice if the auction had landed square on midnight, if only for the poetry of it, but it was almost one in the morning by the time that the preferred buyers started to filter in through the stage doors to check out the merchandise. It was a who's who of all the worst people in the world, and Sully couldn't bring herself to be surprised.

Lord Blackwood was the first through the door, a solid five minutes ahead of any of the other big spenders, showing without a doubt that being British nobility still held some weight here in Hong Kong, even if your lines of credit were extended to their limit just getting a portal into town. He caught sight of Sully and strode over to her with a sinister smile spreading across his face. "Now this is just delightful."

"How's unemployment treating you?" Sully grinned right back. Blackwood had been the British Empire's prize demon wrangler; the man that rewrote the world to put his agenda first. With no extra-dimensional monsters available to cut deals with, he had been left virtually useless.

"I'd wager that my retirement is rather more comfortable than yours at the moment." He examined his manicure. "I assume that you were sent as an agent of the American insurgents?"

Sully shrugged. "Yeah, something like that."

"I would double my wager that those people would not pay a fraction of your worth to get you back." He sighed, peering at Eugene with distaste. "Such an emotional people, too blinded by propriety and public relations to recognize the true value of things. Were you a weapon in my arsenal—as you once were and shall doubtless be again soon—I would have treasured you."

"I bet." If Sully rolled her eyes any harder they'd end up on the floor.

"Whatever your masters may have told you about the British Empire, you must admit that you could at least trust in our honesty," Blackwood wheezed. "We would have put you into harm's way, for such is the life of a weapon, but we would not have made you believe that it was your own choice, or that there was some higher ideal involved. They lie to you, Sullivan."

"Of course, they lie to me. They're politicians, that is their job." She met his watery stare. "I'm hurt that you think I'm dumb enough to believe them."

The old man chortled and turned his back. "You always were droll, Sullivan, regardless of your incarnation. Once all has been set to rights, I believe that I shall seek you out for personal protection during my exceptionally well-earned retirement."

"I don't think there is any reality where I don't end up kicking the shit out of you." Sully called after him as he ducked out of the door, "Feel free to look me up!"

There was another lull before the rest of the crowd moved in, during which Sully stumbled to her feet and did her best to make herself presentable. There was the vague possibility that one of the people coming to bid on Eugene didn't want her dead, so it wouldn't hurt to present a good impression.

The crowd that streamed by Sully's circle over the course of the next hour comprised the very best of international scumbags, and every one of them stared at her like they wanted to check her teeth. Sully had been objectified before—men didn't stop being men just because you had no interest in them—but this was the first time she'd ever felt like a literal object. Even when she was in Pratt's grasp during the war, he still treated her like a person. She had expected most of these bidders, so the few completely unfamiliar faces were all the more notable.

She received a long, deep bow from a local vampire boss, his ponytail falling back over a printed silk frock coat instead of the more contemporary European suits that the rest of the gangsters seemed to favor. She couldn't understand a single word that he was hissing to her, but it all seemed pretty civil.

"HE THANKS YOU FOR FREEING HIS PEOPLE FROM THE YOKE OF THE BRITISH."

Sully had almost forgotten that Eugene was there. She rubbed at the back of her neck, then gave a little bow to the vampire. "Uh, you're welcome."

There was a thin man with a well-groomed beard, a shaved pate, and a military bearing striding around, rattling off notes in curt, barking Mongolian to an underling who looked like he should have been in uniform. They wore the next best thing, plain and formally cut gray suits without collars. As he came closer, Sully could see that he was at least half European, and he had a pair of dueling scars hidden in the upper reaches of that beard. A man accustomed to command, he gave Sully a polite nod as he passed without slowing. "Bianpao."

There was that word again. "FIRECRACKER."

"Jesus, are you my full-time translator now?"

"YOUR KIND ONCE USED TINY EXPLOSIVES TO DRIVE EVIL AWAY." Eugene's voice dipped so low that Sully could feel the vibration in the soles of her shoes. "THEY DID NOT WORK."

One of the waiters that had been rushing around fetching cocktails for the attendees had sidled up to Sully's circle while Eugene was speaking. His head was cocked to one side, his hair was hanging loose from where it had been bound back. "OH hoW The miGHty hAVE FALlen."

Sully rolled her eyes. "I thought Manhattan had some class—you're murdering waiters now?"

"We DO wHAt is NECEssaRy, jUSt as We aLWAys HAVe."

"Necessary?" Sully leaned forward until she was nose to nose with the dead waiter. "You know what? I'm glad I killed all your friends. Ogden and the rest of them? They had it coming."

"YOu DAre to spEAK hIS NAme, mUrDeRer?"

"Murderer, is it? I've killed plenty of people in my time, but every one of them deserved it. And there isn't one man who deserved it more than that bitch. What you people did to get back here, that was evil, and I'm going to be glad when every single Magus that decided their life mattered more than the innocent people you slaughtered is dust on the wind, just like him."

The corpse flung itself against the invisible barrier of the circle and exploded on contact with the magic in a blinding flare of light. That was the trouble with the vessels that the necromancers of Manhattan rode around in—they had to be stuffed to the brim with magical energy just to keep them moving. One spark more and they went pop.

When Sully's vision had cleared, there were a lot of men with guns pointed at her. "Don't look at me, I didn't do shit."

There were an exciting couple of minutes as everyone yelled at each other and the Peninsula's pet Magus swung back around to see if the circles were intact, but then the exploding waiter became just another topic of conversation among the guests, a minor curiosity in a night of grander designs.

Still, Sully was amused to find that all of the other buyers were careful not to come any closer to her circle than the black blast mark on the floor. Representatives of a few imperial powers sidled by without a word, diplomats doing their best to pretend that they had never been here before. Dull people doing the boring work of subjugation on a grand scale. For all their faults, at least the Khanate seemed to take pleasure in their attempts to take over the world.

Standing apart from the rest of the diverse crowd were two flamboyant Europeans, performing a complex dance among the milling evening wear, careful to ensure that they never came into contact with one another.

Sully recognized one of them as Augustus Le Plongeon from the photographs in the textbooks that she had once studied in the Imperial College, and reread during her long period of recovery as she tried to get a modicum of her old magic back. Like most heavy magic users, his aging had slowed to a crawl but even with that assistance, streaks of gray were starting to show in his ponytail, and his elaborate silk scarves were creeping higher and higher to conceal the wrinkles around his neck. Sully was surprised that he was still around; she hadn't heard of any publications from him in decades and for someone who loved attention as much as Le Plongeon, silence usually signaled death.

When he spotted her, he flounced across the room with a wry grin as though she was an old friend. "Madame, it is a pleasure to finally meet with you. If time and fortune allow, I would love to discuss your advances in evocation before we go our separate ways. I must admit with some shame that I never even attempted to solve the Dante's Inferno formula, thinking it fundamentally flawed. You have shown me that the impossible is but a stretch of the mind away, and for this I am in your debt."

"Get me out of here and we'll call it even."

"Hah, very good, Madame. Very good. Have no fear, I shall be bidding upon you heavily when the time comes." Even the curt little bow he gave her managed to be flamboyant. "Assuming that my patron allows for such fripperies."

That was one of them dealt with, and with a crushing inevitability, the other followed soon after, terrified of being left out of the loop. Madame Blavatski wore huge round sunglasses and a fur coat so voluminous it looked like it was consuming her. Beyond the fur, her skin was pasty and deeply lined from a lifetime of sneering. The only point in her favor was that she was shorter than Sully—something of a rare treat.

Blavatski had been a famed demonologist in her day, responsible for some of the most horrific works of the Great War, at least indirectly. After the fall of Europe, there had been a mad rush by all parties to recruit her, but instead she had ostensibly retired to life as a private tutor in the Nordic Kingdoms. There had never been a clear understanding of the limits of the old woman's power, though it was known that she could duel Magi to a standstill if she were pushed.

"The others, they are simple. Humans. They see no deeper than the skin." Her voice was incongruously rich and throaty.

Sully tensed.

"I know you for what you are, Cambion. Your deceptions may serve you well against these blind fools but I am not so blind as you might think."

"YOU MUST KILL HER."

Sully kept her teeth carefully gritted together. She was not going to respond, not going to draw attention to herself.

"The demon in the doll, this is interesting but it is not new. It has been studied by many. It is a simple tool now. A lever." Blavatski lowered her glasses and let her milky white eyes rake over Sully. "But you, darling, you are a first. Unique. What I wouldn't give to find out how you look under the deceptions."

Many people had stared at Sully, imagining what she would look like with no clothes on—some of those people had even found out—but this was the first time that she could remember somebody staring at her and wondering what she would look like with no skin on.

"Alas, it is not my largess that I am here to spend. I come only in service of my benefactor, and they are very particular about their requirements. All I can do is hope that you fall into my hands when the auction is through."

Sully had to suppress a shudder at the thought. Images of vivisections and agonizing binding spells fluttered through her mind unbidden. No matter what else happened, she had to make sure she didn't end up going home with Blavatski. If Blavatski went home in a box, that would be an even better outcome.

The remaining crowd started to thin after a while, the guests filtering out to their seats in the gaping darkness of the auditorium beyond. Eventually there were just a few stragglers from the Caliphate arguing about the age of the dragon's egg with one of the attendants. The oily manager sidled over to Sully with a smile still plastered over his face. "The auction will begin momentarily, Ms. Sullivan. Can I get you some refreshments, perhaps?"

"Can you tell me which way the wind is blowing?" Sully asked.

That gave him pause. "I beg your pardon?"

"Do you know who is planning on buying what?"

He glanced around to ensure none of the guests were about then replied in a low voice. "Most of our smaller ticket items are being entirely overlooked this evening, when each would typically have seen considerable interest. You and the doll seem to be the sole focus of our guests. He is being favored quite heavily at this point, with bids on you being viewed as a backstop. The intention seems to be to use you as a bargaining chip to influence the winner of the top item."

"I'd complain about playing second fiddle to a cuddly toy, but with this crowd it's probably better not to be the center of attention."

"Hah," he replied without a hint of humor in his voice. After a moment of awkward silence, he sidled over to the dragon's egg to move things along.

Eugene was pressed up against the invisible barrier of his circle, his plush flush against it. "NOW WOULD BE A GOOD TIME FOR YOUR DARING ESCAPE PLAN."

"While everyone is watching us?" Sully tutted. "How far do you think we'd get?"

"WAIT A CENTURY FOR RESCUE, THEN PREACH TO ME THE VIRTUE OF PATIENCE," it growled back.

Another local with a flamboyant coif and a slick black suit strode out onto the stage and a spotlight snapped on to follow him. It robbed Sully of her night vision for an instant as he strode by, but while he went through an unintelligible preamble at the lectern, she managed to blink her way back to a state of equilibrium. She could make out individual factions clustered in the seats, all carefully positioned far enough away from one another that there could be no confusion as to who was bidding. She couldn't have asked for a better view of the action.

Finally, either the auctioneer switched over to English or a translation spell kicked in. "Good evening, ladies, gentlemen, and others, it is with great pleasure that the Peninsula Hotel presents these items for your consideration." He gestured to the circles behind him, and the light danced over each of them in turn. Sully was left blinking and blind all over again.

"In light of the limited interest in them at this time several of the items have been removed from the listings in the interest of brevity. The Aetherially Saturated Biological Specimen has been purchased in a private arrangement by the Mongolian Empire. The Egg of Unknown Provenance has been purchased by private arrangement with the gentlemen of the Caliphate. The other items will be withheld until next month's event."

A second spotlight buzzed to life, affixed on Eugene, in his circle. "Given the rarity of this item, and the inestimable value attached to it, we have appraisers on hand to evaluate any non-traditional bids. Who would like to start us off?"

The babble started almost immediately, with every different person in the crowd bellowing to be heard over the others. The auctioneer sighed and held up his hands. When that had no effect, he began tracing a silencing veil in the air with spellfire. That was enough to catch the crowd's attention. "I understand that there is a great deal of excitement about this item, but please, show some civility. Raise your card if you wish to bid, and you will be heard in turn."

There was more muttering and unmistakable grumbling but the screaming match seemed to have been averted for now. Sully rolled her shoulders and settled her messenger bag back into place on her shoulder. "Get ready."

Blackwood's voice rang out from the shadowed auditorium. "One million pounds in gold bullion."

"We have our starting bid of one million." The auctioneer's smile was plastered back in place. "Do I hear two?"

Blavatski sighed. "Two million, diamonds."

"Three million, gold," Le Plongeon barked immediately at her heels.

The Mongol contingent seemed to have been arguing among

themselves throughout all of this bidding but eventually their leader managed to growl, "Manchuria."

The auctioneer held up a hand for silence, then a quick messaging spell darted over to him from the wings and he nodded. "Due to the recent Nipponese contention for that area, I am informed that we cannot accept that bid. We stand at three."

"Four million in precious stones." That was the vampire boss from earlier. Sully dreaded to think what sort of havoc undead gangsters could unleash with a wish.

"FivE MILLion, aETHeRIc CRYStaLs." Funny how after all this time, those mangled voices could still make Sully's skin crawl.

Another long pause and another flicker of magic punctuated the bid before the auctioneer nodded. "We stand at five million from the Magi of Manhattan."

There was a murmur among the buyers. Apparently, the Manhattanites' presence hadn't been noticed before. Maybe Blavatski wasn't as all-knowing as she thought she was.

"Malta." That was Blackwood's voice. Sully hadn't realized that the British had any of their imperial holdings left. She thought for sure that local nation states would have gobbled up the free territories. That was concerning. The island fortress of Malta was in striking distance of both Ophir and the new settlements that were springing up in the ruins of Europe.

The backstage team seemed to be getting their act together. The auctioneer was nodding almost as soon as the murmurs following Blackwood's bid quieted down. "We are taking that bid at an assessed value of 20 million."

The Mongol general slapped one of his underlings into silence, then roared, "Taiwan."

"The bidding now moves beyond cash value, and stands at the island of Taiwan."

Blavatski popped to her feet, far faster than you might have expected a woman of her girth to move. "Iceland."

"We have a bid of Iceland."

Le Plongeon was flummoxed for only a moment before he cried out. "Goethe's Transubstantiation."

The increasingly distressed auctioneer was interrupted by Blavatski's hissing. "You bastard, you had it all of this time?"

"The bid stands at Goethe's infamous Transubstantiation spell."

Breaking free of his wrestling aide, the Mongol bellowed, "Siberia!"

Sully shook her head. She was getting too caught up in the drama of the auction, and it was distracting her from the task at hand. Whatever guards were on duty were hidden out of sight so that they didn't interfere with the ambience. They were trusting in their Magus's circles to keep Eugene and her in line. She couldn't really fault them for that, the circles were expert work. Even when she'd been at the top of her game, she doubted she could have come up with a better containment circle, and hers had held demons the size of trucks without difficulty. She almost felt bad for the staff Magus, putting in all that work for nothing.

As far as escape routes went, she had seen entrances on each side of the stage and she suspected there was another one behind the drapes at the back, but she didn't want to bet her life on it. The real decision was between running across the length of the stage to get to the corridor that she'd come in by and memorized, or taking the closer option of the door beside her, which could lead damn near anywhere.

Out in the auditorium, strange bedfellow alliances were being hastily forged between the different bidders. Le Plongeon and Blackwood were pooling their humbler resources to try to match the bids of the bigger empires. Blavatski had responded by allying with the Manhattanites, whose arcane resources complimented her exotic object bids nicely. The Mongol empire, with their ridiculously deep pockets in terms of real estate, were offering up increasingly huge portions of the Orient to keep up. The battle lines may have seemed like they were being drawn in almost random places but it all came down to the wishes in the end. Some wishes could coexist quite easily in the same reality, while others were direct contradictions.

That was why Sully felt certain Mongolia was going to lose out in the end—they couldn't compromise with the others, not when they were going to be wishing for total global domination. Nobody else would agree to those demands.

The vampires had gotten up and calmly left some time during the escalation. Apparently a local crime cartel couldn't compete with global superpowers when it came to throwing resources around.

"WHATEVER YOU HAVE PLANNED. NOW IS THE TIME TO ACT."

Sully shook her head and was surprised at the heat that crept into her voice. "You don't know these assholes like I do. Every one of these pricks thinks they're the king of the world. They're babies that never learned how to share. The minute that it looks like they aren't going to get their way—"

"WE biD thE SurvIVAL of EVEryone IN ThiS ROom." The voices echoed out from all around the darkened edges of the auditorium. The hidden guards stepped out into the light, their bodies limp and ungainly under the control of the Magi of Manhattan, but still capable enough of using the Gatling rifles that they held ready in their hands.

Sully rolled her eyes. "There it goes."

The Mongolian aides were on their feet with guns drawn before the pronouncement of their doom was even complete. Their leader had some sort of rustic animal talisman clutched in one hand and spellfire trailing out of the other. Blavatski and Le Plongeon had separately activated what looked to be exactly the same contingency spells and were wrapped in flickering shrouds of colored lights. Blackwood had dived for the floor, cured of any shred of dignity that he might have retained after his wartime confinement. Everyone was glaring at everyone else, summoning their power, readying their weapons.

Sully carefully touched the Cold Iron of her ring to the magic circle, then crawled out. Bullets started to fly, the shouting turned into screaming and incantations. She scrambled forward and repeated the same gentle touch with Eugene's circle, reaching up with her stump to knock him off his pedestal and onto the floor, then scooping him up and making a wild sprint for the more distant of the doors.

The doll's body was rigid and silent until she tucked him under her arm. Then Eugene groaned, "YOU ARE DERANGED."

Sully let out a loud bark of laughter. It wasn't like anyone was going to hear them over the rattle of the guns. The corridor had been emptied of any lurking guards by the Manhattan Magi's hijacking, so Sully had a clear run through the service side of the hotel until she plowed headlong into the oily manager as he came sprinting out of a crossing corridor. "You!"

"Me!" Sully shouted gleefully as she hammered her fist into his temple. He went down like a house of cards and she kept on rolling.

From under her arm, Eugene growled, "IONA SULLIVAN, WHERE DO YOU PLAN TO TAKE ME?"

"It's kind of a moving target. I'm less interested in where we are running to and more interested in what we are running from."

The staff Magus was standing between Sully and the open door to the world outside, peacefully puffing something noxiously green in a long clay pipe and staring off into space. The Magus turned her doleful eyes toward the sound of approaching footsteps and for one long glorious moment Sully thought that the brain scrubbing had been so extensive that she was just going to let them pass without a fight. Then the Magus flicked her wrist and a dart of vibrant aquamarine light shot out at Sully's chest. She managed to get Eugene up to block it just in time. The doll yelped. "WHAT ARE YOU DOING?"

Sully ducked under the next flurry of darts with a cackle. "If you don't eat your magic, you'll never grow up to be a big strong demon."

Each one of the Magus's spells was exquisitely crafted, just as the circles had been, but each one ran into the same unpassable shield of Sully's plush little doll. Eugene was leaking light from his seams by the time Sully had closed the distance.

With a grunt, she took the Magus down with a cross to the jaw, her fist passing effortlessly through all the magical shields that the younger woman had flung up. Sully didn't even have time to stop and gloat—there were shouts and the unmistakable sounds of Gatling guns spinning into action behind her. She dived out into the cool night and ran for her life.

JULY 13, 1977

The void was no problem as long as nobody ever looked up. The forest was still glorious and bountiful. The beasts and the flowers still grew as rich and wild as ever. There remained an infinity of forms that each one of the Lemurians could take on as easily as thinking. They had no time to wallow in self-pity or fear when there was still so much to experience. Mu moved gracefully through the trees, face almost human so that she could enjoy the play of colors and light, but body almost entirely feline. In the beginning they had committed fully to each form, devoted to seeing the world as others could see it, but now what had seemed their duty faded in significance in the face of hedonism. Why be less when they were so much more? A living creature may have been more than the sum of its parts, but the Lemurians were free to pick and choose which parts to add together.

Since their fall into the darkness, life had become a kaleidoscope of forms. Each one drawing closer and closer to the oblivion of non-sentience. Even now, Mu was toying with it. The sweet silencing of all thoughts. The purity of just existing without the great sorrow of all that they had lost. When the last of them succumbed to it, there would be nobody left to reinforce the barrier and it would crumble under the weight of the wish outside sweeping over the whole island and blinking them all out, and they would be none the wiser. Could there be any greater bliss than to forget the inevitable?

As she broke free of the tree-line Mu grew a wingspan as wide as she had been long a moment before, furnishing it with feathers and leather in eloquent patterns that the buzzing insects around her could never appreciate. They dipped in and out around her as she rose, trying to suck at her blood and finding nothing but the same tasteless ectoplasm that composed her entire body. She could feel those parts of her being still flitting around once they had been drawn, she could call them back with a flex of her awareness, absorb the biomass of the bugs to add them to her own, but she would not. She had no right to rob them of their fleeting existence, and there was some pleasure to be found in spreading out across the island in tiny motes of self. She imagined that it was how death would feel, if it ever came.

Rising up above the treetops, Mu manifested more and more eyes to take in the entirety of her world. From up here near to the crackling dome the whole expanse of Lemuria stretched out, from coast to coast. Once it had seemed like a whole universe of new experiences but now it was shockingly small. She had been everywhere. Seen everything. Perhaps forgetting it all was the best choice.

Her eyes began to flutter shut, sealing up as they closed. She couldn't bear to see it for a moment longer. She dimmed her vision and turned her attentions inward. The feeling of the wind on her wings. The memory of endless skies to soar through. The sun on her back. Light.

It was all ancient history now. So far back that Mu was not even sure how much of it had been real and how much her own fevered imagination. That was all that was left to them, memories and this short stretch of dirt. Oblivion beckoned, both above and within. It would be so easy to let it all go, to wipe away all that she had been, to let the Atlantean bastards win.

She moved to seal up her final eye when something caught her attention on the shoreline. A shimmer of light, where once there had been only the gray sand. Change. Change had been their god when Lemuria was still in the world and change was what had been stolen from them. It had been so long since anything changed. Perhaps one of her kin had found some new transformation and this spike of excitement would ebb away to nothing, but in those brief moments before the nothing, she knew there would be bliss.

In her haste she shed too much of her wingspan and nearly clipped the tops of the withered palms. Every mistake had been worn away by repetition, so even this accident thrilled Mu. Pain flared through her hindquarters and it was a rare treat before she nullified it and closed her wounds. She landed in a tumble on the beach, reveling in the grating of the sand across her skin. The light came from what was unmistakably a human. It pulsed within this strange man, illuminating the tangled jellyfish of his nervous system with each flare.

"Is this Atlantis?"

It took time for Mu to understand the vibrations of the air against her skin, and longer yet for her to manifest a voice of her own, but when she did her voice came out of her in a growl. "Atlantis did this to us. If you are a friend to Atlantis, I will render the fat from your body and make it into a candle."

The specter jerked up his hands. "No. No. There is no need for that! They are my enemy as surely as they are yours."

"No. Not as surely. Since the sun first rose, they have set themselves against us. Since before your kind came down from the trees, we have waged our war. They are the enemy of all life, and there can be no enemy of theirs greater than Lemuria."

He backpedaled until he was standing atop the surf. Now that she was closer, Mu could make out more details of this man. His hair was long, pulled back into a tail, and he had garbed himself in scarves of silk atop strange garments that Mu could not recognize. Human fashions had never interested her. "I meant no offense, Madame. No offense at all. I come to offer my services in your conflict, that is all. Atlantis has allied itself with my oldest and dearest enemy, and I wish only to provide you with a similar opportunity."

"What use could we have for a human? You are weak. Mortal." As she spoke, she straightened up into a new form. Taller and more imposing, sleek and shimmering. The monkeys were easily impressed. "There is nothing that you can offer us."

"Well, Madame, that is not strictly true. If we were so powerless, why do you think that Atlantis came crawling to that bitch Blavatski for help? Most members of the human race, I will concede, lack anything that makes them at all special, but I am quite another case entirely."

She loomed over him, and to his credit he did not flinch back this time. "What is it that you can do that is so special it was worth troubling me?"

"Why, Madame, in addition to my natural talents as a sorcerer, I am a medium by trade, just as surely as that charlatan Blavatski. But while she is possessed of luck and the womanly skill of listening to the conversations of the disembodied, I have been granted by fate the highest of the intermediator's gifts."

"Spit it out. What do you offer us?"

The shimmering projection could not sweat, for it had no skin, but the pulsing of the nerves grew rapid and irregular as panic took hold of the coward's heart. "Only the provision of your greatest desire, Madame. I can bring you back into the world."

AUGUST 5, 2013

By all rights, it should have been easier to get lost in the streets of Hong Kong. Yes, she had red hair, which was a little unusual, and yes, she was a grown woman carrying a doll, but in the throbbing mob, that shouldn't have mattered. She should have blended right into the mass of bodies. The shouting men with guns, hot on her heels, seemed to disagree.

The first problem was that the crowds were too thin around the Peninsula Hotel. The shadow of the fortress across the water still hung long over these streets no matter how brightly the inhabitants lit them up with neon, and while it might not have had the raw arcane revulsion of the Black Bay back home, the ghost of the British Empire seemed to be enough to put most of the locals off lingering around here like they had by the docks. Sully still hadn't been able to parse Hong Kong's attitude toward the British, and she hoped to be long gone before she had the time to sit still and work it out properly.

The crowd might have been thin here, but it was still enough to make the pursuing guards hesitate. They didn't want to indiscriminately slaughter bystanders, meaning that they were about eight steps up from the usual scum that Sully had to deal with. She'd do her best not to kill any of them if she had the choice. "THEY ARE GOING TO CATCH US."

Sully ducked a pot shot. It rang off a street sign. "Well, why don't you do something about it? What happened to you? You had a reputation as some big-shot malevolent mass murdering mannequin. Where is that when we need it?"

"I CAN AFFECT THE WORLD ONLY GRADUALLY. THE MAGIC IN THIS REALM IS TOO THIN FOR ME TO DO MORE. IT CAN TAKE DAYS FOR MY WILL TO BE WROUGHT." Sully didn't reply. Without the overwhelming crowds of the inner city, cars were flying along these streets with reckless abandon. No law meant no speed limits. But Sully could work with that.

As reckless as the drivers were, they still swerved to avoid her when she dashed out into the shared turning lane in the middle of the street. The air was full of the stink of burning rubber and the shriek of brakes, but even so, the cars didn't slow, just swerved around each other to keep roaring on.

Sully had a clear run along the street and they would have to be mad to follow her, but whatever qualms they'd had about firing into the local pedestrians didn't seem to apply to traffic. The next burst of bullets riddled the car up ahead, setting it fishtailing off at high speed. Sully skidded to a halt. With a ragged breath, she gasped, "Didn't I just pump you full of half a dozen spells?"

"THAT . . . IS A VALID POINT."

Demons used magic in a very different way from humans. There were no spells for them to cast, just a natural and implicit understanding of the way that reality could be rewritten to suit their desires. Working together in one great gestalt of raw power, demons could change the whole universe. The Fae had used magic the same way when Sully fought them, as easily as thinking.

Sully could only remember being in the room once when a wish was granted, right at the end of the war with the Fae, and it pressed up hard against the jagged static in her mind full of things that must not be remembered, but it had felt something like what happened now when Eugene flexed his power.

Time wound down to a crawl. The bullets in the air were buzzing bees. The blurs by either side of Sully slowed into cars. It was easy for her to see everything as it happened. A flashy convertible blew a tire. Careened out of control. Missed Sully by an inch. Hit the oncoming traffic with a deafening crunch. Flipped into the air. Sully could see the driver's mouth stretching into a silent scream as the car made one full rotation in the air before coming down on top of the clustered Peninsula guards with a sound that she could only describe as a splat. Time kicked back into gear at about the same moment that the screaming started. "Holy shit. Remind me to never piss you off."

Eugene rumbled, "WE ARE SEVERAL YEARS TOO LATE FOR THAT WARNING," but he sounded content and smug, so Sully didn't worry about it too much.

With the immediacy of the chase forestalled, Sully had time to realize how sore her legs were from all of that running. She had never been big on running before the war, preferring to stand her ground and die rather than risk anybody thinking that she was afraid of them. Maybe her running was a sign that she was maturing as a person. She was still painfully exposed as she made her way back across the now halted traffic and pressed back into the gathering mob on the pavement. The Peninsula guards had always been the least of her worries. Once everyone in the auction realized that Eugene was somewhere in the city, up for grabs, there was going to be a bloodbath. The next time that she felt like she could take a decent breath was when she found an open-air market and a decent crowd to sink into. Without remorse, she crammed her sweat drenched suit jacket into a trashcan and bought a camel trench coat for a couple of pounds, followed by a wide brimmed hat to keep her hair under wraps and a cup of coffee that tasted like burned water but brought a ghost of life back to her aching body.

She kept Eugene nestled against her side, hidden under the new jacket, but now that they had a moment to speak, she pressed herself into a piss-reeking doorway and lifted a lapel. "You doing all right down there?"

"ALL OF THE PORNOGRAPHY DID NOTHING TO PREPARE ME FOR THE HEAT AND AROMAS OF BEING PRESSED INTO THE SOFT FLESH OF A HUMAN WOMAN."

Sully's jaw flexed. "Who knew that genderless hell-spawn would still be misogynist pigs?"

"PERHAPS I WOULD BE MORE DISCREET IF YOU TUCKED ME UNDER YOUR SHIRT ALSO." It was hard to tell when a demon was making a joke. Intonation didn't work the same when you had a voice like somebody gargling screaming locusts.

Meanwhile, her own frosty tone was pretty easy to read across species lines. "There is still plenty of time to drop kick you into the water."

"AT LEAST IN THE OCEAN THE TIDE WOULD CARRY ME AWAY. ALL THAT YOU ARE DOING IS DRAGGING ME AROUND IN CIRCLES. WHERE WOULD YOU HAVE US GO NEXT?"

"We need to get off the streets, lay low for a bit before we make a break for the docks. The buyers from the hotel will be out in force, but Hong Kong doesn't have cops or local government for them to rope in to search for us." Sully smirked. "Plus, old rich people get tired pretty easily. I figure we can just wait out their first burst of flailing and get to a boat before they get a second wind."

"AND WHERE PRAY TELL, SHALL WE DO OUR WAITING?"

She shrugged. "The pub, obviously."

Sully was a stranger in a strange land, and wearing the Cold Iron ring she had neither translation spell nor guide to help her navigate the intricate warren of backstreets and alleyways that seemed to make up the majority of Hong Kong's real estate. Heading out from the market led to one dead end after another. Mesh fences. Elevated walkways and locked gates. No wonder everyone flooded through the main streets when even the most obvious-seeming shortcut could turn into a barricade without a moment's provocation. At first Sully thought that the stuttering of time was just a symptom of being lost, that her perception of wandering aimlessly was stretching some moments out and condensing others, but when she kicked a can and it spiraled across the alleyway in slow motion, she realized that something was up. Eugene was dragged out by his hair. "What are you playing at?"

When it was surprised, Eugene defaulted to his old habit of playing possum, so that Sully looked very much like a lunatic shouting at an actual doll. She gave Eugene a couple of shakes, then it finally replied sheepishly, "THERE ARE A TANGLE OF WISHES AROUND YOU. VISIBLE NOW THAT YOU ARE NOT SHROUDED BY THE COLD ONE'S TOUCH. I WAS TRYING TO DECIPHER THEIR PURPOSE."

"Oh, is that all?" Sully rolled her eyes. "The British tried to wish me away a half-dozen times, my mother wished something on me when I was just a kid to block that from working, I'm pretty sure I made a wish myself before the Fae all exploded, and I'm damn sure a few other assholes have flung some changes on me that didn't stick over the years. Don't worry about it."

"YOU ARE AT THE NEXUS OF A WARP IN FATE AND YOU TELL ME NOT TO WORRY ABOUT IT?"

"Worrying won't change it." Sully shrugged. "Eyes forward."

Now that she knew what was happening, the changing tides of time became less disconcerting. She never really expected Eugene to stop poking at her just because she said so, and throwing a tantrum wasn't going to help anyone. She just kept on moving, letting her feet take her where they wanted and trying to ignore the insistent tugging as Eugene tried to pull her in the direction of whichever destiny someone else had tried to attach to her. She had almost convinced herself that its efforts would come to nothing when, in some out of the way, near pitch black alley, they came across a neon sign in the shape of fish and the familiar sound of adults trying to drink enough to forget their responsibilities. Just the kind of port that she wanted to wait out this storm.

Blinking to adjust her eyes to the darkness as she pushed through the beaded curtain on the door, it took her a moment to get the lay of the land. The same neon fish was stretched above a mirror-backed bar that was so well stocked with liquor there was scarcely room for a reflection. The few tables crammed into the lounge were full of vampires and their donors, all wearing either evening wear or clothing that should never have left the bedroom. It would have been scandalous in New Amsterdam but it seemed completely normal in this context.

Sully kept her eyes down and turned toward the bar. She didn't want to do anything to draw attention to herself. If she could prop herself up in a corner and nurse a few beers through to morning, she might just survive.

The hubbub of the room had fallen silent for a moment as she walked in, but it was almost back to normal by the time that she got to the bar itself, once she'd shown that she didn't have a thing to say to anybody about anything. It really looked like she was going to be all right, until a very familiar voice shouted out. "Sully!?"

The years might have been moderately kind to Sully thanks to her magic, but they had done absolute wonders for Marie. She had always been the most beautiful woman in the world to Sully's eyes, but all of these years without sunlight had made her into something else entirely. Something ethereal. Her blonde curls had lightened until they were almost white. Her freckles had become the only distraction in a sea of creamy skin. The floral dresses that had populated her wardrobe since before the two of them could even afford a wardrobe were gone, replaced with a slick red silk number that made Sully's mouth dry up. At the center of it all, Marie's eyes were wide with shock, her scarlet mouth hanging open in surprise, showing just the faintest hint of fang.

All of Sully's plans had just fallen apart and she was nothing more and nothing less than completely delighted. A grin spread across her face. "Hey, sweetheart. Did you miss me?"

Gormlaith did not trust the demon, and the demon did not trust her. Through her own dealings with the hell-born, the old woman had learned how emotional and unpredictable the hulking beasts could be. Gormlaith did not trust anyone, of course, but this demon seemed particularly deserving of her mistrust.

All that she wanted to do was to care for Little I with the very generous pension that the Americans were providing. She wanted to enjoy her retirement from political life now that the British were gone. She had earned it, after a lifetime of service to her country. Yet every time that she turned around, the great black crow seemed to have its spider-clustered eyes fixed on her. Judging her.

It was no surprise that the demon did not trust her, not really; it was Iona's beast, through and through. While Gormlaith had taken a more pragmatic view, Mol Kalath had taken Iona's sacrifices on behalf of the cause very personally. It felt that a debt was owed to her. A debt that Gormlaith was not fulfilling. But what could she do, beyond what she had already done? She had healed her daughter's burns and given her shelter so that her mind might heal. She had told all the stories that she knew of Iona's life abroad, omitting the parts that might make her hostile. It was more honesty than the little bitch was due after the way she had discarded her own mother and her own people.

If things had been different, if Gormlaith's goals had not already been accomplished, then this would have been a perfect opportunity for her. Little I was soft and malleable now, in desperate need of care, comfort, and guidance. She could have been reshaped into the perfect tool with just a few well-placed lies. The holes in Iona's memory were big enough to hold a million deceptions without contradiction—her re-creation now would be better than her first childhood. The pain had broken her of her willful ways.

Even now, Gormlaith could have set Iona to a purpose if it wasn't for the damned bird. The girl was brimming over with magic after her journey beyond earth, warping everything around her when her emotions became too fraught. If that energy could have been channeled somewhere, it would have been a great asset. Instead Gormlaith had to watch, day after day, as Iona lounged around, staring into space, useless.

Trudging out along the well-worn paths to the stone circle, Gormlaith was almost spitting with rage at the unfairness of it all. The rain came down in a gentle drizzle, soaking through her shawls and trickling down her neck. She watched her step as she went, careful of the snakes in the undergrowth and the water hidden on either side beneath a thin layer of silt and filth. A thousand pairs of shoes or more had been worn out walking this very path, but her eyes never lifted. She was no fool to trust to memory alone.

Half of the stones were gone now, and the other half were blackened and crumbling. Even the oldest stone could not withstand the power of her daughter's magic when it was fully realized in flame. The magic that Gormlaith had given her. The gift that was now being squandered.

Gormlaith turned her fuming anger on the stones. Half the circle was already down, but she still wouldn't feel completely settled in her own home until the whole thing was gone. Her hands moved slowly and methodically through the spellforms, tracing a fine line of fire with her fingertip. When the spell took hold, the air thickened between the old woman and the stone, then that tension drew down into a razor thin rope of coiling wind. Gormlaith ratcheted the wind back and forth around the stone, throwing up a cloud of dust and lichen with each groaning twist of her arms. The rain fell heavier now, thick dollops of it spattering off her exposed hands, setting the joints aching as the chill crept inside. She was too old for this. Her daughter should have been doing this for her. Caring for her in her dotage. Wasn't that why people had children?

It had been a good circle, hauled up by druids or worse, long before history was first written, and it had served its purpose well throughout all of her casting years, but now that there were no more deals to make and no more wars to fight, Gormlaith found it discomfiting to have a door to the other planes dangling open a stone's throw from her cottage. There were fundamental rules about magic that she had always believed, the first and foremost among them that no creature from another plane could force its way up onto this one, but she had seen Iona arriving unaided with her own eyes.

There hadn't been a rule that she'd laid down for that girl that hadn't been trampled all over. Sneaking off with the other schoolgirls, caught in their bedrooms or behind the bike-shed, earning lashes and bringing shame on their family's name. Then there had been all the trouble with "borrowed" books, broken chains on the library shelves and corrections scribbled in margins. Too smart for her own good. Always looking past the job in front of her to the reason behind it. Every task the girl had been set turned into a clash of wills. Every question she asked had barbs on the back of it. There had been treachery in her heart long before she stopped answering her mother's letters from university. Long before she signed on with the Navy and spat in Gormlaith's face and left her mother country without a backward glance or a thank you for raising her.

Still, for all of that, she could not understand how the universe itself had shucked all its responsibilities to make sense around the girl. Enough magic concentrated in one place could make rules bend, that was the foundation of spellcasting after all, but not break, never break. Little I had always been a cause for concern, always at the center of Gormlaith's plans and thoughts, but for all of that she had never really feared for the bitter little creature that she had made. Now fear was her constant companion. Not just for the fate that would befall her daughter, who she'd never much cared for, but for the fate that the girl might inflict on her own mother if she ever clawed back some recollection of who she was. Spiteful and vengeful, that had always been Iona's way. More like her mother than Gormlaith would like to admit.

The journey back down to the cottage took even longer than the careful walk out to the dwindling stones. Gormlaith was bone tired after her hours of work, and the rage that had propelled her off into the swamp had simmered down to almost nothing. Anger had always been the flame that kept her engine turning and now she was running on fumes. The British were gone. The Fae were gone. There was nobody left to hate, and Gormlaith hated it. She found herself looking at her blank daughter with envy. Iona had no purpose now that the wars had been fought, but she didn't know that she had lost it. Not like Gormlaith, who felt that loss keenly. They said that ignorance was bliss, but Little I didn't seem blissful. She was troubled for all that she was blank. Her body and her mind had been built for a purpose that now escaped her. It was a fitting end for a weapon, to be punished by being made completely harmless.

Something felt wrong as she approached the cottage, and it took her too long to realize that the oppressive presence of the demon was missing. The great nest it had woven itself from the thatch sat empty and dark atop the mossy old stones. Within the cottage the light of the fireplace danced strangely, casting shadows that seemed to stretch further than the light itself. There was a sound just on the edge of hearing. The thundering of great black wings somewhere out of sight.

Exhausted and old as Gormlaith was, she still ran along that last stretch of path, tripping and stumbling over stones that had been rounded under her own heels through the years. The demon was inside the cottage when she slammed the door open. It had compressed itself in through one of the vine-shrouded windows and now it hung over Iona where she lay, that jagged beak laid out across her breast and those green eyes burning bright with unholy fire.

Gormlaith's hands caught alight just as readily. "Get away from my daughter and out of my house, you filthy bird. I abjure ye. You hear? I abjure ye."

Iona's mouth lay open like she was trapped mid-scream, but it was not her voice that came out of it. "NOT A BIRD."

"I've no care what you be. Whether it be demon or beast or—" Gormlaith's hands were shaking as she traced her spells."

Iona's back arched as the demon's words poured through her. "I AM YOUR DAUGHTER. BORN IN ANOTHER PLACE, BUT HER ALL THE SAME. THIS IS MY HOME SO I CANNOT BE ABJURED."

Gormlaith's curse was forgotten in her rage. "You'll go where I damn well tell you, bird!"

"BARKING ORDERS." Mol Kalath scoffed. "THAT NEVER WORKED WITH IONA EITHER."

"I'm telling you one last time, demon, let my daughter be or I shall slaughter you where you lie."

The flames in the fireplace were buffeted by unseen wings, the light danced on the walls, casting huge, strange shadows. "WE SHALL NOT BE PARTED. MY WORK IS NOT YET DONE."

"Work?" Gormlaith spat, "What are you doing to her?"

"HEALING. THERE ARE PLACES WITHIN HER THAT THE FIRE BURNED AWAY. HOLES IN HER MIND. I HAVE SOME OF THE PIECES THAT BELONG THERE. WHEN WE SHARED OUR MAGIC, SHE LEFT SOME OF HERSELF BEHIND. THAT WAS HOW I KNEW THAT SHE WAS COMING BACK. THAT WAS HOW I COULD SENSE HER PAIN ACROSS THE PLANES. RES-ONANCE. WE ARE ONE AND THE SAME, IONA AND I. EVER HAVE WE BEEN, EVER SHALL WE BE."

"Get out of my daughter's head before I clip your wings, demon. Mol Kalath I name ye. And by that name you shall be commanded. Lift your beak from off her heart and get your arse back out my door."

Crow beak and human lips moved as one. "I AM MOL KALATH NO MORE."

"Whatever you call yourself, if you don't leave my daughter be, I'm going to put you down."

"YOU DARE TO CLAIM MOTHERHOOD EVEN NOW? YOU WHO FORGED A GIRL INTO A WEAPON FOR YOUR OWN WARS? YOU WHO LOVED HER FOR NOT A MOMENT, EXCEPT FOR THAT WHICH SHE COULD DO FOR YOU? YOU ARE NO MOTHER."

For the first time, the demon's words gave Gormlaith pause. Those weren't the words of the demon. That was Iona. The truth that she'd always known but never said. If the demon knew that, if it had told Sully . . . She let her magic die down. "How much does she remember?"

"STILL VERY LITTLE. SHE FEELS IT ALL KEENLY, BUT DOES NOT KNOW WHERE THE FEELINGS ARE ROOTED. SHE IS STILL WHO SHE ALWAYS WAS, BUT DOES NOT KNOW HOW SHE CAME TO BE SO. I CAN GIVE IT ALL BACK TO HER IF YOU WILL LEAVE US IN PEACE. I CAN MAKE HER WHOLE AGAIN. BE HER MOTHER NOW, LET ME HELP HER."

Gormlaith felt the full weight of her age on her back. All the years piled up with the weight of those standing stones out in the marsh. Bent nearly double, she made her aching way across to the fireplace and stared into the dancing flame. She clung to the old piece of weathered wood set above the hearth as a makeshift mantlepiece. It was an elephant's graveyard of knick-knacks and augury bones. A memorial to the life Gormlaith had built here for herself. The pistol was almost invisible among all the rest, buried as it was under a stack of letters. She'd never loved guns—they gave too much power to those who didn't deserve it—but every tool had its time and place, and this relic from the war on the Fae was finally needed.

It wasn't so different from aiming an evocation. Gormlaith just pointed and pulled the trigger.

The slug of Cold Iron hit the demon at the joint between wing and body, sending it tumbling away from Iona. The pressure that had been hanging in the air shuddered and let out in one great gust that set Gormlaith staggering.

Mol Kalath croaked. "NO."

"Oh, yes." She tossed the pistol to the ground with a sneer. "You think I'd have a monster like you lurking around without a way to put ye down? I'm nobody's fool, crow."

Ectoplasm thumped out of Mol Kalath's wound in a flood. A demon's body was held together by magic and with that molten ingot still buried inside it, there was no hope of recovery. "MY DEATH MATTERS NOT AT ALL. SULLY WILL KNOW. SHE WILL BE FREE OF YOU."

"She'll know what I tell her, same as she always has. The demon tried to eat her while she slept. She doesn't remember much of anything these days." Gormlaith stalked closer now, certain of her victory but taking no chances. "She probably won't even know your name when she wakes up. But don't you worry, I'll make sure you're well forgotten."

"Mol Kalath." Iona's eyes snapped open. That was a minor inconvenience. Gormlaith had thought she'd have time to drag the crow corpse out and straighten her story before the girl stirred.

"Don't you worry, Little I. That beast'll trouble ye no more."

The pressure that had vanished when the demon had been separated from Iona thumped back into the room, driving Gormlaith to her knees. Such power. She couldn't wait to harness it. Iona hissed as she rose, "What did you do?"

"What needed done, my love, the demon was feeding on you. Sucking away your—"

Gormlaith's jaw cracked. Her bones were old and brittle anyway but even if she'd been young nothing could have held off the vice-like grip of Iona's magic. First the jawbone cracked, then it was crushed. Teeth and blood showered down her front and she let out a squeal. Iona didn't even bother to look back at her as the agony swept in. Scrambling over the demon instead, fingers smoothing feathers and hunting for the injury.

"COLD IRON. IT IS TOO LATE SULLY."

Little I had always had a stern face to her, never letting any of her feelings show. It was one of the few things that had come naturally to her that Gormlaith was actually proud of, but since she'd come back, that had gone to hell, too. Iona was sobbing as she dug her fingers past the gushing ectoplasm. "It isn't too late. Don't say that. It is never too late. I can fix you. I can save you."

"IT IS OVER. SUBMIT TO IT."

Iona dug her fingers and then her whole hand into the gushing wound, pushing against the tide and hunting frantically for the bullet. It wouldn't matter. The demon was done. Its body was already turning to mush from the inside out.

When Iona's fingers found the bullet, the pressure in the air dropped away once more. Gormlaith could move again. She felt her bladder loosen as the ache rushed down through her body, but it was just pain, it would pass. Iona would heal her jaw and set things right once this last tantrum was done. Iona sat frozen, up to the elbow in the demon's side. Her face had gone blank and empty at the Cold Iron's touch, whatever memories she had stitched together from the demon lost along with her magic. Daft girl. Always poking at things that she shouldn't. Things that didn't concern her.

Gormlaith started the slow painful crawl across the floor, knocking her own teeth aside with her knees as she went. Three hundred years those teeth had lasted her, and now they were in the dust over some stupid bird. Children, who'd have them?

Iona turned to the sound of her movement like she was in a dream, senses wired right to the brain stem, stimulation and response and nothing in between. Gormlaith smirked, maybe she'd stitch that bullet into a collar for the girl, keep her like this forever. It'd be a fitting end for her most disobedient servant to end up a brain-dead slave. Iona's hand slithered out of the forgotten demon as she turned, with a sound not unlike stepping in the swamp. The bullet fell from her limp grip.

When the magic came back, it threw Gormlaith across the room with another wet yelp. She was too old to be tossed around like a rag doll; if it weren't for the pain in her face drowning out all the rest, she'd have been in agony all over.

The magic poured out of Sully in a wave of spellfire, filling up the hole in Mol Kalath's side and washing out over the demon's body. It wouldn't be enough. The demon knew it, too. "IT IS OVER SULLY. MY BODY IS TOO WEAK TO HEAL, NO MATTER WHAT MAGIC YOU FEED ME. I AM DONE."

Iona's fire went out like a pinched candle and she fell to her knees. Sobbing shook her. "You saved me. After everything, you saved me again."

The bird's head fell to one side. The glow in its many eyes was fading. "HOW COULD I NOT, WHEN I KNEW THAT I COULD?"

"Then how could you ask me to stop when I know that I can?" She buried her fingers in the demon's wilting feathers.

"SULLY, NO."

Iona smiled. Gormlaith had never seen her looking so soft. It frightened her. "Yes."

Whatever had been flowing between them when the demon nestled on her daughter like an egg resumed, but where it had been a trickle before, now it became a torrent, a tidal wave. All that Iona had been, all that the demon had been, every part of it was being dragged out and swallowed down. Spellfire bled from Iona's fingertips, from her eyes and the old scars that had long since faded. She was enveloped in fire but still she drank in more of the demon.

Too late, Gormlaith realized what she was seeing. Too late, she tried to crawl across the floorboards and separate the nightmare unfolding ahead of her. It could not be done. No human body could contain the power of a demon, nor any human mind contain the demon's mind, yet hollowed out as Iona was, there was space enough for the two of them inside. She tried to call out to Iona, to stop this madness before it was too late, but she choked on her own blood before she could get out a single word.

The flames rose higher and higher, pooling on the roof, encrusting it in a shimmering crust of crystallized magic and then spreading through the room. Gormlaith crawled toward the door, but battered and bruised as she was, she knew that she had no hope of escaping what was coming. As the crow's body vanished into the blinding light, consumed along with the rest, Iona could no longer contain the magic within her. Gormlaith only heard the start of the explosion before death took her at last.

AUGUST 5, 2013

Sully was so stunned at the sight of Marie that she didn't even notice the vamps flanking her until they were already close enough to make a grab. They didn't, to their credit, but she was getting sloppy, letting her guard down like that. Most of the cold bodies pressing in around her were shaved-headed goons—small fry in organized crime always had a certain blank quality that made Sully feel better about hitting them—but there was one face that was easily recognizable in the mix. The vampire boss from the auction, still looking pristine. He must have come straight here after his failed bid. How did he know she was coming here when she didn't even know she was coming here? He didn't move. That was one of the funny things with vamps, their stillness. Marie only seemed to do it when she was sleeping, but even that had been enough to creep Sully out more than a few times. Standing there like a statue, he started rattling off a long speech in the local language while Sully stared at him blankly.

After a few seconds he seemed to register her vacant expression and fell silent. Very carefully, one of the wait staff approached their little huddle by the door and cast a translation spell on her boss—taking the time to telegraph every single movement of her casting so Sully couldn't mistake it for an attack. They were scared of her. She could work with that. "I must apologize for interrupting your heart-warming reunion, but I believe that we have some business to discuss."

Sully wet her lips, eyes still drifting involuntarily back to Marie. "I don't think so."

"Do not misunderstand me, all that we ask is an audience. If you will hear us out, then you are free to leave afterward." He slowly lifted his empty hands to placate her. "Nobody here wants to fight with you. Nobody here wants another London."

"Listen buddy, the only person I want to talk to in this whole city is my girl . . . my ex . . ."

"Young Marie will of course be welcome to join the conversation, and she may leave with you or remain here afterward as she desires."

It was impolite to argue when the undead gangsters were being so reasonable. They shepherded Sully through to a back room and the sleek gangster settled himself beside a card table covered in green felt and rusty stains. Two chairs were produced for Sully and Marie, and they found themselves sitting side by side in awkward silence. Sully's silence was slightly more awkward because of the stupid demon doll playing possum on her lap. At least it kept him quiet.

There was a daring slit in Marie's dress, running almost all the way up to her hip, and the pale exposed flesh seemed to be radiating a chill toward Sully's more sensible trousers. With some effort, Sully kept her eyes on the mob-boss instead of staring at Marie. If she was being honest, it wasn't just about being polite. Marie had always been a middling actress at best, and Sully wasn't sure if she was ready to see the other woman's undisguised emotions. It had been a long time— even for people who would live forever if somebody didn't murder them first—and that had been plenty of time for Marie to change her mind about waiting for Sully to come back from the war. The fact that she'd fled to the far side of the world and left no forwarding address didn't bode well in that regard.

Once the living bar-staff had delivered what smelled tantalizingly like a gin and tonic in front of Sully, they all retreated against the walls of the room, trying to fade into the background. All attention was on the three people and the child's toy sitting at the table.

"May I first apologize to you, Miss Marie. You were not hired here with the intention of making you bait, but it is our policy to perform thorough background checks on all of our staff. When we learned of your connection to Miss Sullivan, and when Miss Sullivan showed up in town unexpectedly, it only made sense for us to keep tabs on you." From this close, the vampire's nature was unmistakable. The younger ones could pass for human more often than not, and they probably still thought of themselves as human, too, but the old ones like this were an entirely different proposition. Skin didn't fade in the eternal night so much as it became more luminous. This one had a golden diaphanous light, while Marie looked more like moonshine in the corner of Sully's eye. The color bled from their eyes after only a few months, leaving a dull red behind, but the eyeshine came later. That tiny reflective flicker when a light played over a vampire's face had been enough to put the fear up many of the vice cops Sully used to work with. More than anything though, it was that same stillness that marked them as something other than human. The world kept on moving around them and they stayed put.

"It's all right, Songling, you've been very kind to me since I've worked here, and I've always known the kind of business you're in. There ain't no offense taken." Marie's voice was like honey to Sully's ears. She had to press her eyes shut to keep the tears from falling. Wouldn't do for the vamps to see her looking weak.

While her eyes were closed, something brushed against the side of her leg. She nearly jumped out of the seat before her eyes snapped open and she realized that it was the back of Marie's hand. Without even thinking, she reached down and took it.

"All right, Songling, you want to talk business, so let's talk business. You know who I am, you know what I can do, so the only question you need to ask yourself is whether you want to get in my way."

"Miss Sullivan, when I saw you at the auction, it was clear to me that you were here in a professional capacity, to retrieve the prize for America. Knowing your reputation, I thought it best to withdraw and wait for you to do so successfully before presenting my case to you here, in the company of our mutual acquaintance."

"And how exactly did you know that I was going to escape?"

"You were entirely too calm in the face of your impending death." Songling leaned back in his chair, a hint of a smile touching his lips at this cutting observation.

Marie let out a very un-ladylike snort of laughter that brought an involuntary smile to Sully's face. "That ain't because she knew she was going to escape, that's just Sully."

If this flustered Songling, it didn't show. "In this city we deal in facts, not technicalities. Whoever the legal owner of the doll happens to be, the reality is that you are the one in possession of it, and it is unlikely to leave your possession unless you give it willingly. A fair assessment?"

Sully reluctantly released Marie's hand and pulled Eugene into a tighter grip. "Spot on."

"As you have demonstrated by your continued possession of the doll, you have no wish of your own to make?"

Sully's eyes flitted involuntarily across to Marie, who caught her looking and had to fight back a smile. "I've got everything that I want."

"Then allow me to represent the interests of Hong Kong to you now. Let us remove any mystery surrounding our use of the wish."

Sully looked directly at Marie now. "You think that a bunch of bloodsucking gangsters represent the best interests of Hong Kong?"

"I mean . . . kind of? When the British bailed out it was chaos. The only ones who stepped up and put out the fires were the Jasmine Society. They're the ones that have kept the lights on over here. I guess they're as close a thing to a government as Hong Kong gets?"

"As Miss Marie says, we merely seek to protect the people of Hong Kong from outside influences that mean them ill."

"And what's so special about Hong Kong that it needs to rewrite reality to stay safe? That little army on the doorstep? The British kept them out for decades."

"The British maintained the peace with ancient wards set in the walls. Wards that now crumble. Our experts give us no more than a month before the bombardment of the Mongolian Empire breaks through our defenses. You were in New Amsterdam when the British came with just one of their ships. You know the death toll that we would experience."

The raw numbers escaped Sully's recollection, but the screams and the gagging scent of burning flesh came back to her in a rush. She crushed it back down before the sense memory overtook her entirely. "Why should I care about Hong Kong?"

Songling didn't sigh—that would have required breath—but he did seem to lose a little of his rigidity. "You have no reason to. I had hoped that an appeal to your empathy might be successful, or that you might feel some affection for the place that has given Miss Marie and so many of our kind shelter."

"This is the only place left for us since the empire collapsed," Marie added. "Sure, they treated us like garbage, but they didn't try to kill us or bury us alive just for existing."

Sully couldn't keep her eyes from rolling. "Because vampires were useful. Because demons couldn't sense you clearly and they needed somebody to fight demons. Not because the British had any morals."

"Does it matter?" Marie did sigh; she was still in the habit of breathing, even though it wasn't necessary.

She looked so tired and defeated when she said it that Sully almost gave in on the spot, but Marie wasn't immune to manipulation any more than she was. She couldn't give in just because they'd turned her girl. "So, you're telling me, Marie, that Hong Kong is the only place on earth that you vamps can live free? Like you're some endangered species and this is a nature preserve that the Mongols want to pave over?"

"Unless something big changes, this is it for us."

"We have created equilibrium here, a society where humans and vampires can live in harmony." Songling insinuated himself back into the conversation. "Nobody bleeds who does not wish to, and in exchange for blood, we provide goods and services of equal value. Not everyone here lives well, but everyone has the opportunity to."

Sully scoffed. "As long as they roll over for your little criminal empire?"

"How is our empire any different than the others? We do violence to those who break our rules. We make trade to support our people. What is it that we lack in your eyes? Does the turn of centuries grant legitimacy? Because in truth, the Jasmine Society has ruled here for longer than either of you has drawn breath."

"The Jasmine Society?" Sully's shoulders hunched involuntarily. "The ones who beat the shit out of me the minute I hit town? That Jasmine Society?"

Songling, the ancient vampire overlord of Hong Kong, looked sheepish. "That was an act committed in error."

"You're damn right it was."

Marie was nonplussed. "Darling, you ain't got a scratch on you."

This was not a subject Sully wanted to get into five minutes after reuniting with Marie. That felt more like a second date kind of conversation. "I got better."

"The parties involved have been disciplined," Songling added.

"You want to use this last wish, turn this place into vampire heaven on earth—hot and cold running blood—impregnable by the Mongols and all other comers. Is that your pitch? Is that the deal?"

Songling and Marie both stopped smiling abruptly. "Sanctuary for our people is all that we ask," the older vampire said.

Sully leaned forward toward Marie. "Must sting the pride a bit, having to come begging to me for help in doing the one thing you're meant to be good for."

Marie looked mortified, and when she hissed her lover's name it brought back a tide of memories to Sully. Her theater friends that Sully had sneered at. The foreign food that Sully had turned her nose up at with the chef just a foot away. Every shitty little thing that she had ever done to embarrass Marie and justified to herself as being her personality instead of a fault hit her like a sledgehammer. She'd been trying so hard to be herself again that she'd forgotten that some parts of who she had been were better left behind.

Before Songling could formulate a reply to the insult, Sully sighed out. "I'm sorry. I've been known to be a bit of a bitch but I'm trying to do better. You don't deserve it. I'm sure I'd be down on my hands and knees if the situation were reversed. I get it. How we feel about what we have to do to protect our people doesn't get to factor in."

Songling didn't realize what a momentous occasion Sully apologizing for anything was. He accepted it with a gracious nod, but Marie looked suitably awed and grateful. That was why it was even more of a kick in the teeth when Sully had to say. "But I still can't help you."

Songling seemed to wilt a little, a single strand of hair slipping out of his tight ponytail to tickle across his face, but Marie looked downright appalled. "You can't be serious."

"Listen, I'm intimately familiar with how wishes work. I've been on the receiving end of more of them than I like to think about. You aren't just changing a few things when you make a wish, you are wiping out the whole universe and replacing it with another one that suits your fancy. One little change and *everything* is different." Sully spoke as softly as she could, fighting to keep the tremor out of her voice. "If you were to wish that the wards were back in place, we'd all blink out of existence and the damn British would be ruling over everything again. Or something worse. Every time anybody makes a wish, big or small, we all die, and somebody else puts on our faces, remembers our memories, and walks on."

Songling nodded slowly. "It is not what any of us would want, but at least we would live on in some way. If the walls fall, nothing will remain."

"I didn't . . . go through everything that I went through just to see it all reset again. There aren't going to be any more wishes. This is the world that we live in, this is the world we need to fix. We can't just rewrite history every time that we don't like it."

"When it suited your purposes, this magic was acceptable, but now that my people are at the edge of annihilation, it has become immoral. I understand you perfectly." Songling leaned in closer. You might have expected him to have breath like a grave or some other nonsense, but instead it was faintly herbal when it washed over Sully's face. "From the stories about you, I could never understand the years that you spent serving the British, but now it makes perfect sense. You are just like them."

Her fist clenched, white-knuckled, but the old anger had long since burned away. "Calling me names isn't going to shame me into giving you the doll, and we both know how this ends if you try to take it by force. I think that we are done talking. Let's go, Marie."

Marie took a hold of her shoulder and eased her around until they were facing each other. There wasn't much point in whispering with a vampire eavesdropping, but her voice dropped anyway. "I don't know if you're listening, but this is the last stop for me. I haven't got any-where else to go, Darlin'. If you still want to be with me, then it has to be here."

Sully swallowed hard but said what she needed to say. "I under-stand, but right now we need to get the hell out of town while all of this blows over. Your boy here has the good sense not to tangle with me, but there are a dozen other idiots chasing after this doll who don't give a damn if they incinerate everything and everybody in Hong Kong to get it."

Marie cupped Sully's face in her hands and it was all that she could do not to melt. "Darlin', you need to listen to what I'm telling you. I ain't leaving Hong Kong."

Sully's own hand was shaking when she reached up to take hold of Marie's, despite all her efforts to let nothing show. "Then I'll come back for you. Same way that I always do."

"With respect, Miss Sullivan, Hong Kong may not be here by the time that you find it safe to return." Songling gently intruded once more. "The Khanate already has agents within these walls, not even counting the general that they sent to bid on your little friend there."

"Buddy, I respect where you're coming from and normally I'd be right there on the front lines with you, but I don't think either of you really understands how much of a shitstorm is on my heels right now. If I stay here, I'm just going to make things so much worse for you, both of you."

"AS MUch aS IT hURts uS to SAy tHIS, sHE IS RIghT."

Sully was up and reaching for a weapon before the first grating syllable was all the way out of the dead bartender standing against the wall. Eugene landed on his head by her feet as she hefted the gin and tonic in a vaguely menacing way, slopping some on the doll. "Will you lot just fuck off back to Manhattan. Haven't you got more important things to worry about?"

The answer came from all around her. There had been more staff in and around this room than she had realized. Sloppy and distracted, again. "VEnGEance iS OuR prIORitY."

"Marie, get the doll and stay between us. Songling, they're no stronger than a regular human but they're coordinated."

A wicked looking blade had slipped from his sleeve, acid etched and straight edged. "Like a flock of birds. I see them."

"All right, then." Sully rolled her shoulders, brought up both her fist and her stump and roared, "Come and get me!"

The flesh-puppets of the Manhattan Magi hadn't learned their lesson the last time and they came at her in a wild rush, planning to barrel right through on weight of numbers. But in this tight a space they didn't have a hope in hell. Her fist lashed out, faster than even Sully could have anticipated, and while it only glanced off a cheekbone, that one touch of Cold Iron was all it took to break the Magi's hold. Sully was making the same mistakes again, too. She didn't need to pound them into submission, she just had to touch them and they'd wither. She opened up her hand and slapped the unnatural life right out of the next one, backhanding another and dropping a third just by catching its outstretched hand. More came on, but she had no trouble holding her ground and from the sound of whistling steel and blood splatter behind her, Songling was doing his part, too.

She held one stumbling corpse off with her stump as it sprayed blood and spittle onto her sleeve from perfectly made-up lips. "ThIS IS JuST thE BeginNIng, SuLLivAN. WE ArE LEgIOn. ThERe IS No end. ONLY US. HunTING yOU. FoREver."

She slapped the life out of it, then pushed the dead girl away with a grimace. "Because I killed some of your friends? So what? I've killed plenty more of my own. It was a war. You all signed up, and death was part of the deal."

"YOu haVe no SHAme." Whatever connection the Magi used to keep control of their victims seemed to be faltering for they were slumping forward now instead of pouncing. They were slurring out their threats. "No HONor. YOU SLAUghTeRED theM liKE ANIMals."

Sully didn't even have to try when the next one lunged at her—she caught the dead man by the face and tossed him aside. "How are you this stupid? Come on then, morons, let's do Intro to Criminology. How do I benefit from killing your people? What was in it for me?"

The onslaught had slowed to a trickle. The one talking to Sully now wasn't moving at all. Who knew that talking worked? "To NEUtER tHE ThreAT to yoUR PRECIous AmeRicAs POWER."

"It's like you've never even met me. Does that sound like something I give a shit about, or does that sound like Leonard Pratt?" The name fell from her lips like a leaden weight. It was kind of fitting that this was how she killed him after all these years of patient waiting. This was the kind of war that Pratt had always waged. Whispers and backstabbing. It was only right that his death warrant was signed by a quiet conversation in a shady bar on the opposite side of the world.

"PrATT." They all fell silent and eerily still. Sully realized with a shiver that technically she was the only living person in the room. Even Songling's blade had stopped singing. For the first time, Sully could hear the screaming going on out in the bar proper.

"Yeah, Pratt. He wanted me to kill Ogden, tried to make it sound like justice. He pulled the same shit on Ogden, making out that I was going to be a threat." Sully sunk back down into her seat, which somehow had not only survived, but stayed upright. "He spent the whole war trying to lever himself to the top of the pile of corpses he was creating. He never cared about any of the big ideals he kept banging on about. He just wanted to be king."

The remaining corpses were moving erratically. The magi could only keep control when they themselves were working in harmony. The minute there was disagreement among them, the whole thing started to fall apart at the seams. When they bellowed, "ThE wish. We stILL NEEd tHE WISh," it sounded like they were trying to convince themselves more than Sully.

"We all lost people in the war—Manhattan more than most—but this isn't the way. You can't tear the whole world apart just because you're hurting. You have to let them go." Sully found what was left of her gin on the felt table and trailed her fingers through it. Unsure why it was so hard to say this while looking right at what was left of the reanimated staff. "All that they wanted was to come home. Don't destroy that home just because they're gone."

The internal confusion was finally too much for the Magi to contend with. The spell lost cohesion and the last few bodies went tumbling down. Marie's mouth was hanging open when Sully turned around to check on her. "Darlin', did you just talk them to death?"

"You can't punch every problem in the face."

Marie snorted. "Who are you and what have you done with my Sully?"

That hit just a little too close to home, so Sully turned her new, unscarred face away before it could show. "Guess she finally grew up."

The room had gone from quiet dignity to a massacre so fast that the space was almost unrecognizable. Doors that Sully hadn't even realized were there hung loose on their hinges, and the pile of dead bodies where she and Songling had been standing was impressive. Every human in the building must have been turned. Songling himself was patiently wiping his weapon clean on the lapels of a dead waiter. "This is not going to make recruiting new staff any easier."

Sully took in the long arcs of blood decorating the ceiling, the walls, and Songling's sodden silk jacket. Pools of it were spreading out from the corpses on the floor, still warm. "At least your dinner is sorted."

With a pained smile, he replied, "I already ate."

AUGUST 1, 2013

Even within the voluminous body that his tailor often complained about, Leonard Pratt could not find any space for a love of bureaucracy. He was well trained and adept at navigating its metaphorical corridors, certainly, as any gentleman who had grown to adulthood within the British Empire was forced to be, but that did not mean that he enjoyed it. Sullivan, for all of her myriad faults, had been quite adept at cutting through the Gordian knot of meetings, consultations, and committees by virtue of her rudeness. It was quite easy to be simultaneously rude and acceptable when you were a short white woman in a society designed to coddle those who looked just like you. It mattered little that the woman contained the destructive potential of a small nation—she appeared to be tiny and harmless so her rudeness was read as amusing and adorable rather than an affront. If he had attempted anything of the sort during his long political and academic career, doors would have slammed shut in his face faster than you could say, "But where are you really from?"

The thought of Sullivan pressed on his mind quite frequently these days, his last great gamble to restore his proper station in the new, tangled alliance of nations that he had forged into a unified country. If there had been any justice in the world, he would have been revered for his role as the architect of the downfall of the British Empire and the foundation of this new democracy. Instead, he was reviled for doing injury to the enemies of that democracy and voted into obscurity by those who owed him their awe. He had always known that children could be intractable but he had never supposed that the same adage might be true of young nations. He was really quite put out.

With his attentions so divided and his desire that the world would be reset to its correct order sooner rather than later still in his heart, it was difficult to focus on his duties fulfilling the will of the government that had so cruelly betrayed him. It should have come as no surprise whatsoever, therefore, that his mind turned sooner than usual toward his luncheon.

Here, too, was the affront of his new social standing all too readily apparent. Where before he would have had his choice of the finest eateries in the whole of New Amsterdam at his beck and call, now he was at the mercy of the lowest maître d'. It was quite intolerable to have a hankering after some Ophiran wat only to be told that he would be put on a waiting list. Even today when his desire ran in a more European direction, his table for one had to be squeezed in between the lunch and dinner services. Whoever had heard of eating French food at three o'clock in the afternoon? It was ridiculous, yet here he was, in the modest town car that his position still afforded him, struggling against the South Bronx traffic in the vain hope that he might get to sup upon a non-Peking duck sometime this decade. He was studiously avoiding any food that might remind him of Mongolia at the moment. His digestion was already troubled enough without constant reminders of Sullivan's quest.

He was dubious about her chances of retrieving the doll, and even more dubious about the chances that she might return it to him, but it wasn't like he had a whole world's worth of agents at his disposal these days. Even old university friends dodged his calls and his publishers seemed to have slipped him gradually down the midlist and into obscurity. It seemed that he was doomed to die forgotten—all of his great achievements and academic contributions forgotten just because he misspoke in the defense of Sullivan instead of condemning the foolish harlot for her destructive habits. It was just as well that he was not a vengeful man, or he might have sent her into a truly lethal situation without support, hoping that she would expire in the attempt to perform this thankless task just because her tangled moral code demanded it. What a terrible outcome that would be. Truly tragic. The catharsis would be extraordinary.

The truth was that he expected her to pull through as she always had. He was nothing if not dutiful, and the threat of seeing his great experiment in democracy overrun by the crass wish of some foreign power irked him more than he cared to admit. There may have been some small pleasure to be taken in the untimely demise of Sullivan, but she was, ultimately, an ideal tool for this particular situation, and if she should deliver the last wish on earth to him as he had requested and paid for then he would doubtless still retain her as a tool for future situations of a similar nature. That was the trouble with the infuriating woman—she remained perpetually useful. Even *in extremis* he found himself trying to retain her at the expense of his other, more obvious, assets. That mistake had cost him the crown, but he remained convinced that it would pay off in the long term. Perhaps his confidence was misplaced, but he had seen that woman beat the odds too often to discount her entirely.

Traffic was usually terrible in this part of town, but it seemed to be particularly overwrought on this afternoon, almost as though there was some disruption up ahead that wasn't being reported. Leonard Pratt sank back into the squeaking leather seats with a sigh. His situation was so dire that he had sworn blind that his meal would take no longer than two hours so that the bistro could reclaim its table in time for the evening crowd. Every minute that he was delayed cut into those precious moments of relaxation. Sighing yet again, he leaned forward to rap on the partition. "Pardon me for asking dear driver, I do not mean to tell you your job by any stretch of the imagination, but is there perhaps a more circuitous, yet possibly more effective, route that we might be taking?"

There was no reply, so Leonard rapped once more. "I say, driver. Is there a better way around?"

The partition rolled down painfully slow, giving him more than enough time to see his usual driver flopping spasmodically in the front seat. For a moment he was frozen in shock, then he scrambled for his phone. A swift call to the emergency services would set this right. "Don't you worry Clarke, I'm calling an ambulance now. You shall have the very best of care, I promise you."

"ToO LATe fOr thAT."

Leonard froze in place again. This time it was not the sudden jab of shock, but the deeper chill of abject terror that rolled down his spine. He had been lucky enough to avoid the worst of the Year of the Knife the first time around but that had done nothing to curb his nightmares. "My dear friends, the Manhattan Committee has my office number; these kinds of theatrics are entirely unnecessary in this more civilized age. Particularly when they cost an innocent driver his life."

"ThERE ARe NO INNoceNTS." Clarke's head shuddered and rotated to face Leonard, like a plucked Caucasian owl. "OnLY those whO ARE NoT YeT GUILTy."

Leonard did not throw himself back in revulsion—he was too well schooled to show his hand so soon—but he did ease back into his seat with a sigh. "Quibbling pedantic points is hardly befitting Magi of your station. Why don't we sit down like adults and discuss whatever is so urgent."

"You BETRayed us PRAtt. YOU tURned on US. ThREw uS INto the MEAT-griNder whEN IT suITED YOur purpose. WiPEd US out MORe surely than CENTURIES of SeiGE."

"My dear fellows, who has been filling your heads with such utter nonsense? The war took its toll on you, certainly, but it was hardly disproportionate. You know, as I do, that those with the greatest talent are the ones who pay the price for politics. The other Magi that the American Alliance secured suffered entirely comparable casualties, I can assure you." He drew a cigar from his pocket and clipped the tip with an expert hand.

"HOW MANy of THEir dEaThs did you ORCHEStrate? HOW MANy of thEm WEre a THREAT to yOUR POWer?"

Taking care to keep his hand from shaking, Leonard reached for the cigarette lighter set in the door, clicking it to life. "Honestly gentle-men, I haven't the first inkling of what you could be talking about. You were deployed in battle as dictated by our dear general, in agreement with the late, great Magus Ogden. I merely provided the logistical sup-port that was required to execute military action."

Clarke's body began pushing its way back through the partition inch by inch, screeching and roaring, "THE SAme STORY, EVen noW? SULLIVan TOLD us EVERYTHING."

Pratt lit his cigar with a roll of his eyes. "Trying to save her own neck from your unique brand of vigilante justice, I shouldn't wonder? My dear fellow, when you put someone's neck in a noose, they will tell you anything to undo the knot. I am merely the most expedient target for her to deflect your ire onto. Of course, she would blame me for her actions, the whole world blames me for her actions. They condemn me for that wicked woman's extravagant, violent excesses, her twisted sense of justice, and the bodies left in her wake. Is it any wonder that she repeats these lies to shield herself from consequences?"

"MoTIvE," the Magi barked.

"I shall tell you her motive easily enough: she understood the political necessity of our alliance but she never forgave you for the brutality you inflicted while you were trying to return home from the far planes. She came to me on the eve of the war's beginning and demanded the execution of your leader, the moment that the battle came to its conclusion. Of course, I declined, but the woman takes the law into her own hands every day, and as you may recall, she was in a position of some authority, capable of placing you and your compatri-ots in harm's way with her orders. Fearing the worst, I contacted your Magus Ogden to give him fair warning of the vengeful nature of his militant counterpart. So that he could countermand any order that might be intended to cause your kind harm." The lighter was still in his hand even as he puffed at the cigar, the flame-rune inside it sizzling in the air.

"DO yOU KNOw WHY we BElieve SULLIVAN, nOT YOu?"

"Oh, I imagine that you have bought into the rather romantic idealized image that she has created for herself over the years—the brave military veteran, the clever policewoman, the martyr. I wish that my public relations team had a fraction of the sway that her fan club of jilted lovers manages to hold over the public consciousness. Well, let me tell you the truth for once and damn the consequences. The woman is a murderer, pure and simple. Each of her different guises was just a mask for the savage impulse that drives her ever onward. She revels in violence and delights in destruction. If some bright morning I were to awaken and find that the whole world had been set aflame by some mad act of magic, I would not have to think twice before pointing to her as the culprit." It was quite the speech, but Leonard knew that if they had reached this stage, the time when a clever speech might save him was long gone. He was really just stalling for time at this point.

"We BELIEVE HEr because SHE HAs no reASon to LIe. ShE dOES NOt FEAr uS."

He couldn't very well argue with that point; he was practically pissing himself at this juncture. Leonard was not a man prone to physical activity of any sort—the only heavy lifting that he performed on a daily basis was hauling himself out of his Egyptian cotton sheets each morning—and the prospect of physical confrontation paralyzed him. Yet finding himself nose to nose with the very horror that he had once devoted a not-inconsiderable amount of his mental energies to combating, he finally found the second half of the equation that a man flooded with adrenaline always faced. When given the choice of fight or flight, for the first time in his life, he chose the former option. He thrust the flame-rune of the lighter into Clarke's slack face and dived for the floor.

It was a curious property of the reanimated bodies that the Manhattan crowd used that the spells involved created a rather dangerous instability. There was so much magic necessary to animate the bodies that the addition of even a small amount more was sufficient to trigger a detonation. Leonard Pratt, for all of his intellectual gifts, had never possessed even a spark of arcane power. It was one of the cruelest twists of fate to mark his otherwise luck-laden life. He did not have the innate power to destroy his attacker, even when it would have taken no more than a mere spark—a spark as miniscule as that generated by a simple fire-rune.

The windows of the town car exploded outwards in a blast of blinding white light and it rocked back and forth on its suspension for a long moment before Leonard was able to pull the door open and eject himself onto the tarmac. Blood was pouring from his ears, his well-tailored suit had been reduced to tattered rags, and burns completely covered his back, from scalp to heels. Yet, still, he lived and his assailant did not. Perhaps this was how Sullivan felt when she was fighting the world and winning. There was elation beneath the pain. He had faced an assassin alone and had come out victorious.

Without proper apparel, he felt rather chilly kneeling there on the road, the open wound on his back seeming to be particularly cold. He didn't worry himself about the injury itself. He had the money and contacts to make little problems like near lethal injuries go away. An ambulance was no doubt already on its way.

He took a deep, aching breath, and pushed himself up to look out at the crowd he was sure was gathering, as New Amsterdam bystanders always did. He was hardly looking dignified at the moment, but the optics of his foiling an assassination attempt would probably outweigh the fact that his arse was hanging out of his suit. The crowd stood eerily still and silent around Leonard, their limbs dangling like unstrung marionettes.

Their mouths were moving, but with his burst eardrums, Leonard was pleased to find that he didn't have to endure another moment of their inane prattle. "Oh, just get it over with. I've nothing more to say."

They fell on him in a wave. Fingers hooked and tearing. Fists flailing. The dead finally bringing their judgment down on Leonard Pratt, the first Prime Minister of America.

AUGUST 5, 2013

Marie had not eaten before her shift started. Her pupils had dilated until they filled her eyes at the sight of so much blood, and she was clearly fighting the urge to drop down on all fours and start lapping up the good stuff. Sully found her glass among the wreckage, inexplicably still solid, and with a little application of pressure on a neck stump, she got it half full before anyone could register a comment. She slipped the warm glass into Marie's grateful hand and plucked Eugene out of her arms.

He sprang to life the moment she laid hands on him, and despite all of the time they'd spent in each other's company—despite knowing that the damned doll was alive—Sully still jumped. Eugene twisted in her grasp. "SOMETHING IS COMING."

"Finally decided to join in the conversation, did you?"

Eugene was flinging himself around so much that Sully nearly dropped him. She'd never seen him that agitated when he wasn't about to burst into flames. "SOMETHING IS COMING. SOMETHING POWERFUL. WE MUST MOVE. WE MUST FLEE."

Sully plopped him onto the table. "Calm down, short-stuff, it's dealt with. Manhattan are out of the fight."

"THE OUTSIDERS." The doll was shaking and swelling against his seams as he glutted himself on the saturation of magic filling the air. "THE OUTSIDERS ARE PRESSING IN. WE MUST ESCAPE."

Songling raised a quizzical eyebrow, and Marie looked askance to Sully but all that she could respond with was a shrug. She'd heard plenty of people called outsiders through the years, but the way that Eugene said it—like it was a name—was new to her. "Who are the Out—?"

The deafening scream that cut her off did not come from anything living. It was the tortured sound of brick and mortar being dragged apart by forces too overwhelming for even stone to resist. The walls, the ceiling, and the floors above began to move up and away from them. From the perfectly straight seam where the building had once been connected to its foundations, plaster dust rained down, lit from behind by flares of dazzling light. Eugene bellowed as Sully snatched him from the table. "THEY COME."

Songling was already in motion, the long blade secreted back about his person wherever such things were hidden and his cultured, composed expression replaced with an inhumanly blank mask. "Smugglers' tunnels. Follow me."

With Eugene under her arm and Marie's hand grasped firmly in her own, Sully chased him through back rooms and corridors that were becoming more and more exposed with every passing moment. Their knees were probably visible from the street by now. They came to what was clearly a sewer grating by a glass-washing station. "What about your people?"

Songling lifted the grate with a strength that would have been astounding if he weren't so obviously a vampire. "They will escape or they will not. My presence makes no difference. What matters is getting the demon clear."

The two of them helped Marie down into the dank darkness. Songling stepped back and gestured for Sully to follow, bringing her to a dead stop. "You're being surprisingly magnanimous about not getting your wish."

He offered her a hand. "I may still get my way. The longer that I keep the wish out of the grasp of our mutual acquaintances out there, the more time you will have to change your mind."

"True enough." Sully pointedly ignored his hand and jumped into the hole.

If she had been expecting sewers or the kind of raw-dirt smuggler's tunnels that riddled the docklands back in New Amsterdam, then Sully was in for some serious disappointment. Beneath the vampire's bar there was a perfectly comfortable little apartment with a side room full of bunk beds in case of unexpected visitors. Somewhere back in the storied history of this place, they'd hooked into the city's galvanic network, lighting it up with harsh—but magically undetectable—bare bulbs.

There was only a moment to take it in before Songling came down with a clatter and shot across to the set of nondescript lockers that hid the next heavily fortified door. Beyond that, the actual tunnels began, the bulbs spaced far too widely for Sully to see much of anything in the shadows between them. The vamps would manage it fine, but she'd be stumbling all the way. "Grand."

Marie took her hand, leading her along through the deep shadows at a pace that Sully could blame for the pounding of her heart. Songling didn't make a sound as he glided along ahead of them, illuminated for only moments in the strobe of their motion. Sully could understand why people used to be scared of vamps when she saw him like that, a nightmare stalking through the night.

Sully did what she always had done when fear tickled up her back. She mouthed off. "What exactly is our plan here? I know these tunnels have to head right for the docks, but the minute they find the open grate back there they'll be along here faster than you can blink. If you blink. Do you blink?"

Songling pointedly ignored the question. "Our tunnels are an expansion of the infrastructure that the British were already putting into place beneath the city. Wherever you wish to surface, they will take us."

Eugene barked. "RUN FASTER. WHY ARE YOU SLOWING? THEY COME FOR US."

Their wild sprint had slowed to a jog, but even that was enough to have Sully puffing away. "Come on, man, it's your town, where would we be safe?"

"Moments ago, I would have told you there was nowhere safer than the Gudgeon, but it has now been destroyed by those that hunt you. I would not bring that wrath down on any of my other holdings." An explosion echoed along the tunnels behind them and a flash of light chased over them. Marie looked stricken. They were out of time.

"THEY HAVE FOUND THE TUNNEL."

"All right, I know a guy who owes me a favor. Which way is the theater district?" Even if it came to nothing, at least mentioning the stage was enough to chase the look of terror off of Marie's face.

Songling led them through the warren of tunnels without ever missing a step. The official and unofficial ones seemed to be almost identical, as though the mobsters had hired the same government contractors to carry out the work. Knowing Hong Kong, they probably had.

Before whatever was making the horrific sounds behind them had managed to catch up, some new horrific sounds started up ahead of them. Songling charged on regardless but the metallic roars slowed Sully's pace. That and the burning sensation in her lungs. She was getting too old for this shit. She gasped out, "What the hell?"

The tunnel opened out into a vaulted chamber. Machinery filled the lower half of the room and smog the upper half, smearing the red brickwork with soot and oil. Sully could taste it on the roof of her mouth. Thick coils of cable grew up out of these machines like blasphemous trees spreading out across the roof in thick bundled vines, branching off in every direction. These were the galvanic generators that kept the neon up above lit, the groaning spluttering heart of Hong Kong. It was deafeningly loud, and so hot it made Sully's skin feel like it was going to peel off, and so overwhelming that she didn't realize that Songling had stopped dead in front of a heap of crates until she plowed into him. It was like running into a brick wall with elbows. She fumbled Eugene and groaned, "Right in the tit."

She turned to Marie, expecting to see her barely containing a laugh, but if anything she looked even more horrified than before. Sully followed her line of sight across to the crates, and then crouched down among them so that she could make out the contents through the oily fumes coming off the generators. Neatly lined up inside each straw-lined crate were row after row of sticks of dynamite, all wired up and ready to go. She started to do the calculations in her head, based on how many sticks would fit in a crate, how many crates were in the stack and just how big a blast that combination of numbers was going to make, but after a certain point it was pretty much academic. This was enough to gut the city, if not destroy it outright. "Mongols?"

Songling had to shout to be heard over the machines. "The Mongols would not destroy the city. They wish to take it as a prize. To gloat about claiming it at last."

Marie's lower lip was trembling as she asked, "The British?"

"No motive." Sully's mind was still spooling through the numbers involved, the time it would have taken to smuggle this amount of alchemical explosives into the city. Something didn't add up. "Killing Hong Kong doesn't bring the British Empire back."

Sully passed Eugene to Marie and crouched down to carefully uncoil the exposed wires connected to the crude detonator. This close she could hear it ticking. "This whole set up makes no sense. It would be much cheaper and easier to just use magic. If you've got enough time to put all this together, you'd have plenty of time to cast something big and destructive. I know that not everybody has Dante's Inferno memorized, but there are plenty of other spells in the world."

"Which leaves us with suspects who cannot use magic." Songling probably would have made a good cop. He already had most of the skillset from being a criminal. While Sully disarmed the bomb, he stood stock still. Marie looked equally paralyzed in the face of so much raw destructive potential. It was a good reminder for Sully that at the end of the day, these were civilians.

She cast Songling a glance. "Vamps? You think your people did this?"

"Perhaps. Some of them may have done this as a last act of vengeance, to be triggered if the city falls, but it would have meant working against my wishes. I believe in their enlightened self-interest too much to suspect that they would do that."

"Great, a mystery bomber." Sully had finally caught her breath. "Just what we need. Can we get back to running like hell?"

That thought was punctuated by a sound like a roll of thunder from the tunnels behind them, loud enough to drown out the machinery and even the thumping of Sully's heart in her ears. Marie stood pinned by indecision for a moment as Songling shot off silently, but Sully waved her off even as she struggled back to her feet. "Get going."

She had never been much good at running, either in the physical or philosophical sense, but even if she didn't have her magic she still had just as much fight in her as she had ever had. Scooping up a fistful of dynamite, she ran back toward the tunnels they had just vacated. There was a decent length of fuse wire on each piece and rat-chewed wires all over the place. It was almost easier to rig a booby trap than not. The only piece of the puzzle that she was lacking was knowing how long it would take whatever was chasing them to arrive, but judging the best she could from the lights flashing and the droning roars echoing along toward her, it wouldn't be long.

There was no way that she could have caught up to two vampires running full pelt if they hadn't waited for her, and Sully was more than a little surprised that Songling hadn't made a grab for the doll while she was out of the picture. Fear of the damage she could do was one thing, but this guy—this gangster—was treating her with something an awful lot like respect. That made her suspicious. Scooping Eugene back before respect lost its luster, Sully crashed into Marie's waiting arms, who spluttered, "What took you so long?"

"I'm not as young as I used to be."

Marie was clearly dubious, right up until the moment that the first explosive went off. Songling's eyes narrowed. "You did not."

"I did. Not the whole stack, just enough to close some tunnels."

Songling turned away in disgust. "The ghosts of those above that you just condemned to death should lie heavy on your conscience."

"They'll have plenty of company." She marched right past him.

This was not the time to wallow in self-pity; the collapsed tunnels wouldn't keep whatever was chasing them out for long, given how easily it had ripped a building from its very foundation.

They picked up the pace again, running too hard for anyone to start a conversation, even if Sully did have some burning questions for the demon trapped very firmly in her armpit. The silence was both good and bad in equal measure. On the one hand, it meant Sully didn't have to deal with any more recriminations from Marie or Songling; on the other hand it meant that every time another piece of masonry was destroyed behind them, they could hear it echoing along after them. When they finally skidded to a halt, Sully was actually willing to take the boost that Songling offered and found herself flung almost to the grating above her head before she managed to hook a foot in the embedded ladder and stop her ascent.

They came out in a nondescript alleyway overrun with trash and graffiti. It felt just like home. Sully stuck her head out into the street at the end and oriented herself fast. They were less than a block from the boarded-up noodle bar. Couldn't have asked for better luck. "Okay kids, stick close and walk briskly. Running people are interesting, brisk people just have somewhere to be."

She turned back to find Songling almost nose to nose with her. "I do not need to hide in my own city."

"Of course, we were creeping through the sewers for fun. Until Eugene is out of town, the usual rules don't apply."

For a moment before she stepped out into the mass of people on the street, Sully was pinned by indecision. With reluctance she handed Eugene off to Marie and draped her coat over the taller woman's shoulders to conceal him. "I need my hand free and if things go south, you're the only one I trust to make the right decision with it."

"DO I GET A VOTE?" Eugene rumbled from the vicinity of Marie's stomach.

In chorus, Marie and Sully replied. "No."

The press of bodies had never felt more oppressive than it did now. Every face that turned toward them as they passed could have been on the lookout for them. Every brush against Sully's shoulders could have been a hand grabbing for her. She spun the ring on her finger nonstop as they made their way right past the front of the shop and around to the narrow alley at its side. The front door would have been too obvious, particularly if the place was staked out.

Monkhbat was sitting on the back doorstep with his head in his hands and a cigarette that had turned entirely to ash stuck between his fingers. Sully kicked him in the ribs, not as hard as she could have—not hard enough to break anything—but hard enough to knock him over. "Surprise!"

He could barely contain himself well enough to speak. "Sully! You escaped!"

Sully dropped herself onto the step where he'd been just a moment before. "You thought I was going to walk straight into a trap without any plan to get out of it?"

"Sully, I am so very sorry. I cannot forgive myself and I would never ask you to—"

"Water under the bridge." Sully shrugged. "I know you'd never do something like that again. You're a good guy who was in a bad situation, right?"

While Monkhbat gaped at her, Sully glanced back to the vampires. "Sorry, I'm being rude. This is Monkhbat, an old friend from New Amsterdam. Monkhbat, this is Songling, who you probably owe that money to, and this is Marie, my . . . I want to say *girlfriend* but we haven't really had a minute to catch up?"

Marie wet her lips. "I think girlfriend will do just fine for now, Darlin'."

Sully couldn't contain her grin. "And I'm sure Eugene doesn't need any introduction."

"THIS ONE HAS FAR SUPERIOR BREASTS. I SHALL REMAIN NESTLED HERE FOR AS LONG AS I AM CONDEMNED TO THIS MISERABLE PLANE."

Marie, incapable of blushing, managed to look mortified all the same.

Sully's grin was threatening to take the top off her head. "What a charmer."

Monkhbat had scrambled to his feet and was halfway into a polite nod before his eyes bugged out of his head. "You brought the demon here?"

Sully's grin started to look sinister in the dim neon flickers of the alley. "That was what I was trying to say before. You're a good guy who was in a bad situation, you were feeling all torn up about handing me over to be sold off and butchered. And that is how I know you'll never pull anything like that on me ever again. You owe me, Monkhbat. You owe me big."

He might have been a nobody in the grand scheme of things, but in that moment, Monkhbat could have caused them all manner of trouble if she had judged him wrong. He already had the cash in hand for selling her off to the Peninsula earlier in the evening, and he already had one hell of a motive to screw her over any way that he could, even if Sully couldn't quite recall what that motive was. Which was why she was so pleased to see his shoulders rise up from their slump and his chin jut out. "How can I help?"

Sully strode over and clapped him on the shoulder. "Can we start with some more of those noodles?"

September 10, 2011

It felt good to be back in New Amsterdam. There had been another spate of what looked like wendigo attacks over on the UN border that had kept Sully searching through forests for what felt like months. It was good to have concrete all around her again.

In the end there was no evidence that it was a wendigo. Everyone was always so afraid it was going to be a wendigo, admittedly with good reason. But there was no sign the bodies were being eaten, just bitten by something with canine jaws. Eliminating wendigo from the suspect list was only half of the problem, of course; there was still something running around the western border provinces shredding hikers.

There were plenty of supernatural creatures with mouths like dogs. There were werewolves and demons and cursed humans and a whole variety of spells that would let a person take on another shape voluntarily. The process of elimination removed the werewolves and demons, as the kills were nowhere near the full moon, and demons were not known for subtly sneaking around in unpopulated areas picking off a couple of stragglers.

Sully had only been back for two weeks before the steady supply of victims dried up. There were no more clues, just a pile of new jobs landing on her desk back in the city. She was a stubborn woman; if the order hadn't come down from on high, she probably would have gone on marching back and forth through that forest until she found something to blow up. As it was, the ability to buy a fresh coffee every block was still a delight, and her official request for information from their neighbors to the west, The United Nations, would probably go unanswered until long after her death.

There was a stack of folders on her desk when she crept back into the office and she stared at them with disgust. Anything urgent rarely made it to the folder stage. Everybody in the office must have been dumping their nonessentials on her desk. She sat down heavily in her chair, and the creak must have been enough to summon the gods of interoffice comedy.

Ceejay stuck his head over the top of his cubicle and gave her a suspiciously friendly grin. "Well, brave hunter? Did you find the mighty beast? Did you lay him low with your barbs and arrows? Are the innocent people of Uncle-Fuck Nebraska safe to go back to their moonshine operations?"

Sully just stared at him. She had never been one for repartee. Luckily, everyone else in the office seemed more than willing to make up for her silence.

Bernard popped his head over the other side of the cubicle, leaping to her defense. "Now, Ceejay, don't go laughing at the girl just because she spent all month chasing coyotes with a bunch of yokels. Laugh at her because she didn't find anything after spending all month chasing coyotes with a bunch of yokels."

When he caught sight of Sully's glare he jumped to attention as if he had just been struck by inspiration. He ducked out of sight and Sully heard steel desk drawers slamming. Then he dashed into her cubicle and dropped a raccoon-skin cap on her head. The tail dangled down in front of her face, and she blew it away irritably as the men brayed with laughter.

After they had started to calm down she finally replied in her best attempt at a western province accent, "Ain't sharing my moonshine with any of y'all now."

That left them guffawing again and gave the blush on her cheeks a chance to recede. The hunt had been a waste of time, but it could have happened to any of them and they all knew it. As bad as she was at small talk, she liked the people in this office. A Superior Agent had a whole set of duties above and beyond being on call for tactical operations and some of them required a desk.

Their office here in Staten Island had that barracks camaraderie she had been missing since she joined the IBI. The Navy had been a nightmare to begin with until she found her sea legs and started rolling with the jokes as much as the waves. Then it had turned into something like this. The rum allowance had helped with the small talk, too.

She took the top two folders off of the stack and dropped one over each side of the cubicle's partition walls. She heard groaning from both sides and called out, "You both knew it was going to bounce back. I am taking care of some of your shit, so don't start with me, boys."

The grumbling quieted and after a few seconds Sully felt Ceejay casting. A long time ago he had gotten his hands on a minor portal spell that never should have been outside the research lab. It made the hair on the back of her neck stand up every time he used it, and now, when he turned on the old radio at his desk, it was tuned to some African rock and roll station that couldn't possibly have been in range. Keyboards started tapping away on either side of her.

Sully flipped open the top file still left on her desk and understood immediately why it had been demoted to a non-priority call. Vampires were being murdered in the city, and for some reason the NAPD thought the problem should be passed up to an imperial level.

She was about to bounce it back to the NAPD with a big red stamp on it when she saw the case had already been officially accepted. The signature on the intake form was the Assistant Director's. Sully cast her eyes up to the ceiling and after a long moment decided not to fight with him. As much as she didn't care about Nova Europa's burgeoning vampire population, the local police would somehow find a way to care less. Vamps had been people once, so she could at least give them the respect a corpse was due.

She pulled on her jacket and headed out the door with the case file in hand before any more work or insults could be flung her way. She liked this jacket. It was black leather, and unlike so many leather jackets, it didn't have a rain repellent enchantment on it.

Unexpected enchantments could interfere with evocation in many hilarious ways, like dousing you in flames or turning your hair green for a month. The black jacket had been a gift from somebody who had, very briefly, been a girlfriend-turned-home-invader. She'd had good taste in clothes, though, and with age Sully had acquired enough wisdom to wear something warm instead of trying to prove that she was tougher than the weather.

She caught a cab down to Brooklyn where the last vamp victim had been found, wrapped in garbage bags. She read through the details of the previous three murdered women. Was it still murder if you didn't have a pulse? The police report danced around the fact that all three of the girls had been prostitutes. That was where every vampire ended up in the end, at least in Sully's experience.

She visited the alley and found it empty. There was no chalk outline nonsense here. She cast a scan but the murder had been more three days ago and any residue had long since evaporated. Her mobile phone chirped while she was walking around the connecting alleyways looking for inspiration.

She frowned down at Bernard's office extension and answered the call with a sigh. "You thought up another funny-funny thing to say, little man?"

He chuckled. "Just thought that you would like to know that you have a fresh victim in Brooklyn."

Sully exhaled heavily. "Where's it at?"

He was entirely too pleased to reply, "A strip club."

She forced joviality into her tone. "You sure you don't want this case? It seems like it's right up your alley."

Bernard snorted. "What? You have a sudden aversion to tits now?"

She raised her voice in mock indignation, "Listen to me, buddy. What I enjoy in the comfort of my own home is not related to the sad sacks that shimmy in those places."

He was laughing again. "All right, all right, don't go all affirmative action, bull-dyke on me. I just report the news, I don't write it."

She spat into a pile of trash. "Well, you could report it with less-obvious glee. Text me the address."

She didn't say goodbye as she hung up; it seemed to be a habit that permeated both the police and the IBI. Everyone said their piece and then hung up. The phone blipped a few seconds later as the call disconnected, and she left the alley to get her bearings. The strip club was only a few blocks away. If she jogged, she could be there before the NAPD had trampled through everything resembling evidence.

After shouldering her way through the inquisitive crowd and waving her ID around, Sully got a look at the corpse in the dumpster. Like the last ones, it had been divided up into separate bags; the limbs were all tangled together in one, the torso alone in another. The head had been left out in the open, peeking around the corner so that the dead eyes were pointed at the clientele going in and out of the club. The cuts separating the parts were ragged and torn. It reminded Sully of the recent messes in the woods.

There was a reporter milling around with the civvies, and it took a few hissed orders that she really had no authority to issue before the police technician on the scene would cast a shroud over the area so they could work in peace.

She cast her scan and found a whole swarm of magical signatures crisscrossing the place. The technician had been recording everything, some of the officers had laid minor sensory enhancement spells, the girls from the club had been swathed in cheap glamours, and there was an underlying vibration that smelled of iron.

Sully narrowed her search down to the magic that tasted of blood. There was some sort of transformation spell in use, possibly with an enhancement blended in. Whatever it was, the spell was well and truly outside of her area of expertise, and it had made the caster physically strong enough to shred a vampire in a couple of minutes, before dashing off toward the waterfront and disappearing into the frenetic city life.

She jotted down as many notes on the spell as she could before collecting second-hand interview information from the detective sergeant. Anything to avoid talking to the employees. She'd had enough experience with strippers to last her a lifetime. The dead vamp had been hooking outside the club for about three months, picking up men with empty wallets who were in need of some extra stimulation. Nobody had seen who she went off with. Nobody ever saw anything. Sully sighed and went to catch another cab.

Hunt's Point was a rough patch in the Bronx, and it just so happened to be the main congregation point for every prostitute in New Amsterdam. Oddly enough, Sully didn't have any problems with prostitutes. Her Navy experience with strippers had been overwhelmingly negative, but every prostitute she had ever met just seemed to be a normal woman who had made a few bad decisions and ended up doing a job she didn't like, or a normal woman who had made a few unorthodox decisions and ended up doing a job she enjoyed.

The girls hanging out by the underpass looked her up and down, and perhaps a quarter of them wandered away. The ones who left thought sex for money was fine but sex with a woman was immoral, or at least weren't desperate enough to bend that rule for a quick buck. The rest of the women started cooing and displaying their wares until Sully flashed her credentials. Suddenly they were all chilly or had somewhere else to be.

Sully experienced some discomfort looking into their eyes, but her usual habit of looking at chests or hair was resulting in some mixed messages. She ended up shouting at them. "I don't want to cause you girls any trouble. Everybody has to work, and I'm not looking for a freebie. I just want to know where the vampire girls hang out."

Immediately a six-foot-tall Egyptian woman in an outfit that must have left her freezing started shaking her head and tut-tutting. "Girl, you need yourself a warm pair of tits to cuddle up to. Those dead girls will give you frost bite. And a real bite. You don't want to get bit, do you?"

There was some giggling among the prostitutes and a skinny

blonde dressed in fishnets at the back squealed out, "I'll bite you, honey. Won't even cost extra. You look tasty."

A couple of the girls at the front made some barking and snapping noises as Sully rolled her eyes. Their attempts to embarrass her might have worked a few years back when she first started out in the city, but this nonsense was old hat to her now. She waited until things had quieted down a little before she tried again to speak. "Listen. Somebody is chopping those girls up, chewing on them. Some real sicko. I'd rather get to him before he decides he wants a warm meal and comes around this neighborhood, yeah?"

That seemed to sober them up, and they gave her directions to the right street corner up in Red Hook. That took her by surprise. Red Hook was where all the city's art galleries were and where the southern singers came up to hold their intimate concerts. She shrugged it off. It made a twisted kind of sense. Prostitutes and artists had a long and sordid history together. While a lot of the artistic types in New Amsterdam lived along the Black Bay near her crappy little apartment, the ones up in Red Hook were the ones who were making it, the ones with some money to throw around. The fact that the girls were vampires added that gothic aspect that a lot of the southern artistes seemed so hooked on.

Sully had to walk a good few streets away before she could flag a taxi down. None of them would pick up too near to the streetwalkers in case they ended up in jail for a miscommunication. She made it up to Red Hook before lunchtime and found her way to a gutter-side sandwich cart. It wasn't fine cuisine but it was cheap and familiar. After the bland, greasy nonsense they served up as food over in Dakota, something as simple as pastrami tasted like wafer-thin heaven.

She strolled along, munching happily and taking in the sights. As predicted, the whole street was nothing but art galleries and coffee shops but, here and there, practically invisible to polite eyes, she could see parasols bobbing along. It was close to midday and there were no shadowy alleyways to lurk in, so the vamps had to be out and about, advertising their wares.

Sully tailed a few of the parasols as they started to gather together. She followed them along the streets as they meandered around, stopping to peer in dusty gallery windows when the group slowed or halted altogether.

There had been a time when humanity was afraid of vampires; when they were the terror in the night, killing children and stealing life a mouthful at a time. They had been apex predators then, feeding on the scared and the lonely and the lost in the dark. Now they were being stalked by a woman still suffering from jetlag who was munching away on a sandwich without their even noticing. They led her, as the day passed by, to the corner where the living prostitutes had directed her. When they were all lounging around outside the corner deli, Sully made her approach. "Excuse me, ladies. I wonder if we might help each other."

They all turned to face her, heads snapping around like owls. It took Sully a moment to realize what was so uncanny about their faces. Their eyes were all the same strange color. At first she mistook the irises for a pale brown but, now that she was focusing, they were clearly red. A porcelain-white girl who looked like she was in her early teens cocked her head at Sully and mechanically fluttered her eyelashes like the wings of a moth. "Give you a lick for a suck, Miss Irish. I like the color of your hair. Reminds me of rust in the water at the bottom of the bay. What do you say? Best offer of the day."

Sully shook her head in disdain. Did she smell of sexual frustration or something? She tugged out her credentials and began. "There have been a series of murders. Girls like yourselves have been attacked and killed around town. I'm here because I want to stop it, and to give you fair warning that there is somebody out there who might wish you harm."

The teenager looked as though she was laughing, but only a faint dry wheezing came out. The others still had Sully fixed with their unblinking eyes. The girl's face snapped back to neutral with whiplash speed. "Just lovely. Everybody wishes us harm, Miss Irish. Every living soul in this city would rather we were gone and buried, never to return. You want to ask us some questions, want to know if there have been any johns ruffling our feathers or knocking us around? That's what we're for, Miss. We take the beatings and beat them off afterward because we can take it. We get a free drink and we're back on our feet or back on our backs all over again. Now, we haven't seen anything stranger than us, so kindly piss off back uptown so we can get back to business. We can take care of ourselves."

They turned away from her all together, resuming their conversations and reminding Sully of a flock of birds; all preening their feathers and chittering away to one another. What a waste of an afternoon.

Sully turned away from the pack and headed along the street again, pausing to peer down the alleyways now shrouded in shadows. There was movement in some of them. She caught glimpses of exposed skin and hiked up skirts that made her turn away with a little flush in her cheeks. She moved on, looking for an alley with only one occupant. Hoping to corner at least one vampire and work her over for information without the rest of the swarm enforcing solidarity and silence.

Only a few alleys down the line she heard one of them call out to her. "Give you a lick for a suck, darlin'. What do you say?"

There was something in that lilting southern voice that stopped Sully's next question. The vampire crept forward a little. Waves of peroxide blonde hair cascaded around her face and freckles stood out like ink spots on the papery skin. She asked again, "What do you say, little lady? Want me to make you feel good? I'll do it for you real nice. All I want is a little warmth. You've got plenty to spare. What do you say?"

Sully whispered into the alley's mouth, "Marie?"

Sully did not drag Marie out of the alleyway. Neither did she throw her into the taxi and haul her down the bay to her apartment. If she had done either of those things, there would have been witnesses and not just a string of people deliberately looking the other way. The streetwalker was obviously just assisting an officer of the empire in her duties. Marie had tried to speak once or twice in that taxi, only to be silenced with a glare. Sully threw her through the door of her apartment and slammed it shut before turning on Marie and readying the first round of screaming. She looked smaller than Sully remembered, and all of the wind left Sully in a sigh. She looked at her old lover and felt nothing but numb.

Marie was staring at her feet. Whatever predatory menace a vampire was meant to present she didn't possess in this moment. Sully leaned back against the door and asked, "What the hell happened?"

That predatory edge suddenly returned, and she snarled at Sully, "*You* happened! *You* happened to me over and over until everything was fucked beyond repair."

Sully was finally on the defensive. "What? What did I do?"

Marie snarled again. "You left me. You came storming in and blew everything apart again. What do you think happened to me after my husband got exploded? Do you think things went swimmingly? The police took me in. I was in jail, Sully. And where the hell were you?"

Anger rose back up in Sully, sweeping the numbness away in a sweet rush. "*You* left *me*. We were going to get married, and *you fucking left me*. We had everything in the world to look forward to, and you threw it away for some cock. So screw you and your sob story. You could've had me in your corner, and instead you went off with some greasy piece of crap with a magic mirror and the brains of a sturgeon."

There was a guttural quality to Marie's voice. "You left me all alone."

The vampire started sobbing, and Sully couldn't meet her eyes. Marie went on between gasps. "I was all alone, and I couldn't get a job, and I couldn't find anywhere to live. I was starving, Sully. I was on the street and I was starving, and I was freezing, and some guy came along and took the pain way. I mean yeah, I'm thirsty right now, but it's so easy to get a drink."

Marie's sobs stopped abruptly and she licked her lips. She let her eyes run up the length of Sully's body and purred, "So easy and so good."

Sully couldn't help but smile. "Nice to see some things never change."

Marie's purr turned bitter. "Everything has changed. You don't want me. I don't breathe anymore. Why can't you just leave me alone? Every time you come near me everything just gets worse."

Sully snorted. "How much worse can it get?"

Marie gave her a dead stare. "What do you want, Sully. Why did you come poking your nose into my business?"

The first part of her day suddenly came back to Sully. "There is somebody killing off vamps in the city. I was trying to get in touch with the community. Give you all a fair warning."

That brought the argument to a grinding halt. Marie exhaled. "Shit."

Sully gritted her teeth and asked, "Do you have somewhere safe to stay? I'm looking for this guy, but even I can't get him instantly."

Marie shook her head. "I live on the street. Which you already worked out. Why do you have to make me feel like . . . ?"

Sully cut her off with a raised hand. "You can stay here until it's over. I—I can't have you in harm's way."

Marie scowled. "I can't. Even if I was willing to take your charity, I need to drink."

Sully looked her up and down. She was paler than she had been and she had shed a few pounds but otherwise she looked as good as she ever had. Sully quelled her nervousness and smiled. "Let's do business."

It was worth everything else that followed just to see Marie's eyes widen in shock.

AUGUST 5, 2019

"I figure we've got about twenty minutes before somebody thinks to track Eugene by magic instead of tracking me, so I'm open to ideas."

Monkhbat's eyes were bugging out of his head, but whatever fear was gnawing at him was doing so quietly. His hands had no tremors as he sliced and diced together a meal for Sully and himself. The other two had politely declined food, but appreciated the invitation to come inside. Eugene was placed on the bar and Marie had her arms crossed over her chest, as if that could fend off the perverted stares of those painted eyes.

Songling's head cocked to one side. "You have no plan?"

"I don't know if you've noticed, but my plans tend to rack up a body count. If there's a way to get out of this city with nobody else dead, I'll be a lot happier." Monkhbat pressed a bowl into her hand and she took it with a wink and a grin.

Marie laughed. "Iona Sullivan, running away from a fight? I never thought I'd see the day."

"Oh, they'll get theirs eventually." Sully slurped down her noodles between words. "But right now we're sitting on a powder keg and I'd rather not fling fire about."

"I watched you disarming the explosive." Songling's placid face drew into a frown.

"Figurative powder keg. *The wish*. You know, the destructive force capable of wiping out our whole reality. On that note, Eugene, what the hell was chasing us?"

"THE OUTSIDERS. WE HAD THOUGHT THEM IMPOTENT IN THE FACE OF OUR GATHERED POWER. WE WERE WRONG."

"They're people. People and creatures that were wished away hundreds, no, thousands of years ago. But even though you wiped their universe out, they were able to survive." Sully's eyes had slipped out of focus. The noodles hung limp and dripping from her fork and there was a croak in her voice as she remembered against her will. "They had magic like we couldn't even dream of nowadays and they protected themselves against the change. They've been stranded in their own little pocket realities all this time, trying to get back. How are they coming back?"

Eugene had swiveled to face her. His sudden movement left Monkhbat cowering against the stove. "HOW DO YOU KNOW OF THE OUTSIDERS? NO MORTAL KNOWS OF THEM."

Sully already had a lie on her lips when Marie interjected, "I'm more worried that you went from knowing nothing to being the damn expert quicker than you could say boo."

She didn't want to lie to Marie. She really didn't. But they didn't have all night. "I . . . my memory is still spotty sometimes. It just came back to me."

"I CAN TASTE YOUR LIES, WITCH."

"You'll taste my fist in a minute, Eugene."

Songling's voice was soft as a sigh. "Keep your secrets, we have more pressing concerns. How do we destroy these Outsiders? How do we escape them?"

"THEY ARE THE GREATEST WIELDERS OF THE ARCANE TO EVER WALK THIS EARTH. SOME SO ATTUNED TO MAGIC THAT THEIR VERY FORMS FLOW WITH THEIR THOUGHTS, THE OTHERS SO RIGID IN THEIR CONTROL THAT THEY CAN CONJURE WITH THE VERY FUNDAMENTS OF CREATION. THEY HAVE NO MATCH ON THIS PLANE. EVEN MY KIND WOULD NOT HAVE CROSSED THEM IF IT COULD HAVE BEEN AVOIDED."

Marie finally turned her eyes away from Sully. "So why did you?"

"IN THOSE HALCYON DAYS, THIS WORLD WAS SPLIT IN TWO. TWO GREAT KINGDOMS WAGED WAR ON ONE ANOTHER FOR TOTAL DOMINANCE. ATLANTIS AND LEMURIA. EACH AS UNLIKE THE OTHER AS COULD BE IMAGINED, BUT UNITED IN THEIR DEVOTION TO THE OTHER'S DOWNFALL. ON ONE FATEFUL NIGHT—"

Sully cut him off. "Jesus, we're in a hurry here. They both cut deals to wish each other away and the demons took them up on it because they figured it would be easier to sneak past lowly shlubs like us and take over."

"None of this tells us how to defeat them," said Songling.

"They'll burn out. They're in the same position as Manhattan was before they came back, but unlike Manhattan they haven't been dumped on top of the source of all magic. Just maintaining contact without manifesting is probably burning through whatever supplies of magic they've got left in their little pocket planes. We just have to stay out of their way until they go dry."

Eugene rocked on the spot, but said nothing, which Sully took as agreement. "So how do we get out of town without anyone spotting us?"

"The tunnels showed the most promise, but with those creatures down there, it seems inadvisable." Songling drooped onto a stool.

Sully was glad the conversation was moving on, even if Marie was still staring at her far too intently. "Well, the streets are out, too. You might keep a tight leash on your gang, but everybody else out there is just one phone call away from a world of trouble."

Monkhbat opened and closed his mouth, then returned to nervously consuming his noodles. So much for local knowledge.

Sully had finished with hers. The food that had been delicious earlier sat like ashes on her tongue now. "Unless somebody has a better idea, then I guess we're getting a cab down to the docks and fighting our way through as best we can."

Both Songling and Marie looked like they were about to tell her just how stupid that was when they both suddenly cocked their heads around like dogs. Marie hissed, "There's somebody coming."

Sully yanked a knife off the magnetic strip on the wall and stalked over to the door. "Give me numbers."

Songling was pressed against the boarded-up window, peering out, before Sully had even seen him move. "More than twelve. Semi-automatic weapons. They are not my people. The Peninsula Consortium from the auction trying to reclaim their lost property?"

"Makes sense that they'd look here." Monkhbat had stripped off his apron, set down his empty bowl, and was ambling toward the door. "Have no fear. Monkhbat will speak with them."

Marie yelped, "No!" at the same time that Sully and Songling barked, "Absolutely not!" and "No way!", respectively

"Sully? You still don't remember, do you?" Monkhbat scoffed.

She held out her hand to him. "Whatever happened in New Amsterdam, we can work it out. Don't go out there. They'll tear you apart to get to us."

"You found out my secret. Everyone knew what I was. Everywhere I went. Even here, everyone knows. Everyone but you."

His eyes were inky black amidst the folds of his face, and there was a rumble in his voice. Something that spoke of deep forests and dark caves. Something that touched the primal parts of Sully's brain and set her skin crawling. Songling hissed, "He is Yaoguai. Why didn't you warn us?"

"What the hell is a Yaoguai?"

Fur swept over Monkhbat's face, as rich and dark as his eyes. His nose and mouth jerked forward, jagged teeth shining yellow between his parted lips. All the while he swelled larger and larger until the buttons of his jacket pinged off and the mass of dark fur within spilled out. Only when he had fallen onto his forelegs did Sully finally understand what she was looking at. "A bear? A werebear?"

Monkhbat reached the size of any normal bear and kept on growing. The claws that had burst out of his once chubby fingers in a rain of blood had twisted into brutal hooks the length of Sully's forearm. Marie had to dart forward to catch Eugene before the expanding fur knocked him from his perch. Still the werebear showed no signs of slowing. His muzzle swung toward Sully and his lips curled back. The aroma of beef noodles swept over her as he chuffed out a breath. She didn't think that he would be able to talk in this state, but she felt him speaking like a rumble in her bones. "After this, we are even, gwailou."

Without thinking, Sully reached up and stroked his muzzle. The fur was stinging hot to the touch. "Thanks, Monkhbat."

He knocked her from her feet as he charged out through the barricaded shopfront. The Gatling guns of the gangsters spun to life with a dreadful whine, but before a single round was fired the screaming started. Sully scrambled across the floor, caught Marie by the hand and dragged her off toward the back door. Songling was already in the alleyway, scouting their exits.

The gunfire echoed around to them, a steady staccato that Sully knew all too well. Marie caught her by the sleeve. "You can't just leave him here to die for us."

"You figure any of those guns have silver bullets in them? All they're going to do is piss him off."

Whether Songling believed Sully or he merely wanted to get them moving again was unclear, but he nodded his agreement and urged them on.

"THE WATER IS TO THE SOUTH. WE SHOULD HEAD THERE. YOUR PET WILL BE DRAWING UNWANTED ATTENTION." It was impressive that Eugene could sound so demanding when dangling by one foot from Marie's manicured hand.

Back in New Amsterdam, Sully could have told you the way to damn near anything. Even taking the backstreets and ducking through markets and kitchens like they were doing now, she would have known where everything was. Hong Kong was so familiar in so many ways but that just left her feeling even more lost when the turns she wanted to take led to dead ends and the instincts screaming at her to head one way swiveled just a street over. She couldn't even look up at the night sky for guidance. The glare of the neon reflected by the smog hid any stars that were lurking up there. Even if she could have seen them, the stars were all wrong. This unfamiliar sky was no friend of hers.

It wasn't often that Sully was envious of Marie's condition, but when they stepped out onto a crowded street and paused for a moment in front of a mirrored window to reorient themselves, she got a glimpse of herself, red with exertion, heaving for breath, and slick with sweat. She was starting to remember the real reason that she never ran. Running was bullshit.

Songling and Marie looked as picture perfect as the moment they had first started. It wasn't fair. Even Eugene looked pretty smug, although that was probably because Marie had him cradled against her chest again. Sully was looking forward to slam dunking him directly into hell.

She had barely caught enough breath to speak before they were moving again in a tight cluster. Songling strode along like he owned the streets, and they followed in his wake. Marie's hand found Sully's as they walked briskly on, and despite their impending doom that same goofy smile found its way onto Sully's face. "Back in Ireland . . . I just want you to know . . ."

"You couldn't see me." Marie batted her lashes. "I worked it out, Darlin'. Doesn't take a detective. You went wherever those Manhattan folks went, and when you came back vamps like me were invisible, same as we are to them. I figured you'd solve it and come find me, and here you are."

Sully gave her hand a squeeze. "Sorry it took so long."

"Darlin', we've got all the time in the world. Just knowing you were out there, coming for me one of these days. That was enough to keep me bobbin' along."

They ducked under the cover of a tattered tarpaulin overhang, crammed in so tight they were almost touching, as a posse of suit-clad gangsters strode by on the other side of the street. "What happened in Ophir?"

"What do you think happened? Somebody figured out what I was and I left town before they could put me in the dirt."

Sully looked down. "I'm sorry. I thought that Ceejay would get you somewhere safe."

"There ain't anywhere safe for us no more, Sully. That's what I've been trying to tell you—Hong Kong is the last stop for us."

Songling had already moved out of the cover, but Sully hesitated for just a moment. "I understand. As soon as Eugene is out of the picture, I promise you I will be here. I will fight for you. I'll do whatever you need me to do."

Marie's grip tightened on Sully's hand as they moved out into the street once more, hemmed in by the swarming crowds. "Sully, that wish could save us all. Not tomorrow or the next day, but right now."

Sully sighed. "Honey, there's nothing on the other side of a wish except death. It doesn't matter what gets promised. Everything that you were, everything that you are, it all dies when somebody makes a wish."

"ThEN DIe."

The Magi of Manhattan were getting better at their body snatching shtick. This time they'd taken control before the bodies hit the floor, but out here in the night crowd full of vampires the few powerless humans that they could snatch were scattered. The same crowd that had kept Sully trapped in place now blocked them from getting closer. Sully slugged the closest corpse in the face as it lumbered at Marie and had her hands up ready to dance with the rest, but they never arrived.

She had to shout to be heard over the screeching crowd. The vampires seemed to be freaking out that their dinner dates had just dropped dead. "I thought we'd settled this. Pratt is the one that—"

"ANd hE HAS paiD FOr his CRIMeS aGAinst US in blOOD. WE HAve no quarREL WITh YOu, SuLLIVan. JusT GIve us thE DOLL."

"Come on, guys. Don't do this. I gave you the guy that screwed you over. There's no need for this."

The dead moved through the crowd at a crawl. "We NEEd OUR

PeopLE back SULLivan. We did nOT SURVive FOR aLL those YEars AMONg thE FAE just for tHEm tO DIE heRE. It IS not RIghT."

"It isn't. It isn't right. But this isn't right either."

If her words gave them pause, there was no sign. They lumbered ever closer. There was no need for them to hide what they were now, not while they were trying to intimidate her into surrendering Eugene. Every one of their vessels—every one of the people that they had just killed as an afterthought—was a broken puppet, battering through the crowd of vampires as if they weren't there. "WE wiLL MAKe it RIGht. WhEN we haVE the POWer. WHEn wE haVE the DEMon."

Songling barked something out in a harsh Mongolian tongue that Sully didn't recognize. Some dialect or slang that the translation spell wasn't rigged for. The Magi steering the dead didn't seem to hear him. But the crowd did. The vampires fell on the animated corpses with the frenzy born of lifetimes of careful restraint. A half-dozen of them latched on to each of the Magi's vessels, draining them dry with long luxuriating gulps. The blood must have still been warm enough to be a treat. It was over so fast that Sully couldn't believe it.

Terribly aware that she was the last one in the street with a pulse, she whispered to Songling. "What the hell did you say to them?"

"That their friends were already dead, so we might as well feast in their memory. It loses something in the translation."

Sully nodded. "Are you two going to do me like that when I get dropped?"

Songling's shoulder twitched up in what may have been a shrug. "Waste not, want not."

"Never even crossed my mind, darlin'." Marie smiled beatifically. "I always figured there wouldn't be enough of you left to eat, the way you carry on."

Sully fought to hold back a laugh. "Christ, tell me how you really feel."

Lights began to flicker above the buildings to the north, like a storm was gathering down in the streets, just out of sight on the muggy horizon. "THE OUTSIDERS."

They had been drawn like moths to the flame of the massive amount of magic that Manhattan had just expended for no good reason. Sully dragged in another breath and willed the aches in her legs away. It was time for more running. Her favorite thing to do.

SEPTEMBER 11, 2011

The next crime scene was a lot more gruesome. It was in Red Hook just as Sully had predicted, in an alleyway beside an artisan sweet-tea cafe. The vampire must have fed just before this happened to her; there was too much blood splattered around the place for it to have been otherwise. The body wasn't cut or clawed this time, though. It had been dismembered. Afterward, somebody had scooped up some of the blood and tried to leave a note.

Sully sniggered to herself at the thought of the all-points bulletin she should be sending out. *Crazed, super-strong killer—enjoys finger painting.* The local police looked at her in horror, staring at a ruined corpse and laughing. You either learned to laugh or you went mad in this business.

Sully examined the word on the wall, still bright red and fresh under the forensic spotlights. She had a pretty good education, all things considered, but she had never heard of a "Manitou" before. Some translation spells were hanging in the air around her, letting her clearly understand the angry Spanish conversation going on inside the cafe thanks to all the sensory enhancements the forensic Magus had dumped on her, but they were doing nothing to the word. Which meant it wasn't a European, African, or Asian language. She supposed some of the Australian dreamers might have popped up over here without anyone realizing, but they had never shown an interest before. Maybe it was a name.

She snapped a picture on her phone, sent it to her office email and then flinched as she brushed against the bandage on her thigh as she slipped the phone back into her pocket. She waved her thanks to the technicians and dispelled all the enhancements before she walked into a wall. She wasn't ready to go back to her apartment yet, even if she was off duty. The longer that she made Marie wait, the hungrier she got. It was a lot easier to deal with Marie, hungry and desperate, than Marie, fed and sullen.

Sully picked up some iron tablets and blood builders from an all-night pharmacy, getting a dismayed scowl from the girl behind the counter. Apparently, blood loss was a common complaint in this neighborhood. Sully spotted a little group of vampires waiting for her by the street corner when she emerged. They had lost a lot of their cool, and some of them were pacing.

Sully gave them a much more polite nod than they had given her earlier in the day and tried to walk past them. They pressed in around her like hens around dropped corn. All hissing at her and talking over each other until she held up her hands, trailing sparks, and startled them all into silence. She let the tingle of magic slip away and sighed. "See? Somebody is killing vampires. I was trying to warn you. Have you seen anyone new? Seen anything weird?"

They all started chattering over one another again until Sully pinched the bridge of her nose, and then they fell silent. She pointed to one of them at random, a girl who looked to be about ten and who was quick to answer. "The girl that died tonight. Her name is Marie. She went missing this afternoon."

Sully had to bite back her immediate anxiety and the stupid response it would have prompted before calmly replying, "Marie was taken into protective custody this afternoon because she was at particular risk. Is anyone else missing?"

Another vamp butted in, a pretty boy with hair slicked down over one side of his face. "Why was she at risk? Who is a target? Who is doing this?"

Sully groaned at her own stupid mouth. "She was at risk because she had a personal connection to the investigation. The killer has shown no pattern so far except for attacking vampires. We don't have any information to share at the moment."

The buxom platinum blonde in the middle of the group spat some blood at Sully's feet. "A nice warm citizen dies and you can't move for all the cops. Ten of us die and you have no information."

Sully rolled her eyes. "Look, it isn't safe on the streets. Have you got anywhere to be for a few nights until I catch this guy?"

The boy sashayed closer. "You gonna put us all in protective custody, honey? Got a nice clean cell with an east-facing window for all of us? Fuck you, lady."

The other vampires nodded in agreement and started to drift away. Sully called after them, "Have any of you heard of somebody called Manitou?"

The crowd kept on dispersing until only Sully and the little girl were left. The girl looked just about ready to run but Sully stayed completely still and waited. Knowing when to shut up was a key investigative skill. The girl seemed to lose whatever fight she was having with herself and blurted out, "We are Manitou."

Sully raised an eyebrow and stayed silent until the girl groaned and went on. "I went across the border into the UN once for a special party. Vampires are illegal over there so it was all hush-hush. There was one guy. An older guy. The whole time that he was . . . doing his thing. He kept calling me that. I think it's the Native Americans' word for us. Vampires. It's not British."

Sully gave her a little smile. "Thanks, kid."

The girl tutted in disgust and walked away. "I'm a hundred years old, *kid*."

After three hours of unproductive phone calls to the UN embassy, Sully went home with her eyes closing. Marie jumped on her before she was even through the door, jaws snapping and skin pulled far too tight over her bones. Defensive spells sprang to life. Marie did a slow orbit around her and then smashed into the whiteboard. Shrieking and hissing. She tried to spring up again, and Sully cast a quick blast of ice to catch one of her feet. Marie sprawled on the floor. She caught

Sully's startled expression and changed tactics immediately, licking her lips and trying to arch her back despite the odd angle at which her leg was twisted.

Sully couldn't help but giggle. Marie would have flushed with embarrassment if she'd had the blood. As it was, she just looked quietly angry like she had every other time Sully had come home late. It was too sharp a memory for Sully. She pointed a finger at Marie and whispered, "Bad vampire. No blood for you."

Marie pasted on her most placating expression. "But you promised."

There was a distinct feeling of déjà vu happening. Sully dispelled the ice, and Marie crept slowly across the rug toward her, like she didn't want to startle her. It was like watching a kitten attack your socks. Sully knew she should stop it, but Marie was just too cute to look away.

Eventually, when Marie was on her knees right in front of her, looking up at her with those big blue eyes, Sully gave in. "All right. You get to top yourself up. But you owe me one."

Marie grinned. "Owe you one what, darlin'?"

Despite herself, Sully blushed and Marie giggled.

"Oh. Is that still your favorite way to wake up? I suppose I could do that for you since you're treating me so well."

Sully put her hands over her face and tried to will away the blush. Marie's cold hands fumbled at her belt buckle and she muttered, "How are you enjoying having your own personal sex slave, Iona? Do you like owning a person?"

Sully caught Marie's chin in her hands and tilted her face up, Marie had lost the puppy dog eyes, and her pupils were vertical slits. Sully squeezed just a little too tightly and hissed, "You could have left any time you wanted, Marie. Dead or alive, you are just the same as you always were." She bent at the waist until they were almost eye to eye, smiled sweetly and whispered, "My bitch."

Marie jerked back, need warring with anger on her face. This close, the heat radiating off of Sully was bringing a flush to her pallid cheeks. Being this close to the living could make vampires feel like they were still alive.

Sully smirked at her. "I've changed my mind. I guess I am in the mood after all. Come to bed and work for your treat."

Marie stood there, wavering for a long moment, as Sully stripped and walked away. Then she gave in.

AUGUST 5, 2013

Streets were starting to look more familiar as they blurred by. Maybe they were getting closer to the docks. Sully wondered if you could learn the geography of a city by osmosis. She'd never tried consciously to learn her way around New Amsterdam, and now she knew it considerably better than the back of her own hand, since all the old scars had vanished after the war. Maybe time in a place was all that it took.

That ominous glow on the horizon didn't seem to be abating, the further that they ran, so either these Outsiders were burning brighter or they were getting closer, still on Eugene's tail. Sully knew which option she'd put her money on. She needed to get her cadre off the streets until things cooled down, and they needed to go somewhere that nobody would expect. Songling nearly yanked Sully off her feet when she caught ahold of his collar. "In there."

"You cannot be serious."

Sully shrugged. "If I was hunting me, it's the last place I'd look."

It wasn't really a proper church. They'd banged out some of the upstairs windows in the scabby looking block and slotted in some stained glass, but the building was still a big slab of ugly concrete. There was a cross above the door, plain and generic without any of the good old-fashioned Catholic gore that Sully was used to. Still, if there was going to be a single door left unlocked in the chaos on the streets tonight, it would be this one.

Inside there was a moment of blissful silence after the constant roar of the crowds. In a city of sin, you couldn't find anywhere quieter than this. The pews all sat empty, the altar was unadorned. If there had been anything of value, it probably had been stolen by now. Vamps weren't known for their religious leanings, what with the church's typical approach to them involving a whole lot of hellfire and not much of that fabled forgiveness. Sully walked down the aisle, scoping the place as she went. For all that it was a modern building, they'd recreated all the dark nooks and crannies of a big gothic cathedral, and with only a few candles burning it was hard to make out much of anything in the flickering shadows. She stepped up to the altar, and stared down at the Gatling gun lying there for one long moment before she heard Marie's yelp and spun around.

It took her a second to recognize the preacher from the day of her arrival, mainly because his ragged overcoat had been cast aside and tonight he was bristling with munitions. If she was being honest, she hadn't paid too much attention to his face, but his demeanor was unchanged. Shoulders back, his frame radiating self-righteousness. "How dare you bring these abominations into the house of the Lord!?"

Guns or no guns, Sully couldn't help herself. "Which abominations in particular?"

"The dead have no place walking the earth, as well you know. They belong in the ground, awaiting their final judgment."

He was staring too intently at Marie for Sully's comfort. She needed to hold his attention. He probably wouldn't shoot her just for existing. "I've been thinking about this a lot since the last time we met, and I think I've finally figured it out. It's the sex thing, right? You religious nuts can't get laid, because that would be a sin, so you've got to get all that energy out somewhere else. You can't blow your load, so you want to make everybody else just as miserable as you are."

That did the trick. He advanced on her, bellowing. "You dare to belittle my holy purpose, to drag it through the filth of your own iniquity, here in the house of the Lord? You should be on your knees, begging his forgiveness!"

Sully rolled her eyes and leaned back on the altar. Her fingertips brushed the gun. "Yeah, nothing sexual about that. Get on your knees. This is my body, shove it in your mouth."

The leather of his face flushed puce. "How *dare* you?!"

"How dare I? How dare *you*? You think you know what your god wants? You haven't even worked out how shit works on this bitch of an earth and you're already trying to tell us about what's up above it. If your god is in the house, he'd better speak now or forever hold his peace."

The silence in the church was deafening, broken only by the sound of the preacher's gun cocking. "Take your blasphemy outside."

Songling was silently circling around behind the whack-job. Sully just had to keep him looking at her a little longer. "Who's going to make me? You?"

"You know nothing of the power that I wield. The power that God has granted me to punish each and every one of you sinners and abominations." He was almost frothing at the mouth.

Sully wet her lips. "Are we talking about your peashooters there or the bomb under the city?"

That stopped him dead in his tracks. Unfortunately, it stopped Songling too. The preacher didn't say a word, but the widening of his eyes gave it all away. Amateur. "I was trying to work it out. Who didn't have magic but wanted this whole city leveled? Who could slip in and out with all those explosives without anyone paying a blind bit of attention? Who was beneath notice?"

"They shall all take notice soon enough. This den of sin shall be razed, just as our Lord—"

Sully grinned. "I disarmed the bomb, dumbass."

Now that he was closer, the tremors of fury running through the preacher's arms and fouling his aim were clearly visible. Even with the spray-and-pray Gatling gun, Sully would give good odds on the fool missing her. As well as bugging out, his eyes were darting all over the church as he tried to work things through. "This is not the end of my crusade. Oh, no. I shall lay you to rest, then return to my holy workings. Prophecy has foretold this. The city of the dead where the anti-Christ shall rise. The unholy trinity made flesh. It cannot be abided. The Order of Iscariot shall purge this sinful land through flame and—"

"The Order of Iscariot? Holy shit, I thought you guys were a joke that somebody in anti-terrorism made up." Sully cackled. "I've got to get a picture for Ceejay, he'll never believe this."

"We are burdened with the most sacred duty. To purge the—"

Whatever he had planned on purging, Sully never found out. He was still mid-sentence when Songling leaped onto his back. Marie hit the dirt as the two men struggled, but Sully had nowhere to go except over the top of the altar when the preacher's convulsing hands rattled off half a drum of bullets in her direction.

Somewhere in the tumble, instinct took hold, and she came up from behind the altar with the preacher's backup piece aimed squarely at his chest. But by then he was done. Songling had his fangs hooked in the old bastard's neck and his eyes were rolled up in ecstasy. It was the first honest emotion Sully had seen on his face since meeting him.

She ignored the moaning and stalked down through the church to find Marie curled up under a pew. A raised thumb popped up as Sully approached. "Nicely done, sweetheart."

The door was not easy to secure. Like most of the furnishings it was made out of something closer to cardboard than wood and it took considerably more effort and noise than Sully would have liked to get the heavy stone baptismal font tipped over in front of it as a barricade. The building probably had a back door or three, but if anyone out on the street had heard the rattle of gunfire, this was where they'd come.

"I wouldn't worry about that, darlin'." Marie was back on her feet with Eugene held upright by the time Sully got back to her. "Folks round here don't fret about a few bullets, as long as they aren't being slung their way."

"Maybe, but that bomb didn't feel like it was a one-man operation, even if they only left that one idiot behind to detonate it. If there's more of that weird cult in town, I'd rather not tangle with them."

They waited politely for Songling to finish, and another moment for him to produce a handkerchief to clean the worst of his dinner off of his face. "Apologies."

"Don't worry about it, we've all got to eat." Sully shrugged.

Marie slumped down onto the front pew, dumping Eugene beside her. "How long do you reckon we've got before the next posse rolls up?"

"NOT LONG."

The vampires both jumped, and Sully had to bite back a laugh. "How do people keep forgetting you're alive?"

"PRACTICE."

"All right, Eugene, you and your demon senses are up." She crouched so she was at eye level with the doll. "How long do you think we have before the Outsiders catch your scent?"

The doll grew still, and from the way that Marie shivered beside him, Sully knew he was doing something with his magic. "IF THEY KNEW WHERE I WAS, THEY COULD BE HERE IN MOMENTS. THEY ARE STILL SEARCHING FOR US. THEY CANNOT HAVE MUCH FOOTHOLD IN THE WORLD IF THEY ARE SO BLIND."

"Give me a ballpark here. How long can we stay still?"

"MINUTES RATHER THAN HOURS."

"I'll take it." Still squatting, Sully ran a hand over the smooth poured concrete of the floor. "Songling, drag all this furniture and the carpet to one side. Marie, go look for some chalk up by the psalm board."

Marie frowned. "What are you going to do?"

"I'm going to do the calculations for a portal to hell."

Songling was already moving furniture, but that stopped him. "You mean to rid us of the demon?"

"Eugene is what they're chasing. With him gone, all the trouble fades away."

He paced closer, hands folded behind his back to keep from fidgeting. He was riled. "As does our opportunity to protect Hong Kong."

Sully had closed her eyes to concentrate on the numbers in her head. "If we can get rid of Eugene here and now, I won't need to leave town. We can move on to the next crisis without Outsiders and Manhattan and all the rest stomping around."

Even with her eyes shut, she could hear him pacing. "With all due respect to you, Miss Sullivan, I fear that you have begun to believe your own mythos. You are but a single witch. A single witch cannot defeat an army nor defend a city."

"Tell that to the British," Marie called back from the pulpit.

Even Eugene decided to weigh in. "SHE IS NO MERE WITCH, COLD ONE. SHE IS AN ABOMINATION. SHE IS THE THREE IN ONE. SHE IS—"

Sully's eyes snapped open. "She is going to kick your ass if you keep running your mouth."

"I do not approve of this plan."

She met Songling's dispassionate stare with a glower of her own. "Good thing I'm not looking for your approval."

"Miss Sullivan, my people are going to die. We are going to be wiped out of existence. Is this the future that you want?" There was something very like emotion in his voice now. An edge of what, in a lesser man, Sully would have called pleading.

She couldn't let it influence her. "If you aren't going to help, could you just shut up? These calculations are complicated, and if I get them wrong, I tear the universe a new asshole."

Marie drifted between her boss and Sully with a stub of chalk held up between two fingers. "You're sure about this?"

"Nope." She plucked the chalk out of Marie's hand. "But we're all out of options."

The circles were the simplest part of the procedure, and with no magic flowing through her, Sully didn't feel the little uncomfortable tug when she passed over them. With those interlinking lines complete, she began laying down the runes and sigils that would light up with spellfire when the time came. Every student of magic, from the highest Magus to the lowliest street witch, knew how to summon a demon. It was so notable in its absence from their formal education that you could almost see the shape of the ritual by the hole that was left, and the one thing that united all students of magic across the world was a desire for secret knowledge. Sully would have been amazed if a single graduate had made it through their university years without some sly senior sneaking them the details. Throughout history, all that had been required was the tiniest pinprick to be opened between the planes and a demon would practically fling itself through. Nowadays, they were fairly content to stay put so the portal that Sully opened would have to be large enough to cram the doll down.

The calculations became more complex as a result of those changes, and the casting grew even more difficult because she had none of her usual senses to feel when things were going awry. It was a feat of pure calculation, made all the more difficult by her fragmented memory and the constant count that she had running in her head. When it ticked past the five-minute mark, she began to sweat.

After each new component of the spell was marked down, she forced herself to lay down the chalk and stare at it, to think through every next step. With all the enemies breathing down their neck, even the slightest delay could mean death, but Sully realized on her third rewrite of the same spellform that she was procrastinating. Marie was watching her intently, and Sully didn't know if she wanted to be seen. With a growl, she snatched up the chalk and scribbled out the rest of the spell without pausing.

What Sully wanted had nothing to do with the situation that they were in. How she felt had always been secondary to what needed to be done. She had made a career out of ignoring the things that she wanted in favor of what was necessary—with the odd detour into what was right—and this was where all of that had led her, on her knees in a church in a vampire town, trying to throw a demon doll into hell before one of the millions of people who wanted her dead finally caught up to her. She read over the spell one last time to be certain, then she stood up with a grunt. "I'm ready."

"Miss Sullivan. Do not do this." Songling was standing so close behind her that the hair on the back of her neck stood up when he whispered. "Listen to reason."

She didn't turn, but she did glance over to Marie to get her read on the situation. Just when Sully thought that her lover couldn't get any paler, Marie proved her wrong. "We don't have time for this."

"Only if we follow through on the course that you have set. If we take a different path, then there is time enough for all of us." This close, Sully was finally able to identify the familiar undertone in Songling's voice. His words didn't come out silky smooth, they came out like the rushing noise of sand dunes shifting.

"I AM IN FAVOR OF THIS PLAN."

"You want to put it to the vote? Eugene and I want him back in hell now. You want to keep ahold of him. That just leaves Marie. What do you say, sweetheart?"

Marie's mouth fell open. "What?"

"Do you want to send Eugene back to hell now, or keep him? And I don't want to rush you, but the longer you take to decide the more likely it is that we all die horribly."

Songling seemed to be just as surprised as Marie. He actually fell back a step. Marie looked terrified. "Why are you asking me?"

"Why should Songling and I get to make the decision? You're here. You've been through this with us. You're just as important as either one of us." Sully gave a little shrug. "What do you want to do?"

"I don't know, darlin'. And it isn't that I don't trust your judgment, or that I think what you're saying ain't right. It's just . . . this is big. This is real big. How can folks make decisions like this?"

Sully gave her what she hoped was a reassuring smile. "Just say what you feel."

Songling came at Sully so fast she didn't have time to turn before he hit her. She didn't even feel it happen. She just went from standing to the floor with a sound like a gunshot echoing in her ears.

By the time she'd blinked away the darkness from the edge of her vision and let the ache encircle her whole head, Songling already had Eugene. "This is not a democracy."

She struggled upright, legs like overcooked noodles. "No, it isn't.

I just wanted to make sure my girlfriend wasn't going to be too pissed when I did exactly what I was planning to do from the beginning."

They stood very still. Each waiting for the other to make their move. The quiet of the church became almost deafening until it was split by the soft click of Marie flipping the safety off of the preacher's gun. "Put the dolly down, boss."

Sully grinned. "Guess we know who she's voting for."

Songling's eyes darted back and forth between the lovers. Calculating his odds. Sully smiled. "You could probably get to me before I cast, and you could probably get to her before the Gatling spins up, but you definitely can't get to both of us."

"If you're dead, there is no witch to complete your spell. I only need to get to you."

"You think she'd let you kill me without blowing you away? You'd be just as dead as me." Despite everything, Sully couldn't help but dart a glance at Marie's resolute face. Her stubborn pout. It was just as perfect as she remembered it.

Songling's face was less expressive. "Many things are more important than the life of one man."

"Not sure that getting shot to pieces just so that one of those other bastards out there can pick the doll off our corpses is going to make you into a martyr for the cause."

Songling was always still, but he completely froze when Eugene rumbled. "EVEN IF YOU SURVIVED YOU WOULD STILL NEED A WITCH TO SEND ME BACK ONCE YOUR DEAL IS STRUCK. AND YOU WOULD NOT SURVIVE."

The silence kept ticking on. Songling was paralyzed. Eventually Sully couldn't bear the waiting any longer. "Listen, Songling, I owe you for keeping an eye on my girl. I need Hong Kong to survive just as much as you do. You don't know me, you sure as hell don't trust me, but at the end of the day, you've got nowhere to go. Toss me the doll, let me get the whole damned world off our back, and then I'm with you all the way."

He wet his lips with the tip of his tongue. "You will not be enough."

Sully very deliberately relaxed and held out her hand. "Maybe not, but it's me or nothing."

Songling threw her the doll.

Her fingers had just closed around Eugene's nasty little face when the stained glass exploded inward.

Madame Blavatski came through the shattered window frame in a nimbus of crackling light. It wasn't the flying spell that Sully knew, but it seemed to be doing the trick. Marie panicked and sprayed the old woman with bullets, but not a single one made contact. Sully had used protective spells to curve incoming shots away from her in her crime fighting days, but she'd never been powerful enough to just stop them dead in the air like Blavatski had just done. "Demon. Vampires. Cambion. Such a delight to see you all again."

"KILL HER." The voice echoed inside of Sully's head and almost without thinking, she began to ease the ring off her finger with her thumb.

Songling actually gave her a little bow. "Madame Blavatski. The pleasure is all ours."

She drifted slowly down toward them with a fake smile painted thickly onto her face. "What manners, such a darling. Perhaps you will survive all of this unpleasantness unscathed. I have no reason to be less than magnanimous. After all is said and done, I have both of the prizes that I coveted right here before me, and nobody to stand in my way."

Sully growled. "I'm standing right here."

"Oh no, my pet, you are an object of interest, but you do not play the game with enough skill to be considered a contender. If it were my will, you would already be dead where you stand. Only the fact that you are a curiosity preserves you."

Marie had tossed aside the gun, but she was still looking cocky. "Darlin', knock that mouthy bitch out of the sky. She clearly don't know who she's dealing with."

Blavatski let out a dry cackle as her toes brushed the floor. "Such faith this one has, it warms the heart. Shall we break that faith?"

The air around Blavatski thickened as she twisted gossamer-fine threads of spellfire from her fingers. Sully's ears popped as she braced herself for whatever was coming.

It was nothing complex when Blavatski finally cast it, or rather it was a very complex version of a very simple spell. Instead of a single bolt of shimmering blue light leaping toward Sully, the spell fragmented into a dozen smaller motes that flew in at her from all angles. Eugene sucked in and swallowed as many as he could, but the rest hit her skin like a spatter of gentle raindrops. The church started to dim, even as Marie screamed her name.

Down in the deep darkness where she sank, there should have been peace and rest, but instead there was the voice. Echoing in from all around her. "WAKE UP."

She groaned. "Give me a break."

"WAKE UP OR WE WILL DIE."

Sully tried to roll over and go back to sleep. "Don't I deserve a little rest? It's been nonstop."

"YOUR MATE IS IN DANGER."

Sully's eyes snapped open.

Marie was the one hanging in the air now, coils of shimmering light pinning each of her limbs out like she was a butterfly in a collection. Blavatski wasn't even looking in her direction as the spell stopped merely restraining her and began to pull her apart at the joints. Marie was a tough girl who'd been through a hard life, but there were limits to anyone's reserve. Her scream cut right through the fog and dragged Sully up by her guts.

Blavatski was looking down at Eugene with the first genuine smile that Sully had ever seen on her face. She was layered with so many protective spells that it was like walking through molasses just to get to her, but whatever hold they managed to get on Sully fell apart when they came into contact with her ring.

With three lumbering steps, Sully closed the distance and she got to see the look of surprise on Blavatski's face before her fist slugged into it. Immortal or not, powerful or not, Blavatski was still an old woman, and she folded up like a paper bag when Sully hit her.

Marie dropped from the air with an agonized cry and Sully fell to the ground right along with her. Gasping for air as the spell that was meant to render her unconscious kept trying to slow her heartbeat. Standing up again was out of the question, but she couldn't stop until she knew that Marie was all right. Sully inched her way across the floor of the church, crawling until her fingers brushed over the cool silk of Marie's dress. "It's all right, Darlin'. It's over. We're all right."

Songling brushed past Sully, the tail of his coat tickling over the back of her head as she lay there. "You, Marie, have dislocated both shoulders and one hip. You are far from being all right."

He moved back over to Sully and examined her with the same dispassionate expression that he'd maintained throughout their night together. It did not escape her attention that he was holding Eugene. "You are fighting the curse. It will stop your heart if you continue to do so."

She was slurring her words so badly she doubted he could even understand her. "Saves you the trouble."

Songling cocked his head to one side, then carefully laid Eugene down on top of Sully. "You have been nothing but trouble."

His fingers were frigid as they slipped around her throat and started to squeeze. It was a professional grip, none of the amateur-hour nonsense where the windpipe got crushed or there was any possibility of twisting away. Just the firm, unbreakable pressure of his fingers on the sides of her neck, cutting off the flow of blood to her brain.

She clawed at his arms, but she didn't have any strength left to struggle. She could barely keep her eyes open as it was. Her hands convulsed on Marie's skirts, and she felt their fingers entwine before she slipped back down into the familiar darkness and the embrace of the demon waiting there for her.

SEPTEMBER 12, 2011

Sully had spent too much time in conference calls to the embassy, searching for related cases. Just generally wasting her time until something came up to put her in the right place at the right time. She had considered some sort of sting operation if one of the vamps could be convinced to help out but dismissed it just as quickly. There had to be another way to come at the problem other than tossing relatively innocent creatures into the path of a monster and hoping you could pull them away in time. Sully had never liked fishing. She was still aching from the rough repayment she had received the previous night. There were scratches down her back that probably should have been bandaged as much as the matching bites on her thighs were. She wore them all like trophies.

Sully was not an old-fashioned kind of witch, but there were a few of them still out there in the city. Wearing no shoes. Wandering wherever their intuition led them. Obeying some mystical and esoteric rules that only they knew, and that they couldn't possibly explain. Rules that made them superior to the common people with their permanent addresses and their sanity.

Sully could wander aimlessly with the best of them. But she had to get a coffee to keep her hands warm first. No matter where you wandered in New Amsterdam there was always a coffee shop in sight when one cup ran out. In about an hour, she suspected she was being followed. An hour later, she caught the person following her. She turned into an alleyway, dumped a few enhancement spells onto herself and then leaped up the fire escape and rushed onto the roof.

Blood was thumping in her ears as she tackled the coyote. They tumbled over the rooftop and it whimpered and snapped at her, teeth never quite making contact. Sully managed to get her feet under her and then, strong as the coyote was, it was in trouble. She got a knee wedged into its hip, pulled one of its forelegs out wide, and however it howled and snapped, she did not let go. Finally, it went limp beneath her. It submitted and Sully rolled to her feet, letting the enhancements fade. Her next spell would be something lethal and explosive. She had seen those teeth up close enough to know that she didn't want them coming at her again.

Eventually, feeling more than a little self-conscious, she asked, "What are you supposed to be, then?"

Waves of magic started pouring off the coyote and a thin line of light stretched out along its back.

Sully expected something like this, but she still had a killing spell crackling between her fingers while she waited. Nothing happened in this city without somebody seeing it. There were just too many people. If you killed somebody, even a vampire, you would be seen by somebody. A man emerged from the coyote skin, golden-skinned and naked as the day he was born. He didn't show the slightest hint of discomfort now any more than he had while he was an animal.

Sully wasn't interested in naked men as a general rule, but this one was a work of art. He had long black hair flowing smoothly in a way that filled Sully with bitter memories of a tugging hairbrush all through her childhood. He spoke in tongues now, using the inverse spell of the one she had employed earlier on the killer's graffiti. "I have come to find the one who kills your monsters. I have come to bring her home before she provokes war. You will tell me what you know, and you will stop harassing our diplomats."

Sully let out the breath she didn't know that she was holding and took a moment to think. "You understand English?"

He gave a one-shouldered shrug. "Well enough."

Sully crossed her arms. "How about you tell me what you know and I don't send you back over the border as a nice rug?" His face remained placid as he waited for her to talk, confirming all of her suspicions. She shrugged. "All right. The killer I seek is one of your people. One of your police. Somebody like me who hunts monsters. But somebody who has been doing it for too long and has gone a bit too far. You haven't reported any of this yet because it's your partner or something. Right?"

He still looked calm but his tone was breathy. "They warned us that your magic was powerful. That we could not win a war of spirits. They did not warn us that you could pluck thoughts from our minds."

Sully rolled her eyes. "You really are a terrible liar. Now give me what you have on this person, and I will try to take them alive."

"I would not deliver a dog to your justice. You have the stink of the Manitou on you. You would feed her to them if you could."

"All right, so she's a native, trained in your weird animal-changing magic. She hates vampires. She doesn't trust witches. She obviously doesn't trust you since she went on her mission without you. Tell me about the spell that lets you become animals. Any special requirements or ingredients?"

He finally scowled. "I will not share my people's secret magic. All of your torture will not force me to reveal it."

Sully scoffed. "Well, the animal skin is still here so I guess that's a requirement. Is there an upper or lower size limit? Can you alter your mass?"

His brows drew down, and he began to shiver slightly. "We call our power, we make our break from humanity, and we become whichever beast we are touching the hide of."

Sully uncrossed her arms and stretched. "Don't suppose you have a name for her? Any idea of where she likes to hang about?"

He tutted. "I will not give you her true name. I know how your people use them. She will stay close to her prey. As close as she can without startling them."

Sully nodded. "Red Hook. Good to know. Piss off back home then."

He cocked his head looking more like a dog than ever. "I am not familiar with that phrase."

Sully shooed him. "Go back to where you came from. I'll see to your partner. Nobody wants you getting caught on this side of the border. I can't stand when things get political."

She hissed the last word as though it was poison, and for the first time she saw a little smile appear on his face. Some things were universal, it seemed. He opened his mouth to reply, closed it again and then crouched down to pick up his coyote skin. He gave her a polite nod before he changed, and she gave him a less polite pat on the head, setting him growling, before she climbed back down the fire escape.

AUGUST 5, 2019

It took Sully a moment before her mind spooled up to full speed again. If there was some separate hell where dead people went for being naughty, she was pretty certain it couldn't be worse than floating in eternal darkness listening to Mol Kalath bitching her out about all the mistakes that she'd made. She didn't pop up right away even after consciousness had returned. There was a lot you might overhear when people thought you were a corpse and the odds were that nobody would try to kill her as long as they thought she was dead. Wherever they'd stowed her was quiet; the sounds of the streets were muffled, and a tickle of breeze told her she hadn't been buried alive. She listened carefully for any hint at what was going on around her and twitched involuntarily when Marie whispered.

"Your breathing changed, Darlin'. We know you're awake." Fucking vampires. She opened her eyes. They were in a car—which was a pretty ballsy move on Songling's part—but the engine wasn't running. They were parked up in some side alley, although Sully couldn't have even begun to guess where. The vampire in question was in the driver's seat, with a wide brimmed hat pulled low over his face as though he was napping. Maybe he didn't have the guts to face her after his little bout of attempted murder. Eugene was lying on her chest failing to comment on her tits, which was concerning. Her hand was pinning him down, and Marie's was on top of it, keeping the ring pressed against the demon's fabric body. That was one way to hide his magical signature from their hunters, although he was not going to be happy about it.

With a groan she eased out of Marie's gentle hold, Eugene still clasped tightly. All the aches that adrenaline had been keeping down were here to say hello. "Where are we?"

Marie's frown deepened. "You don't want to know what happened?"

"The sleeping spell was killing me because it couldn't knock me out, so chuckles here knocked me out instead." She patted Songling's shoulder with the stump of her left arm. "Saved my life. Much appreciated."

Songling didn't move. "We are south of Hill Twelve. A distance to the docks. Twenty minutes if the streets stay clear."

"We're still headed for the ships? I thought you didn't like that plan."

"You can make my wish just as easily from anywhere in the world, and there is too much attention on Hong Kong right now. On this we are agreed." Songling tilted his head back to take another look at the empty road in front of them.

Sully grinned. "I won't be making any wishes."

"We can discuss this later. For now, we must focus on the task at hand."

There wasn't a hint of trouble outside that Sully could see, but she didn't have vampire senses to rely on. With the ring on her finger, she barely had any of her usual senses at all. "Eugene isn't going to be happy about you putting Cold Iron on him. The way I hear it, demons can't stand the feel of it."

"We are all suffering for his freedom, I can discern no reason that he should not suffer for it, too."

Sully chuckled. "Oh man, you'd better hope we get him back to hell. If he's still here when this is all over, you're going to have a really bad time."

In answer to that, Songling abruptly started up the car and peeled out into the road. This part of town wasn't nearly as built up as the rest. It was all residential properties with what looked like abandoned university buildings dotted in among them. Some of the architecture looked original up on the lower slopes, Mongol built instead of being an imperial addition. Run down, but infinitely more interesting than the bland gray slabs that the British had thrown up everywhere.

They made it a couple of streets before running into the usual Hong Kong traffic, and a couple of streets more before they rolled to a complete standstill. Marie sat rigid with tension beside Sully, staring out into the crowds like a startled meerkat. "What's happening?"

Songling's gaze in the rear-view mirror was chilly. "Monday night in Hong Kong."

"What do you think, do we ride it out or bail on the car?" Sully nudged Marie with her shoulder, earning her a glimmer of a nervous smile.

"We'll make the same time either way, but the car offers us concealment."

It was hard to argue with that. If the windows were tinted like the vamp bus that the NAPD vice squad used to run around in collecting hookers, then they were pretty much invisible behind that mirrored shine, and if the windows weren't tinted, it was still better than wandering the streets, conspicuous as they were. None of that logic did anything to quiet the straining anxiety that built up in Sully the longer they sat still. She wasn't as twitchy as Marie, but she could feel the same nervous energy churning in her gut. She would have called that sensation instinct before the war, but the long slow road to recovery had muddled up so many of her reactions that she couldn't be certain what was real and what was some unrelated bad memory rearing its ugly head.

A thick fog rolled up the street toward them faster than the cars were creeping down, yellow tinted by all the pollution. It brought a smile to Sully's face. Fog came from the sea; the fact that it was here meant they were nearly home and free. She gave Eugene a little squeeze, like she was a kid with a doll. "Nearly there."

That was when the first car up ahead of them flipped over.

Metal shrieked. The next car lurched to one side. Sully knew she should have dived right out with the doll, so she was surprised to find that instead she was flinging herself on top of Marie, as if her body could shield Marie from what was coming. Songling was shouting something in a dialect that didn't translate. Marie was hyperventilating despite needing no air to live. The car didn't turn over. Instead, it tore in half.

The roof lifted clean off. Sully caught ahold of Marie and tried to drag her free, but like the good girl that she was underneath all the makeup, Marie was wearing her seatbelt. The chassis leaped up beneath Sully and she tumbled out onto the tarmac with a grunt. The car was on its side, metalwork screaming against the road as it was dragged along. Marie had her hands out toward Sully, her mouth contorted in a scream, but she was already out of reach.

There was no tell-tale flare of light and magic, there was no sign of any construct. All Sully could see was the fog, formless and coiling everywhere. It seemed to thicken into tendrils as it came down toward where Eugene lay in the middle of the road. Sully scrambled forward and flung herself on top of the doll just as it was lifted away from the tarmac. "Not on my watch."

"IF THE COLD IRON TOUCHES ME AGAIN, I SHALL WEAR YOUR ENTRAILS LIKE—"

Sully stumbled, punch drunk, to her feet. "Why bother? They found you anyway."

The fog reached out for Eugene all over again, and Sully had to twist the doll from the grasp of the impermanent fingers of fog. She'd never seen a spell like this. She'd never even heard of a spell like this.

Marie was screaming her name in terror, but there was no pain in her voice, so Sully couldn't spare any attention. Not while whatever shredded their car was out here. She strained every one of the senses she had left for any sign of trouble, but between the screaming and the fog there wasn't much she could make out. The fog coalesced into something denser but still amorphous. Something huge and fluid in its form. Even if she'd had the vocabulary to describe it, a moment later that description wouldn't have fit.

The streets were finally starting to clear as people fled for their lives. That was what sane people did when faced with something huge, unknowable, and terrifying. Sane people ran in the opposite direction as fast as their legs would carry them. Sully strode forward.

As she came closer, the fog withdrew, pulling in tighter and tighter around a central core that was now completely concealed by the coils of smog. Sully hoped like hell that she was looking at fear. "I'm betting that there's somebody in there who understands me, so understand this. If you come at me again, it will be the last time. I've been screwed with all over this town and I've had enough. Nobody is getting Eugene. Nobody is making a wish."

From the center of that roiling cloud, the very heart of the beast, a weak voice croaked out, "Help . . . me."

Clattering heels drew Sully's attention away for just an instant. Songling and Marie had cut their way free of the wreckage and were heading toward her. She barely had time to raise her arm in warning before the fog exploded outward once more, bowling her over. She wrapped herself around Eugene and rolled as wave after wave of force pounded against her. The fog scrabbled at her clothes, dug into her joints, ripped at her skin with hooks so tiny they couldn't be seen, but Sully would not let go. She could hear Marie and Songling's voices beyond the tempest. She was close enough that she could cry out for help, but what good would that do?

A tentacle of thickening fog dug its way in between her arm and Eugene and tried to lever her off, but when she wouldn't relent, the tip split open into a hissing serpent's head that struck at her face again and again. The teeth did not cut into her flesh the way that real ones might have, but the sting was the same. Her face was sticky where the serpent struck, but it was not her own warm blood leaking down her face. It was a translucent fluid as cool as the fog that had spawned it. Ectoplasm.

"DO NOT LET THEM HAVE ME, IONA. YOU WOULD NOT LIKE THE WORLD THAT THEY WILL CREATE."

The pulsing waves of fog had slowed to the odd rise and fall, but more and more stinging extrusions were raking over Sully's skin. If they thought that they could hurt her to get what they wanted, they really didn't know who they were dealing with. The eye of the storm had shifted closer to her, dragged in by all of the energy being expended on ripping Eugene from her grasp. Despite every other sensation, she could feel the presence of a body behind her, hanging in the air. That same rasping voice came again, barely heard over the whipping wind. "I beg you, Madame. Let them win . . . they are . . . killing me."

Unseen claws plucked at Sully's lips as she gasped, "Le Plongeon? What the hell did you do?"

"It is not . . . . it is the Lemures. I thought that I could harness them as Blavatski uses the Atlantean magics . . . but it is they who ride me. Their will, it is greater than mine."

Another impact washed over Sully and she rolled with it, looking up into the chaos swirling above. Le Plongeon was suspended in mid-air, his long hair whipping around so wildly that it took Sully a moment to realize why he looked so wrong. He was withered to little more than a skeleton and skin. Every drop of moisture had been drawn out of his body to give the Lemurians their gaseous form. Sully had heard of physical mediums who could give temporary flesh to disembodied spirits, but after the life that she'd led, she had made a point to avoid learning too much about ghosts.

If all of this fog was nothing more than Le Plongeon's vaporized fluids, then fire would solve the problem quite promptly. Sully had gotten pretty good with fire magic through the years. Evocation had always been her specialty, but there was something about fire that just felt right to her, an affinity. That was what had drawn her to Dante's Inferno in the first place, all those years ago when the thought of actually casting it couldn't have been further from her mind. She could cast it now. The spell wasn't among the memories that she had retrieved; it was right at the center of her biggest and most painful mental wound. But she knew that if she slipped the ring off of her finger and she reached for that memory, then the words would leap to her lips as readily as breath. All she had to do was slip off the ring and all of this could be over. "DO IT. END THIS CHARADE OF HUMANITY."

Eugene struggled in her grasp, as if he could hear the voice inside her head. "IONA?"

The next time that the Lemurians jerked on Eugene, Sully let them. Without her body to act as a shield, they hauled on the doll so hard that it lifted both of them up into the air.

Eugene bellowed, "SULLY!" as she let him go. A few stray coils of fog still snatched at her as she fell back down, and they slowed her descent just enough that she could catch hold of the emaciated remains of the man still dangling in the air like a puppet.

With one arm, she dragged herself level to his face. "Le Plongeon?"

He hissed, "What?"

"Sorry." She hammered her head forward into his hollow face. It practically caved in at the point of impact. Sully was surprised a plume of dust didn't come out as his nose inverted with a gristly crackle. Unconscious, if not dead, he collapsed onto the road in a dry heap.

For a few awful seconds, Sully lay on top of him and nothing happened, then the fog convulsed around her and was dragged shrieking back inside of the old medium. He inflated beneath Sully like a life-jacket and the sensation was too unpleasant for her to tolerate. She stumbled to her feet just in time for Eugene to plummet down and land beside her. "OUCH."

Sully scoffed. "Can you even be hurt?"

"I CAN BE DAMAGED."

She picked him up and looked him over. "Are you damaged?"

"NO."

"Well, all right, then." She tucked him under her arm and went to look for the vampires. The street was desolate now that the fog had cleared; they would be around here somewhere. She knew Songling would never leave without the doll, and she hoped Marie wouldn't leave without her.

In an uncharacteristic bit of pleasantry, Eugene asked. "ARE YOU DAMAGED?"

Sully laughed. "Usually."

They carried on in amicable silence for a while as Sully peered under flipped cars and into torn doorways. "I don't suppose those amazing demon senses—"

"IT IS DIFFICULT FOR MY KIND TO PERCEIVE THE COLD ONES EVEN WHEN THEY STAND BEFORE US. I CANNOT HELP YOU."

Sully turned in a circle, marking the absence of both vampires and clues with a long, spiraling, "Shit."

Anywhere else in the world there would have been sirens and crowds rushing at her by now, but in this lawless town there was nothing at all. She took a deep breath, faced to the south and started walking. She was always going to leave town. That had been the plan since the moment she saw the embassy burning. Of course, she'd been planning to leave with Marie, not alone. Sully swiped at her face with one tattered shirt sleeve as her treacherous eyes started to prickle at the corners. Marie and her boss had probably done the smart thing and gone to ground. She couldn't expect everybody to run into the eye of the storm with her. It was better that they had pulled back to somewhere safe, and they knew she was headed for the docks. They were probably just around the next corner. Probably.

These streets were close enough to the docks that they were starting to look genuinely familiar. Stragglers from the usual crowds swayed drunkenly here and there, every one of them eying Sully warily when they could get their eyes to focus. With the doll dangling from her hand and her partially shredded suit, it was hardly a surprise that she was drawing unwanted attention, but she couldn't bring herself to care. She was tired, beyond exhaustion and out the other side into some strange placid place where all of her troubles seemed distant. Raavi probably would have said she was in shock, but he always said that after she'd waded her way out of the latest bloodbath.

Sully lifted the doll up to face level so they could talk like equals. "You know what the really crazy thing is?"

"WHAT?"

"I'm starting to like it here."

SEPTEMBER 13, 2011

She went to the office early, starting on a far more productive round of phone calls to the local constabularies. There had been a couple of thefts and one assault of interest in the Red Hook area. An antique shop had lost a few taxidermies, and there had been a pimp assaulted in a very professional way outside one of the worst boarding houses by an unknown woman that the victim had described as being "brown-looking."

It was enough to have Sully tearing her way across town in a commandeered unmarked car. She was browsing the reports on her phone as she went, trying to find the vital information. A bobcat, a bear, and a golden eagle had been stolen. After reading back and forth a few times, Sully was convinced that that was all she had to worry about.

A sensible agent would have assembled a team and had animal control on call, a redcoat response team swarming all over the place, and a sensible agent would have lost the native girl as she turned into a bird and flew away. Sensible was not a term often found in the copious paperwork that Sully generated in her wake. "Bold" appeared in the more flattering ones. "Suicidally overconfident" had come up more than once in internal memoranda.

She crept up the stairs, stepping over a passed-out addict reeking of piss, and cast a shrouded spell of ice on the substantial lock attached to a thin wooden door. Then a quick tap with her boot was enough to shatter the metal, and she was pouring into the room in a cloud of her own power. She had defensive spells swirling around her. Her eyes were glowing with sensory enhancements. And the room was empty.

It was halfway to rotten, just like so many of these almost abandoned buildings. There were no furnishings except the rusted husk of a refrigerator and a flattened mattress in a corner with a few torn garbage bags spilling out their contents. The bear fur was easily recognizable among them and Sully hit it with a tight ball of fire that incinerated it instantly. No point risking that coming back to bite her later. She dug through the melted plastic bags with the toe of her boot, looking for anything else that might have been a skin. If not technically empty, the room really was unoccupied now.

Sully swore under her breath. The window was open. Could these shapeshifters fly if they were wearing a bird skin? Could you even skin a bird? She should have asked the taxidermist some questions. She quickly killed all of the spells that she could, both to stop the drain on her resources and to prevent immediate detection. Coyote boy hadn't cast while he was in animal form, but there were a dozen little enhancements that you could cast before changing shape that might carry over and let you see latent magic.

She slammed the door back into place and repaired the inside chain with a rub of her fingers. She should call for backup if she was trying to set up an ambush; that was procedure, but nobody cared about these vampire girls dying. There was a big difference in the competence level of a cop who cared and one who didn't, and she had the bit between her teeth now.

She closed her eyes and took a deep breath. She always did better on her own anyway; the bandaged throbbing pain on the inside of her thigh attested to it. She bumped something with her foot as she turned back to the room. It was just part of the general junk that seemed to accumulate on the floor of places like this; a roach motel. The top of it was ripped open, and there was something inside. Sully crouched down to look closer. It wasn't a roach, not a whole one. There was a sticky yellow mess just starting to dry out inside the box. That was when Sully got hit with the fridge.

* * *

Afterward, Sully was able to piece the order of events back together. The skinwalker had shed her chitinous shell underneath the fridge and used the force of the transformation, or maybe some other strength enhancement, to lift and throw the heavy block of enameled steel. She'd had the sense to wait until Sully had dropped her defenses and turned her back, and it absolutely would have killed her if the contingency spell hadn't spun it aside just an inch before it struck. Consequently, it only knocked her shoulder out of its socket instead of breaking her back.

The impact ripped the breath out of Sully's lungs and dropped her to her hands and knees. Sully didn't have the air to speak, let alone cast. So with her hands still wreathed in impotent spellfire she couldn't do a thing as she watched the native woman stalk out into the center of the room. She moved like she had muscles in places humans didn't have muscles, but her voice, deep and throaty, was human enough as she cast a lethal spell, flinging it from her hand at Sully with obvious contempt.

The dart of red flame roared as it flew toward Sully. It was some panicked instinct that saved her, rather than rational thought. Sully caught the dart in her hand, still wreathed in licks of her own green spellfire. She met the shapechanger's golden gaze, and then she crushed the dart out of existence. Sully saw the woman's eyes widen. She saw the fear there for the first time, and that gave her the energy to rise up and suck a burning breath down her throat.

Sully growled. "Nice try, bitch," and her face cracked into a grin.

The shapeshifter dived for the scorched mattress, and Sully got enough breath gulped down to prepare a spell. The mattress was flung up against the wall, and there was a thick mat of fur underneath. Sully could have kicked herself. Hidden under the mattress. She got off one spell, not lethal unless you really messed up afterward. A shimmer of silver crossed the room and the skinwalker's hands were frozen to the floor where they were tangled in the mess of fur. Sully took a second to catch her breath—she really needed to go to a hospital—and then staggered over to the woman where she was squatted down, straining against the ice with all of her strength.

When Sully came into sight, they locked eyes and a growl started deep in the would-be beast's throat, eventually resolving into a bitter exclamation. "You do not know the things that we have to do to fight the Manitou. The things we must become. To break free of the limits of humanity, we must cast aside the things that make us human. Only to know that on the other side of some line drawn on a map the monsters roam free and grow to mastery. Here the Manitou live better than we do. Dead things walking among you, eating your children. And you care nothing. Nothing!"

Sully leaned gingerly against the wall, careful not to disturb her shoulder, and sighed. "I get it. I really do. I've seen plenty of people go off the deep end in this job. But I can't let you kill my people. So you've got to go home before you start a war, or I am going to have to put you down. But since we are both on the same side most of the time I'm going to let you choose which one you want."

The woman snarled. "You have no prison that can hold me. You have no shackles that can bind me. If you do not have the courage to murder a real person for the Manitou, then set me free to finish what I have begun." She paused in her ranting and sniffed the air. "I can smell you hiding back there, Keme. Do you still lack the courage to face me?"

A moth that had been doing orbits around the bare bulb on the ceiling split apart, and the man from before landed with practiced ease on his feet. He ignored the trapped woman and spoke to Sully. "My thanks for your service, witch. I will take her home to face our justice."

Sully raised an eyebrow and pretended that her whole body wasn't screaming in pain. "You promise me that she'll get home safe and sound?"

He finally looked at the woman with nothing but pity on his face. "If she does not fight me, I will force her into the form of some small prey animal and carry her in my jaws."

Sully forced a smile. "Great. Have fun. Have your embassy send my office some lies for my report."

The woman broke free of the ice. In a swirl of hair and fur and snowflakes, she became a huge coyote and lunged for Keme's throat. He staggered back a step, but it would not have been enough if Sully hadn't caught the beast by its tail and tugged for all she was worth. The coyote landed and spun to snap at her, but she spun just as fast, staggering around the room kicking up the mess of furs from under the bed. She ran from those snapping jaws, still dragging on the sandy tail and hoping like hell Keme would do something before this ended in her getting eaten.

The man caught one of the furs as it was thrown through the air and twisted inside it. He became an animal Sully didn't recognize, looking a bit like a badger, and then he leaped on the coyote's back, digging his claws into the other shapeshifter's hide. Blood started to flow, and Sully was relieved to see that despite the snapping jaws, the blood seemed to be the woman's.

She let go of the tail and staggered away from the flailing mess of tooth and claw. She got some distance and prepared a lethal spell of coiled lightning, but in the whirl of close combat there was no way to pick one target from the other. She weighed the last few days in her mind, good and bad. Then she unleashed the lightning on both of the fighting animals with her living hand.

When they died, they didn't go back to being human. But underneath the fur, where the lightning had burned it away or their own claws had torn it, there was human flesh. Politics was coming like a tidal wave. Sully could already feel it.

When she left the room, both bodies were heaped upon the furs and the whole pile was burning. It should die out before the whole room was burned, and it would definitely stop before the slum burned to the ground. She was not taking any chances of the whole story being found in those bodies. The last thing she needed was new mandatory training to learn how to become a cat. The report would have the word Manitou in it, and she would describe some foreign monster that could explain the remains. It wasn't perfect, but it was enough to keep the people in her city safe.

After the hospital, she went home instead of to the office; she didn't like to use her "injured in the line of duty" time too often, but this seemed like a worthy occasion. Inside the apartment, Marie was sitting on the bed reading a magazine that Sully was damned sure she had stolen from somebody else's mailbox in the hall. She tossed the girl a bag of blood with a shrug of the shoulder that wasn't trapped in a sling and called out, "Honey, I'm home."

Marie looked from the blood bag to Sully's bandages and before she remembered to slap on an expression of hate she was on her feet, rushing over and cooing, "Oh, my gosh! Are you all right?" She was almost touching Sully when doubt clouded her features. Her cold hands dropped to her sides, and she bit her lip.

Sully pretended not to notice; the pills for the pain had helped give her a swagger again. "Just a little present from the hospital."

Marie raised an eyebrow. "They ran out of flowers?"

Sully pointed a finger in Marie's face, still in a morphine haze, and snapped, "Hey, I do the witty comebacks in this house."

When she dropped her hand, Marie wasn't laughing. "I suppose that you being all beaten up as usual means that this nasty business with the vampire killer is over and done?"

Something cold and wet inside Sully's chest shifted as she saw how this conversation was going to go.

"You can get back on the streets whenever you want to."

Marie had wanted to be an actor for as long as Sully knew her; it had been what brought her to the big city. She had planned to put in some time on the stages of Grand Avenue before moving on to a film career back down south, once she had proven her chops. But none of that had happened and she couldn't fake a smile worth a damn.

"I'll just be rolling along, then; wouldn't want to keep cluttering up your lovely home."

Sully didn't know how to get through the minefield of this conversation. She was smart enough when it came to her areas of expertise, but outside of them Sully wasn't good at talking, not really. She preferred doing. She caught Marie by the wrist as she tried to walk away and spun her around. Then she crushed their lips together before Marie could get a word out. Marie's fangs pressed against her lower lip, and Sully's heart thumped hard enough for both of them.

Finally, when she had to break away to breathe she whispered, "Stay."

AUGUST 5, 2013

Despite her bravado, cold dread had overtaken Sully. There was no way Marie would have left her behind willingly, she knew that in her gut. Songling might have taken whatever path presented the least resistance toward his goals and his survival, but not Marie. Never Marie. Sully kept moving forward because there was nothing else that she could do.

The braying bar crowds from down by the docks reared up ahead, the most living breathing humans that Sully had seen since she arrived in Hong Kong. Out of towners, sailors and revelers all. She should have been pleased to have a crowd to blend back into, she should have been relieved that her long journey across Hong Kong was over, but the cold would not abate. She ran through her suspect list as she pushed into the mass of bodies. It couldn't be Manhattan, the Magi wouldn't even be able to see Marie, let alone abduct her; it was one of the unfortunate side effects of the saturation that they'd suffered in the far realms. Blavatski had the form for grabbing Marie, but she wasn't exactly subtle, so if she was back on her feet there would be fireworks. The Peninsula Hotel crowd seemed to understand the mechanics of abduction and ransom pretty well, but they would have tried to make a grab at Eugene instead, if they'd been close enough to take Marie. That left two options, neither of them easy to stomach. Either the Iscariot losers had grabbed them to get revenge for Sully's disrupting their plans and killing their preacher, or Songling had betrayed her and grabbed Marie as a hostage.

After his performance in the church, Sully was inclined to believe in the latter option. Now that they were in spitting distance of the finish line, Songling had to be getting nervous that she was showing no signs of changing her mind. She'd been the best shield that Eugene could ask for, so it made sense to save her earlier, but now . . . not so much. It pained Sully to walk away, but if nothing else, they had established that Songling was as logical a man as any bloodsucking fiend could be and he wouldn't risk making Sully his enemy by doing Marie any harm if he had any other option. If she could follow through on her plan, get shot of Eugene, Songling would probably hand the girl back without any need to mention it again.

Sully slipped out of her reverie when someone ran by close enough to clip her shoulder and set her cursing. The whole bar crowd, the whole of the dockside, seemed to be coming toward her in a slurring, stumbling stampede. "What now?"

There was a gentle concussion, not unlike the spell that Sully used to fling around for crowd control. It rocked the runners forward and gave them a little more impetus to run faster. Any attempt to push against the flow of bodies would have been futile, but Sully managed to sidle sideways and cling to one of the flickering old streetlights until the bulk of the bodies had passed. If she had been as smart and mature as she'd been telling herself, then she would have run, too. Whatever was waiting down by the boats didn't have to be her problem. She had enough to deal with.

In the end, all of that maturity and hard-won wisdom lost the battle with the simple fact that she was tired. She had been tired of carrying the weight of the world for so long now. When the war was over and she had given everything that she had, she'd hoped it had been enough. Once she remembered enough about herself and the world to be more than a vegetable, she'd been quietly delighted that she had been out of commission for so long and the wheels hadn't fallen off the figurative bus. She should never have come back to all this. "Why couldn't you have just pissed off back to hell when you had the chance?"

"ARE YOU SPEAKING TO ME?"

She hauled the doll up to eye level. "You see anyone else around here? Why couldn't you find yourself some shmuck with a bit of chalk and a bit of magic and get out while you had the chance? Everyone else did."

"I WAS LOST AT SEA WHEN YOU WERE BROKERING AMNESTY WITH THE HELLS. AFTER ALL YOUR KIND HAD DONE, I WAS EXPECTED TO THROW MYSELF ON THEIR MERCY? I LOOK UPON YOUR TAWDRY WORKS NOW AND I DESPAIR. LOOK WHAT YOUR PEACE HAS BROUGHT ME."

Sully bit back a snarl. "Have I ever done anything less than I could for you? Has there been a single moment throughout all of this when I didn't give you all I could give?"

"YOUR GIFTS AMOUNTED TO NOUGHT BUT PISS IN THE WIND; AND I AM NOT TO BLAME FOR YOUR FOLLIES."

All the old anger that Sully had tried so hard not to bring back when she pieced herself together was still simmering somewhere down inside her. The unfairness of this whole situation burned. She couldn't even be mad at Eugene, because it was right. Expecting Eugene to trust a human would have been like expecting her to trust a scorpion.

Now when Sully hunched her shoulders and strode into the mass of fleeing bodies, the crowd parted. Her clothes were just as tattered, her magic just as absent, but now they shied away from her as though it had been the rage that had sheltered her all through the years instead of her power. Vampires, sailors, drunkards and citizens looked into her eyes and turned themselves away. She started to pick up the pace. She was almost jogging when she broke free of the crowd and saw the Mongols waiting for her at the bottom of the slope.

There were still only three of them, the bald bearded bastard now wearing a proper military jacket and his henchmen sporting the season's fashion of pistols and hostages. Songling had not gone quietly; his jaw was hanging loose on his face, all that pretty symmetry smashed with one pistol whip. He'd been bound with some quick and nasty spell, too, some brutish metallic tasting curse that had his limbs all locked up. For her part, Marie was still looking almost picture perfect, just a little dusty after the Lemurian storm they'd all just waded through. Sully smiled at her, despite everything. "How'd you get here before me?"

Their leader, who Sully had mentally labeled Scarface back at the hotel, had cast a quick translation spell to make negotiations smoother. "We did not stop to look for anyone."

Sully slowed her stroll to an amble, keeping her distance without looking like she was keeping her distance. "And why'd you tip your hand and scare off the crowd?"

"Manhattan."

Sully shrugged. "Fair enough."

"This will be a simple exchange. You will give me the doll. I will return your lover." Apparently Mongolian Intelligence was paying attention to her social life; that wasn't creepy at all.

"And Songling?"

Scarface glanced at the struggling vampire mobster with blatant contempt. "If you want it, it is yours, I have no use for vampires."

Sully sighed. "Are you new at this? You really need to sweeten the deal a little. Promise you won't wish me out of existence, offer me money, something like that."

"What use would you have for money?"

"None really, but it's the principle of the thing." She spun the ring with her thumb, working it down toward the knuckle. "You've got to sway me."

"I have a gun to your lover's head and you need further encouragement?" Scarface sniggered.

Sully could only spare a brief glance at Marie's terrified eyes before putting a brave face on. "She's a vamp. It will hurt, but she'll heal."

He raised a gloved hand and pointed to the sky. "Not once the sun rises. You new in this town? We have less than nine minutes. Then both of your friends die with no effort at all on my part."

The ring was resting on Sully's knuckle now, just a flick of the wrist and it would be down in the gutter. "If I give you the doll, they die regardless."

Scarface had yellowed teeth, and it was less of a smile and more of a sneer, a display of aggression. "Not if I give you assurances of your safety after my wish is granted."

"You think I'd trust your word?"

"You can trust that their deaths mean nothing to me, and you have only eight minutes left to decide."

Marie's eyes were wide and darting. First to the horizon, then back to Sully. Over and over. A vampire could survive direct sunlight for a few minutes without dying. They'd get one hell of a sunburn, but they'd survive. That gave Sully ten minutes at most to get her free and get her under cover. She couldn't afford any more delays. She had to move now.

She licked her lips. "How about a different deal?"

"I have offered you favorable terms." Sully was getting really tired of that sneer. "You do not have the leverage for more."

"You seem pretty on top of current events. How's London doing right about now?"

That drew a chuckle from her. "Threats? I expected more. All of that reputation. All of that power. Did you think that I would come unprepared?"

"I count two peashooters and one caster down on the docks with his dick in his hands. Even if you're the best evoker in the Mongol army, which I doubt, you still aren't going to be a match for me. Le Plongeon and Blavatski both took a swing at me tonight. They were the best in the world. And I'm still standing here. You really want to try your luck?"

With an economy of movement that made Sully jealous of his skill, Scarface coiled out a spellform and cast a ball of blazing blue flame right at her chest. She caught it in her hand and crushed the light out of it. Maybe it was a good thing the ring was still on.

He gave her an appraising look. "You misunderstand me. I am not here to match magic with you. They are."

There was a spell woven into the walls of Hong Kong way back when it was first being built. A ward against traveling spells within the city to prevent any covert attempts at invasion. In the fortress out on the water they had a dedicated portal room below sea level that they could flood at the first sign of trouble, but here in the city, if you tried to teleport yourself around, all you were going to get was a headache. All of that meant that when the air seemed to tear around Sully and a half-dozen withered looking Fae emerged into the neon lights of the street, they were not coming from somewhere else. They had been here all along, wrapped up in veils of magic and shadow, just waiting to come out and play.

Even after all this time, they still touched some primal switch for revulsion in Sully's brain. Their spindly limbs spoke of spider-legs and their pellucid flesh was like something that you'd find under a rock at the bottom of the ocean. Nothing good looked like that. Nothing good moved through the world in those convulsive shudders.

The six Fae that Scarface had brought along were looking a lot healthier than the specimen back at the Peninsula. They still had some of the otherworldly luster that they carried with them from home. "You may be the best in the world, Firecracker, but my allies are not from this world."

Instinct made Sully try to back away from the monsters as they emerged, but they had revealed themselves on all sides. There was nowhere to go. Scarface was still running his mouth. "Give me the doll, and you shall not be harmed."

The Fae's huge almond eyes seemed to look right through Sully. They locked on to Eugene where he quivered beneath her arm, but Sully herself seemed to be as invisible to them as they had been to her just a moment ago. The Cold Iron might pull her through again.

It took all of Sully's strength to keep her adrenaline under control and the quaver out of her voice, but she managed it. "Your pets can't touch me. They can't even see me. Vampires either. You've brought them to the only place on earth where they're the prey instead of the predators."

Scarface looked very briefly intrigued. "Is this so?"

The Fae's voice echoed into her head from so close by that it brought bile stinging at her throat. "*We see you, flame-bringer. The wishes that entangle you are like a beacon to those who can feel the warp and weft of fate.*"

"Fuck it then."

Sully swung for the nearest of the Fae, and when her ring made contact, it left a putrid gray scar across its hollow bird chest. It was like hitting a leather cushion. No bones and just a little too much give. The pain was enough to punch a hole in their circle and Sully didn't hesitate to dive through.

Shots rang out from down at the docks, but Sully was relieved to hear them pinging off the brickwork by her head as she went for an alley. As long as the attention was on her, Marie was all right for about another five minutes.

Sully leaped over a trash-heap, took a sharp left and came out in another of the warren of backstreets just a little closer to the water. One of the Fae chasing after her overshot the entrance and had to grab on to the corner to drag itself back. "KILL ME BEFORE YOU LET THEM HAVE ME, IONA. I BEG YOU."

"They aren't getting you. They aren't getting anyone else. Not ever again."

It came for them, bouncing from wall to wall like a ten-foot-tall toddler with only rudimentary control of its body. All the supernatural grace that had been their hallmark was gone. Their bodies were no longer vessels for their godly power; they were prisons that they hadn't learned to navigate. There was something else new about the Fae that Sully hadn't been able to place out there in the sight of their new master. A desperate hunger. It didn't cast, or strike at her—all that it wanted was Eugene.

Sully was so surprised at its bounding leap that for the briefest of moments, it touched the demon doll, bowling them all over. By the time Sully had kicked it off, the glow had returned to the Fae's hand and Eugene was limp in her grasp. They were feeding on magic. The

Khanate must have been spoon-feeding them Magi and artifacts to keep them alive all this time. It was a monstrous kind of genius. Sully stuck her finger in her mouth and yanked the ring free. There was no more time for clever solutions. No more time for dancing around the truth. No matter how she tried to deny it, she was a weapon. When the Fae lunged again, she spat the ring in its face.

The lights went out. It may have just been the generators finally giving out under the strain or perhaps the sudden rocking of the over-head powerlines when every single bird perched upon them took flight at the same time. But for just that one moment before the dawn, the whole of Hong Kong was pitched into abject darkness.

All of Sully's senses returned in a rush. The flow of magic through the air. The gaping vacuum within the reaching Fae. The pulsing life still buried deep within Eugene. She felt them all. She caught the Fae by the wrist and ripped its magic right out of its body, swallowing it all down without spilling a drop. It was nothing but skin and ash by the time that it hit the ground. Sully caught her ring on the first bounce and all the lights in town flickered back to life.

She'd never seen Eugene moving any distance on his own. It was kind of hilarious to watch him now, bumbling around on his stuffed legs. He backed up against the smooth concrete of the alley wall. "WHAT ARE YOU?"

"Shut up Eugene," she snapped.

"I DISBELIEVED WHEN THE OLD ONE CALLED YOU CAM-BION, BUT NOW IT ALL MAKES SENSE." Eugene was edging away toward the road and the Fae. "YOU KNOW THINGS NO MORTAL COULD KNOW. YOU DO THINGS THAT NO MORTAL CAN DO."

Sully scrambled to her feet, fumbling the ring back into place. "We don't have time for this right now!"

"NO WONDER YOU HIDE BEHIND THE COLD IRON. ABOMINATION!"

She was running after the demon doll now as he headed right into the arms of their enemies. "I'm getting really tired of your shit, Eugene."

"MONSTER!"

The doll was almost out into the street before she caught him and her momentum carried her back out into the line of fire. Another bullet clipped by her as she scooped up Eugene, and he tried to wrestle out of her grip. She held the doll above her head like a white flag. "Don't shoot or the demon gets it."

Both pistols were trained on her, but no bullets were forthcoming. The remaining Fae came boiling back out into the streets from the tangle of alleys and straightened up abruptly when they came into Scarface's line of sight. He was as pristine as always.

Scarface had his arms crossed over his chest and a good frown going, but if he planned on staring Sully down, he was out of luck. She'd gone at it with the whole bureaucracy of the British Empire before; this guy just didn't have the staying power. Eventually he grunted, "I wish for her death."

The Fae started casting before Sully could even think of responding, the smooth swooping motions of their spidery hands leaving ripples in the air as they rewrote the universe. As wishes went, it was a small one. Something that even these weakened Fae could muster if they worked in concert. Their fingertips, tracing ripples in the air, began to crumble to dust as the last of their magic left them.

In the breadth of a heartbeat, Sully had to make a decision. The distance back to the Fae was too great to interfere and even if she shed the ring, there would be no stopping a wish. That left only one option. She charged at the Mongols but the soldiers didn't even bother to squeeze off a shot. She was already dead as far as they were concerned. She was within a few steps of Scarface's smug little grin when the ripple of the wish washed over her.

Nothing happened.

Surprise could wait. She kept on going, tossing Eugene at the Mongols' feet and using her momentum, deliberately now, to carry one hell of a haymaker right into the jaw of the man holding Marie. He went down like a ton of bricks. Scarface started barking orders, but nobody seemed to hear them. Sully was cackling as she closed the last few steps. He held up his hands. "If I fall, my army will rush the walls. Hong Kong will burn tonight if you kill me."

Sully kicked him in the crotch, hard enough to lift him off his feet. "Why would I give a damn about Hong Kong?"

With his concentration quite thoroughly broken, the spell holding Songling fell apart. He turned on the other soldier before the man could aim his gun, tearing out his throat and then dropping the remains of the man's windpipe onto the boardwalk with a splatter. It took the vampire another moment to lock his broken jaw back into place, then he fell on Scarface like he'd gone a week without supper. It was gruesome; even Sully had turned away before it was done.

The Fae were all clustered together like lost little lambs. "*An anchor. We did not foresee this.*"

"You should have. I've had it all my life. My old hag of a mother didn't want her precious little weapon getting wished away by the British so she cut a deal with the demons to keep me here." Sully was surprised at how much that recollection still hurt.

"*It is not the shoddy work of demons.*" For creatures without emotion they sure as hell sounded contemptuous. "*Their clumsy weavings, we could unravel without effort. This was wrought by one of our own.*"

"Why would any of you want me kept safe?"

"*Safety was not its purpose. Your emotions tangle all things, even intention. They add complexity where there should be none. It is one of the many ways in which we are your superiors.*"

Sully scoffed. "Yeah, you look real superior, cowering over there."

One of them had managed to parse the wish, seeing things with those big black eyes that humans couldn't even grasp. "*Happiness. That was your wish. Not for yourself, but for another. One who cannot be happy without your existence. A clever ploy, but easily undone. We can see the ties that bind you.*"

"There was no clever ploy. There was no plan." Sully reached back and caught hold of Marie's cool, shaking hand. "When I went down to wipe out your whole miserable species, I never expected to come back. I never wanted to come back. To live with the memories of what I'd done. To remember all the dead I'd made. Who would want that?"

Marie's grip tightened and her voice came in a whisper. "You wished that I'd be happy?"

Sully squeezed back. There was no world in which Marie could be happy without her. She had empirical evidence now that the two of them were meant to be together. That in every possible version of the universe, *they* were meant to be. Joy cracked in her chest, fierce and unexpected. "It must be love."

Songling passed the wriggling demon doll off to Marie with a polite nod. "Any fool could see that."

Sully couldn't tell which of the Fae was speaking. Their voices all sounded the same, emotionless and blank, echoing in her skull. *"Then she must be eliminated."*

When the rage cut through Sully's rosy cheer, she was taken aback by its intensity. The Fae were just as surprised. They flinched back from her expression. Her breath was ragged, but her words came out in a purr. "How do you figure that's going to play out?"

They seemed to be shrinking before her eyes. The failed expenditure of their shallow reserves of magic had drained them beyond the point of being simply withered. They looked like they were moldering from the inside out. *"With her removed . . ."*

"You know they call me a genocide because of what I did to you vermin? Maybe I should make it true. There are so few of you now, and you are so pathetic. I wouldn't even have to break a sweat this time around."

They tried to draw themselves up, to look imposing again. *"Threats. They have no effect. We do not fear as you do."*

Sully took one step forward, letting Marie's hand slip out of hers. "You don't need to be afraid, you just have to understand that I'm going to give you one chance to run, then I'm going to put what is left of you in the ground."

The biggest flaw in the Fae had always been that they could only think of themselves. That was how Sully had been able to truss herself up like a bomb and walk right into their home plane; they couldn't conceive of anyone being willing to die for a higher purpose. Now that same problem manifested in half of them trying to run and the other half trying to cast. If they had worked together, they'd probably have won, even if a couple of them paid the price for it. As it was, Songling closed on them before Sully had even brought her finger to her lips.

He tore through them like paper. They didn't bleed, but there was a clear jelly inside of their rotting hides that smelled faintly of antifreeze. It probably wouldn't have been palatable to vampires. He hared off after the duo that had run before the other three had hit the ground.

It was oddly polite of him to give Sully and Marie a much-needed moment alone. They both opened and closed their mouths a few times, smiling and laughing at their own inability to say anything. It turned out that when there was physical evidence that the person you love can't be happy without you in their life, nothing else needs to be said. Sully closed the tiny distance between them, pinned the demon doll between their bodies, and kissed Marie for the first time in this new universe.

There were no fireworks, but there was a shudder of explosions from over by the city's eastern wall. The Mongols really were trying to break through, throwing magic and artillery shells at the old wards, focusing all their efforts on one location. Apparently, a tattered Eugene was a better prize to crow about than an intact Hong Kong. Marie's lips moved, and all those thoughts faded from Sully's mind in a rush of sensation.

Sully hadn't dug too deeply into these kinds of memories from the past. The memories that brought anger had made her feel guilty, but the memories of this comfort had left her with tears she couldn't explain running down her cheeks. It all came flooding back at the first brush of Marie's fangs on her lip. It ran in a jolt right through her body, and all the little stories that her senses had been whispering to her ever since she set eyes on this girl suddenly made sense again. It was the closest thing to love that Sully had ever known, and she never planned on letting it go again. Not for anything.

"KNOWING THAT ONE OF YOU IS AN ABOMINATION AND THE OTHER A COLD ONE RUINS MY ENJOYMENT OF THIS CARNAL MOMENT."

"It isn't for you." Sully drew back just far enough to drop him in a puddle of blood, then leaned back into the kiss. She wanted it to go on forever. And then the sun came sizzling over the horizon.

FEBRUARY 11, 2010

After so long on the ship, New Amsterdam was a sensory overload of epic proportions. It was chaos, pure and simple. On the destroyer, everyone had their place, everyone had their orders. She could tell the time of day from the position of the sun and their heading, but just as readily from which man was complaining about which minor inconvenience. She had no idea what time it was here in this bar, and the gin was only partially to blame. Daylight worked differently in this strange new place, the sun never rose and it never really set, blocked from sight by the looming walls or reflected back and forth between the gleaming towers. They had warned her before she turned in her papers that the city never slept, but so far she hadn't wanted to, either. Being drunk all day, every day was like being half asleep anyway; she was never really tired, never really rested. But land had always been a state of limbo for her, so this was nothing new.

She didn't have the gentle rocking of Mother Ocean to ease her into sleep each night, so she was on the hunt for some other woman to help with relaxation, but her usual prey was proving elusive. Maybe it was the way she'd been slurring her words, maybe it was something else. It probably said something about her that she found it so much easier to hook up with a girl who didn't even speak the same language, in some backwater on the other side of the world, but she didn't want to examine that thought too closely. Introspection had never made her happy and it wasn't going to start now.

Maybe it was something to do with losing her commission. Maybe she'd been strutting around with the word *Navy* emblazoned on her forehead all these years and that was why the dames had been so quick to drop their panties. They had known she was only temporary, passing through, and each of them had been just a port in the storm. Maybe that was all that she was good for.

Another shot of gin drop-kicked that thought out of her head and refilled her waning confidence. She might not have been a fighter anymore, but that didn't mean she wasn't hot stuff. There was a fresh burn on her cheek that twisted one side of her mouth up into a little smirk, traced there by a stray ember from the last tiny port town they'd burned to ash in Mongolian Indonesia. Chicks loved that sort of thing. Sully had never come into town to drink away her medical leave and gone to bed alone. It was just a different crowd here, she wasn't used to the rhythm and cliques of New Amsterdam yet. She'd get there.

It didn't help that every girl in here was drop dead gorgeous. Sully couldn't look people in the eye at the best of times, and some of these actresses, she couldn't even look them in the face. Park Slope had more bars per square foot than anywhere else in New Amsterdam and that alone was enough to draw in all the arty types from Red Hook and all the starlets from the stages about town. Strippers rubbed shoulders with opera singers. Big name actors shared drinks with charcoal sketch artists who spent their days scraping together pennies forging caricatures on the South Shore. Usually when Sully walked into a bar there was one girl, one pretty girl, that she'd set her sights on and pursue until she got her way, but here it was like she was constantly spinning on the spot. Like she was too thirsty to stop and take a drink.

There was a sprinkle of laughter from the far end of the bar, delicate and high enough for Sully to suspect that it might be her kind of crowd. She peered through the smoke, barely able to make out the sleek forms of women and flashes of bare skin. Whoever invented the cocktail dress had done humanity a great service. A crowd of girls didn't necessarily mean anything in a place like this, and straight girls in a pack could be vicious, so Sully edged along the bar in stages. First, she stopped to buy a cigar, then stopped to light it, then to savor the last dregs of her drink. By the time she had the actresses in clear sight, they'd bought another round. That cut off her opportunity to send something over, but it also made things more casual if she tried to just ease into the conversation. A few months back there wouldn't have been any creeping around the periphery, she would have walked right up to the hottest girl in the establishment and laid her cards on the table. Now, all the near misses of the last few nights had made her gun-shy.

Nerves. She'd never been nervous before, not in a firefight, not in a bar-room brawl or an academic pissing contest. Guts had always been her defining characteristic, even when good sense wasn't. This didn't feel right. She needed to go find a hotel somewhere to sleep off this funk, and maybe in the morning she might find a clue as to what she wanted to do with the rest of her life. She raised her empty glass to the barman. One for the road, to keep her warm through the winter chill still rolling in off the Black Bay.

That was when Sully heard her. The southern accent wasn't uncommon in this part of town, particularly among the arty set, but there was something in the lilt and bubbles of this girl's voice that turned Sully's head. She was perched on a barstool at the outer edge of the herd, her blonde hair cascading like a honeyed waterfall to the middle of her back, and from there a sundress took over. A floral print sundress in a Park Slope bar, like she was straight off the train from farm country.

None of that mattered when she glanced Sully's way. The freckles, the eyes, the pout; this was the mistake Sully had making since arriving in New Amsterdam. She'd been looking at all these pretty little things as if they were all worth pursuing. They weren't. The arena might have changed but the rules of engagement hadn't. It had just taken Sully a little longer than expected to find the single prettiest girl in town.

The cigar fell out of her mouth and landed on her lap but she didn't notice until a hole had burned clean through her jeans. She scrambled to her feet. Stupid. When she looked up, the girl was laughing at her. Looking right at her and laughing. Sully had thrown men overboard for less than that, but the musical laughter and the stretch of the girl's throat as she tossed back her hair turned the heat of that rising anger into something else entirely. Sully met her eyes and smiled, second degree burn forgotten. It wasn't how she would have tried to make a connection, but she'd take it.

It took a minute to push through the crowd to get to the girl, and every little jostle tightened Sully's fists. That was something else they'd warned her about when she handed in her papers, making sure she didn't bring the war home with her. When she'd enlisted—fresh out of the Imperial College—she was pretty sure she'd already been at war back home. Nothing had changed except the scenery.

The girl was still smiling when Sully arrived, which was a good sign, and she'd been edged out of the multicultural thespian love-in happening at the corner of the bar, which was probably an even better sign. Her smile was dazzling. Real movie star shit. "Darlin', you ought to be more careful with yourself."

Sully shrugged. "I've had worse, but it's nice to know you care."

The girl reached over and traced the scar on Sully's cheek with her fingertips. "I can see that, darlin'"

The touching was another good sign. A really good sign. She had to stop herself from leaning into it. "Plenty more where you *can't* see them."

"Ain't you a cheeky little thing? How come I haven't seen you around?" The flush on the girl's cheeks ran all the way down to her chest, but she wasn't acting interested, not exactly. Her eyes kept drifting over to her friends, like she was trying to see if they were watching.

"Fresh off the boat."

The girl cocked her head, trying to place the stripped-out remnants of Sully's accent. "Ireland?"

"Navy."

That earned her a throaty laugh. Too practiced for Sully's liking. "The Navy? Oh, I love a man in uniform." Sully stared at her blankly until the girl seemed to realize her mistake. "Woman. A woman in uniform."

Her eyes darted to her friends again and a picture started to form in Sully's head. The hip cosmopolitan crowd, the country girl who was new in town, trying to establish her chops, proving that she was just as worldly as her new friends. Sully weighed it for a moment—eyes raking up and down the tight body under that sundress—then decided that she didn't object to being a formative experience. Time to move things along. "Listen, I'd love to stick around and chat, but I think I'm going to need a little medical attention here. It was nice to meet you . . ."

"Marie." She stuck out her hand to shake, and Sully took it without really thinking. Rubbing her thumb over the girl's knuckles.

"Sully. Maybe I'll see you around some time." She stood up, still holding on. Waiting for the tide to turn.

"Maybe I should help you? I'm feeling a bit responsible."

"You caught me staring?"

Marie giggled. "I'm sorry, it was adorable."

Sully looked down at her feet. Genuinely mortified. Marie squeezed her hand, and waited until Sully looked back up to her perfect face. When Marie stood up, she was almost a foot taller than Sully in heels that matched her dress. Her hair fell forward like a curtain around their faces; like they were in their own private world. "Want me to kiss it better?"

She looked so nervous that Sully wanted to kiss her right then and there. At least they were making fools of themselves together. It made her feel weirdly protective of this stranger. "Why don't we get out of here? Take a walk? Then you can decide what you want to do."

Marie's face split into the first genuine smile Sully had seen from her, showing too much tooth and wrinkling the corners of her eyes. Every time Sully thought the girl couldn't get any prettier, she did. "I'd love that."

AUGUST 5, 2013

Sully's hands twisted out the shape of a barrier spell ahead of the rising sun, but without spellfire it was just so much waving. They ran for shade or shelter, but the best that this stretch of boardwalk had to offer was a newspaper stand with a west-facing wall. Sully tucked Marie in against it and then started looking for options.

Without the press of bodies, the docklands were surprisingly bare. There were the ships themselves, but they were too far for Marie to reach without some sort of cover. If there had been a convenient umbrella left lying around before the Mongols had shown up, their concussion spells had blasted it off into the sea. Sully stomped over to pick up Eugene, feeling like a traitor with every step away from Marie.

"YOUR LOVER SHALL BURN."

Sully threw the doll at the side of the paper stand. "Thanks, that's really helpful."

Marie was already looking flushed. Her silky white hair was crisping at the tips. "It's going to be all right, darlin'. You don't have to worry."

Sully dropped down to her knees in front of Marie with tears prickling her eyes. "I can fix this."

"Darlin', I never doubted that you could." Marie reached out to take her hand, then flinched back as the sun crept a little higher. "What's the but?"

Sully let out a little snort of laughter that nearly carried through into a full-on sob. "What?"

"The but. What's the but? I can fix this but . . ."

Sully dragged in a wavering breath and almost gagged. She could smell Marie's flesh cooking in the indirect light. "I can fix this, but it's going to mean . . . It's going to change things for us, for everyone. It is going to be loud. Everybody in town is going to come running. I'm going to have to fight again, the way I used to. The way I've been trying not to."

She couldn't believe how calm and quiet Marie was as she burned. "If you do it, can you win?"

Sully couldn't look her in the eye. "Winning has never been my problem."

"If you do it, will you come back to me after?" Marie was speaking so softly now that the waves beating on the docks were almost louder. They'd come so close to making it out. Sully could spit into the sea from here.

She hunched forward to give Marie a little more shelter from the rising sun. "I don't know if you'll want me to."

Marie's face was so close that her cool, rust-tanged breath was sweeping over Sully with every word. "Darlin', I'm about a hop from being charcoal right now. It might be a little late to worry about appearances."

"It isn't about what it looks like, it is about what I am. What I really am."

Marie reached up to cradle Sully's face in her hands. "Show me what you really are and I'll love you anyway."

Tears could fall later, there was no more time for reluctance or self-indulgence. Sully slipped her Cold Iron ring onto Marie's finger with as gentle a smile as she could muster. "I'm coming back."

Marie lunged forward and kissed her. A brush of the lips that lasted only a moment before Sully let go of the Cold Iron and was alone on the docks. The city fell silent. The background buzz of distant voices, of lives being lived, it all faded away to nothing as the vampires slipped beyond her perception.

All that was left was the roar of war beyond the walls. Shadows swept out behind Sully. Silhouettes of great black wings spreading behind her. A halo of black feathers. Then the fire came. Spellfire spilled out from her fingertips and her eyes. When she opened her mouth to scream, sparks danced out from the tip of her tongue. Without the ring to restrain it, Mol Kalath rose up inside of her, filling in the spaces where her memory was missing, making her whole once more. She didn't need to remember a college education or decades of study when the demon's instinctual understanding of magic blended with her own. The flames coiled out into spellforms on their own.

No wonder everyone was afraid of a Cambion, all the worst and best of human and demon combined, all that willful ambition bound to an engine of creation powerful enough to fulfill every desire. Raw power rolled out from her in a wave, flooding through the streets of the silent city, like blood in the water for any caster worth a damn.

Everything that made Sully herself burned away in the spellfire, all of the little slights that she clung to as if they mattered, all of the little pleasures that made her life worth living. Her love for Marie, Mol Kalath's love for its mate, its love for Sully herself, they all melted and merged until she couldn't unpick the interwoven threads. All the lies that she'd told herself were exposed, naked in that blinding light. This was what she had feared, more than Marie flinching away or the whole world coming hunting her as an exotic beast, this erasure of who she had always been, replaced by who she was now. What she was now.

Sully rose up into the air on the beating of unseen wings and stretched her hand out to the east. The spell coalesced around her, more intricate and perfect than any she had ever been able to wield before the war, so dense that she couldn't have parsed it with her conscious mind. The old wards of the city throbbed beneath her and she rooted this new spell within them, navigating the layers of protection without thought, pushing all of the heat and the light bleeding against her fingertips down into the old walls and the old spells so that they would live on for another hundred years without maintenance. Sully wouldn't have known why she did these things. Mol Kalath wouldn't have known either, but would have done it all the same because it felt right. The wards were starving, crying out for power. It felt like that was where the magic wanted to go, so Sully sent it there. She wondered for a moment about wishes and fate, about how much of this sense of rightness was coming from the same root source as Eugene's and the other demon's ability to read causality like a book.

When every piece of the spell had swung into place and the tension in the web of magic made the very molecules of the air tremor in agitation, Sully opened her burning eyes and closed her fist.

The sun blinked out.

Marie could have been lying down there, burned to death or she could have been up on her feet cheering. She could have been running for her life at the sight of Sully wrapped in fire and shadow, or basking in her majesty. She could have been anywhere in the world, doing anything that she wanted and all that Sully had was the hope that Marie would still be there when she came back down.

Hong Kong lay before Sully in all of its glory for the first time, every one of her senses laid open to it and every one of them overwhelmed by the heaving energy of the place. Even without the vampires it was brimming over with hidden activity. The crackling neon was just a ripple on the surface. Magic was everywhere in Hong Kong—more than in any other city that Sully had ever seen—so many different kinds that she couldn't name the half of them that actually had names. The whole world had passed through this port town and left little parts of itself behind. It should have been a cacophony of clashing spells, but instead it was a symphony. Her own magic was a part of it now, woven into that great song, feeding all the light of the sundown into that great conflux and filling it up with fresh life.

She had been noticed. That was inevitable, but the response time was still pretty impressive. There were two distinct and wildly powerful forces rising up from the streets of Hong Kong, dashing against each other, turning away and then flying headlong to the docks. Maybe there were some major players in town that Sully didn't know anything about, but she doubted they'd have waited until now to take a swing. There were a few other pinpricks in the dark; Magi, and curses with enough longevity to register, but they faded in comparison to Blavatski, Le Plongeon, and the respective patrons that were wearing them like hats. If she'd been able to see what she was really up against when she'd been wearing the ring, Sully might have rolled over and given up.

Mol Kalath's voice was gone now, blended smoothly into her own thoughts, but there was a familiar tone to them that sounded more like the demon than her, and that part was saying "NO YOU WOULDN'T."

She didn't recognize the voice that whispered from her crystal dusted lips. "No, I wouldn't."

The Outsiders clashed over and over as they rushed across the city toward the sea, flinging curses and evocations—ancient and alien, literally unearthly—that deflected and rebounded as their respective wielders went through the motions of warding them off, as they had a million times before. The oldest dance on earth. It would have been beautiful if it hadn't been for the fallout. The concrete towers that made up the backbone of Hong Kong's residential blocks melted away like butter under a blowtorch as Blavatski passed by. The tarmac of the streets bubbled up and lashed about like tentacles under Le Plongeon's shadow, reaching for him, then her, then anything that moved. Sully couldn't sense the vampires, so she couldn't guess at the body count, but the city itself was buckling under the pressure of the primordial duel.

Sully fell back to earth. She had to end this now. With the ring, Eugene had looked like a doll, like nothing but detritus on the boarded street, but now he was lit up like a Christmas tree, a vacuum drawing in all of the magic around him. He started to scramble away as Sully approached, but his kneeless legs weren't meant for running. "Stay still."

"WHAT HAVE YOU DONE TO SWEET MOL KALATH?"

"I haven't done anything to Mol Kalath, and Mol Kalath hasn't done anything to me." Back here on the ground Sully's shadow had grown massive and monstrous behind her, a dozen pairs of wings spreading out to surround her. "This is the natural end when shadow twins meet. It is inevitable. We are one."

"YOU EVEN SOUND LIKE MOL KALATH. DEVOURER. DEFILER."

Sully bent low over Eugene and savored the way that the little bastard was shivering. "Your time here is done, little doll. Let us send you home."

Casting a circle and opening a portal was usually a laborious work involving long hours of precise linework and calculations, but not for a Cambion. The sigils and circles coiled out from Sully in gentle spirals of flame, charring the wooden boards as they drifted down. The whole city rocked on its foundations as the Outsiders did battle in the sky, but not a line was out of place nor a rune misspelled by the time that Sully was done. All the power of a demon, all the precision of a Magus.

With the circle cast, Sully poured power into it. Coming up from the lower planes was nearly impossible if you didn't have some sort of foothold, but punching down had always been simple, almost too simple. Over and over and over, the world had been remade and rewritten to the whims of the powerful. Through demons or Fae, deals had been struck and the truth bad been washed away. Never again.

Sully set her feet on the boards and pushed at the veil between worlds with all of her considerable might, in her hurry eating into the reserves of magic that she had carried back with her from the far realms. The boards within the circle shook as the nails that held them in place struggled against the forces being exerted, then all at once the old wood snapped down. A void gaped in the hole where the water should have been, as deep and dark as the place inside Sully where she had buried Mol Kalath for these past few days.

Eugene tried to resist the draw of the darkness, scrabbling at the boardwalk with his fingerless hands, but the pull was too much. Inch by painful inch, Sully dragged him back to hell. When he came to the edge of the circle, he started bellowing. "I WILL NOT FORGET THIS INDIGNITY, ABOMINATION. ALL THE HELLS WILL KNOW

WHAT YOU HAVE DONE TO OUR KIND. MOL KALATH'S MATE WILL RISE FOR YOU. THE ARMIES OF HELL WILL RISE WITH IT. YOU SHALL KNOW NO PEACE. YOU SHALL KNOW NO PLEASURE. EVERY MOMENT FROM THIS UNTIL YOUR LAST WILL BE SUFFERING AND FEAR. THE PAIN—"

"You are welcome." With one last pulse of magic that rippled out across the sea, Sully cast the demon back into the pit.

She should have closed the portal then and there, but there was something in that aching blackness that called to her. Just as it had felt right to conduct the magic of the city, it now felt right that she should return to hell. She took a step closer, felt the vacuum drawing at her hair and her skin. Unnatural sensations. Her feathers should have been ruffling in the breezes of pandemonium. Her wings should have been spread wide to break her fall into the darkness.

At the edge of the portal she came to a halt, torn between the rightness of going home and the wrongness of this body to carry her there. With all the city breaking and burning at her back, she stood staring down into the nothingness for too long, and she might have stood there a damn sight longer if she hadn't felt the ghost of a touch on her hand. "Marie?"

Through the spellfire that wreathed her face, Sully felt a kiss brushing her cheek. That was all that it took to remind her that who she had been before and who she was now were entirely different. She wasn't Iona Sullivan any more than she was Mol Kalath, she was both of them and neither. Both of her old selves and now her new. All three in one.

Closing the portal was easier than opening it, there was no ritual or pomp involved. She just had to stop feeding power into the circle, and that was as easy as breathing. Air rushed into the gap where the hole in reality had been, dragging at the flames around Sully as she reached out to hold Marie, though unseen, away from the danger. Where salt had stained the boards before, they were now rimed in crystallized magic, shimmering and unnatural. Sully could see Marie's footsteps as they formed, heading away from her toward the ships and shelter.

Marie was alive and she would be safe; that was all that Sully would have wished for, if there had been any wishes left.

The Lemurian fog rolled out over the docks, drawing moisture from the air to thicken the bloodstained cloud that was still being drawn from Le Plongeon's dangling husk. At some point he and Blavatski had stopped tearing at each other to rush down to the waterfront, trying to catch Eugene before it was too late. Now Sully turned to face the two of them and the destruction that they had caused with a smile. It was over. The doll was gone. There was no more reason to fight.

Her smile didn't take long to falter. With Le Plongeon, the domination of his patrons had been abundantly clear—they were ripping the very fluids from his body to give themselves form—but Blavatski's possession was more subtle and more insidious. What Lemuria had accomplished with brute force, Atlantis had managed with barely an effort expended at all. The Atlantean spells had woven through Blavatski's power, subverting and twisting it into the shape of their own, like mistletoe strangling an oak. From outside, she looked the same as she always had, but her will had been cored out to feed the parasites.

"You have crossed us for the last time, Cambion. We will not suffer your interference in our affairs again." Blavatski's voice, but someone else speaking through her, like a relay. It was uncanny.

Sully spared a glance for Le Plongeon amid the roiling tempest of beasts and monsters. He really looked dead in there. "Does she speak for you, too?"

The swirl of beasts took on the shape of a great jagged maw. The man's flesh was too desiccated for natural speech. Lemuria spoke in a whisper. "In this at least, we are in accord."

"Millennia of war put aside for us." Sully eyed them both carefully. "We feel honored."

Blavatski lunged forward in the air, looming over Sully and wrapped up in fresh protective spells that did nothing to keep the infiltrating tendrils out of her mind. "Soon you will feel nothing at all."

"As threats go, that isn't exactly fearsome. I mean, 'you'll feel nothing but pain,' that's a classic, but 'nothing at all'?" Sully didn't move an inch despite all of the posturing or the frankly terrifying shapes that burst out from Le Plongeon as they spoke.

A new mouth lashed out toward her, filled with whirling lamprey teeth. "Live under the threat of oblivion for long enough and you will know that pain is better. Anything is better than the hungering dark."

She didn't have anything to say to that little glimpse of madness. "Guys, we don't have to do this. The wish is gone. It's over."

Even as Sully said the words, she knew they were a lie. A comforting lie that Mol Kalath might have believed, but never her. She knew better than most the wild road that vengeance could carry you down. It was always going to end this way. It always ended this way for her, no matter how she tried to change her fate.

It wasn't Blavatski's voice that hissed out, cold, calculating, bitter. "It is over because of you. All of our hopes wither on the vine, because of you. You are nothing and you have ruined everything."

Before combat begins there is a tipping point that every fighter has to reach. The moment when they convince their body that this is really happening. It is no easy thing for people to throw themselves into a situation that they might not return from, and while experience may make the willingness to do harm to others a little easier to reach, it also brings a legacy of pain along with it. Someone who had never been beaten and broken would jump into the fight much faster than someone who knew just how badly they could suffer.

Blavatski moved first. A quick and dirty curse that would have left Sully in six even pieces if it hit. Sully barely had time to get a shield in place to deflect it before Lemuria joined the fight.

Given the choice of any animal that had ever lived as their form, they had chosen the apex predator to end all apex predators. Water was dragged up in hissing spirals from the ocean to add mass to the great gaseous dragon that was already snapping for her.

Sully leaped aside as it plowed through, scattering the boardwalk into splinters. She snapped three darts of white flame off at Blavatski to buy some time, but the old woman had more sense than to throw up a shield, letting her flying spell drop her to the dirt instead.

The dragon was already rising with flames that were all too real boiling up out of its jaws. Sully stumbled away from it, trying to cast a barrier, but there was no time. White-hot heat rolled over her as the dragon disgorged a titanic plume of flame and Sully answered in kind. Pure spellfire, the raw stuff of magic, poured out of her hand, matching the dragon's breath. Holding flaming death at bay by burning through her own reserves. Gambling she could outlast a dragon.

A real dragon probably would have won that bet, but this one was made of steam. The hotter that it got, the more that it struggled to maintain its shape. With one last spluttering glut of flame, it flinched away from Sully and took flight.

Victory was short-lived. When the flames cleared, Blavatski came on, and as fast as Sully could cast by will power alone, she was still no match for the complex patterns of spells striking down at her. First bolts of lightning shaped like nightingales darted at her from all angles, deflected by her shields, but only barely.

Spheres of pearlescent light followed after, slow and sluggish compared to the nightingales, but simmering with untold destructive power. These Sully didn't dare to meet with force, lashing out rapid barriers around each sphere and tossing them out to sea without a backward glance at the icebergs they were making in the bay when they broke through.

With both of those weapons thwarted, Blavatski unleashed wave after wave of invisible force, no one wave enough to knock Sully down, but every one of them enough to buffet her off-balance. A distraction. She looked up.

The dragon plunged back down from the sky, trailing clouds behind it and spreading its jaws impossibly wide, past the breaking point and on, until it was obvious it had no intention of biting—only of smashing straight down onto Sully with all of its weight and barbed teeth.

Sully threw her hand up out of muscle memory, and the spellform for her concussion spell traced in the air above her, growing more and more intricate with her every breath. Down the dragon came, thumping its wings furiously to drive past terminal velocity.

Her spell completed an inch ahead of the dragon's teeth.

The blast dispersed the Lemurian fog and sent La Plongeon tumbling up into the sky like a rag doll. It broke Blavatski's concentration and ended her onslaught, but it also punched Sully through the boardwalk and into the icy waters below.

There was no smooth curve of sand leading out to the sea, just the man-made expanse of a concrete wall on one side and a channel deep enough to comfortably house the bellies of the Navy's destroyers on the other. By the time Sully hit the rusty beer cans on the bottom, she wouldn't have been able to see the sun even if it had still been alight.

Spells of flight were useless underwater, but Sully wrapped one around herself anyway, while she had the time. It pulsed in time with her heartbeat and the flutter of the shadows around her. Her clothes were waterlogged, and swimming to the surface would take longer than the burning breath in her lungs would hold. Good thing her magic was back.

She pointed down, closed her eyes and pushed.

The surface of the water roiled. Steam rose from beneath the piers and a new fog began to rise from the surface, refracting the colors that were dancing in the deeps. Blavatski had drawn closer, spells spinning around her in a broad phosphorescent orbit. Sully exploded from the water too fast for the old woman and her older Atlantean passengers to react. Icicles shot down from the center of the spell-swarm, but Sully melted the vicious daggers away before they could come close to scratching her.

Once she was inside the orbit of the spells, Blavatski didn't have a hope in hell. The white-hot spellfire trailing from Sully's fist collided with the first of the onion-layers of protective spells and rebounded, but not before the curse hidden within her fist could spread out across the whole surface in a ripple of light. Layer after layer of protection burned off—blazing brighter and brighter each time—until the whole of Hong Kong was illuminated by the pyre of the Atlantean barriers. Sully herself had to turn away or risk blindness, so she dreaded to think how Blavatski was faring in the middle of the flare that consumed her.

The Lemurian dragon had pulled itself together again before Le Plongeon could leave the atmosphere, but the Outsiders were wary of Sully's power now. The serpent circled in the sky above, out of reach of most evocations and with plenty of time to dodge around the few artillery shots that could clear that range.

Mol Kalath longed to soar up into the darkened sky, and now, as loathe as she was to admit it, Sully was Mol Kalath. The air sang against her skin, beckoning her up. Who was she to say no?

The silent city spread out beneath her as she rose, neon sputtering and dying everywhere that she looked. What it had taken three empires and countless centuries to build was falling apart after just one night of the real players hitting town. All the people that filled those buildings, vamps or living, deserved better than this. The whole world deserved better than to be a playground for the old powers that still thought they owned it.

Sully might have accepted becoming what she was now, and the loss of herself, to save Marie. Mol Kalath, ever the moralist, might have accepted it to save the world, but all of the destruction and death that they faced now was for nothing, just a tantrum because the Outsiders had been denied. Raised on different planes of reality with wildly different viewpoints on all things, Sully and Mol Kalath had always had this one trait to unite them. Righteous anger.

Lemuria's dragon saw Sully coming from a mile off and spun down to meet her charge. Everything about the beast was too eager, too hungry. Sully didn't trust it for a second. Flames flickered to life in its jaws as it came for her, and it seemed all too obvious what it planned to do. If she went on meeting flame with flame, eventually they could wear her down. Her reserves weren't endless.

Flame lanced down at Sully, but she had already twisted in the air, still gaining speed and altitude, shooting right past the monster toward the stars above. The dragon tried to follow her but gravity dragged at it, the very mass that made it so imposing becoming its enemy. In the end it had to abandon all cohesion and reform around the black nucleus of Le Plongeon, who was facing in the wrong direction entirely to pursue her. That bought her more time.

Still Sully rose, the air growing thinner and the stars growing nearer, plunging through clouds and emerging in shivering steam on the other side, but never ever slowing. The dragon couldn't breathe fire at her now without it washing back in its face. More time.

Whatever plan she'd made to gain distance to cast at her pursuer fell away in a wash of demonic instinct. There was no need for a plan now, only the desire for flight. All that she had to do to survive was to fly higher and faster. The flight spell began to stutter with the power overload that she was pouring into it, but that just made her pour in more to make up for the lost thrust.

Stroke by dreadful stroke of its wings, the dragon gained distance on Sully, swallowing up the clouds to add yet more to its mass as it passed through them. Yet no matter how much wider it spread its wingspan, it still couldn't catch Sully. Even as her spell groaned and splintered away from her in a shower of sparks, the dragon still couldn't quite catch up.

A dragon did not have the same facial expressions as a human, and the Lemurians were far from human to begin with, but even so, Sully was pretty certain she could pinpoint the moment that the dragon went from confusion to realization. It was just before its wings stopped flapping and the ice locked them firmly into shape. However many millennia the Lemurians had been flapping around as dragons didn't matter, they didn't know how the world worked anymore—they didn't know that when a body composed of nothing but water flies too high with no sun to warm it, it freezes.

Flying spells were all about resisting the inevitable draw of the earth. It was no trouble at all for Sully to rig one up in reverse to fling herself headlong onto the great falling ice-sculpture that she had made.

Beneath the frozen surface of the dragon, she could see the swirling mists of Lemuria, twisting, trying to break through, but brute force meant nothing in the face of the ice.

Skittering and sliding over the frozen surface as the dragon spun slowly through the air, Sully stared down into the chaotic clouds, looking for the tell-tale shadow. No matter how mighty any ancient power was, if it wanted to live in the world now, it had to be tethered to a human being, and if Sully knew one thing about humans, it was that they were fallible, breakable things.

It took more than a thought but less than a spell to draw a blade of fire from the palm of her hand. The wind whipped Sully's words away as she spoke them. "Le Plongeon, I don't know you, but if you're in there, I'm sorry. You shouldn't have climbed into bed with the monsters."

Sully punched into the dragon's icy shell and the spirits of Lemuria came out through the crack in a geyser of fog. If she'd had any footing to start with, she would have lost it, but as it was, she just had to pulse more power into the spell drawing her down faster and faster to slam right back into the ice. That moment away from the hollowing remains of the dragon was all it took to see that the ground was coming up fast. The last of the spirit-clogged smog was still trying to force its way out of the ice, but it was trapped in place, still pinned to the source that the great Lemurian beast was using as its entrance to the world of the living.

Le Plongeon was pinned inside the ice, straining to pull his body through a gap the size of his hand. When Sully thrust the flaming blade down into his chest, it wasn't murder. It felt like mercy.

There should have been a great explosion when the man at the nexus of so many magical energies died, but real life was rarely as dramatic as Sully expected it to be. All of the liquid that had been drained from Le Plongeon's body started to rush back inside the desiccated husk, making blood and bile squirt up from his wound, but it was short-lived before even that gave out and the clouds just drifted away.

Sully had time for one sharp bark of victory before she hit the ground.

Down in the deep darkness, there was no demon waiting. Sully and Mol Kalath no longer had that separation. She was alone with her own thoughts. Alone, forever. This was hell.

Without the crutch of Cold Iron, this was all she would ever have. Marie was gone. Mol Kalath was gone, too, woven into herself so seamlessly that there was nowhere to pick them apart. Completely alone, but never herself again. She hadn't thought twice about making the ultimate sacrifice before she did it, she never did, but now she had to live with the consequences of being changed forever. Literally forever. Whatever aging she had done before, was all that she would get. There would never be a fresh scar or a new wrinkle. No matter how she changed on the inside, the outside would never reflect it.

Pain cut through the darkness and she forced her eyes to open. A great jagged shard of ice was sticking up out of her guts. The flames around her were guttering in the breeze, her bones were broken and twisting her skin out in terrible directions. When she tried to laugh, blood bubbled up past her lips. She'd had worse.

Magical healing came with a price, and for Sully that price had always been pain. Maybe it was different for full-blooded demons, but when she reached for Mol Kalath's memories they were oddly blended with her own. Scraped knees in the schoolyard and the arcane explosions of the street war in London were one and the same. She screamed as her bones reset. She writhed as her body closed around the ice until the fire inside her melted clean through it. As her organs grew back, she couldn't even draw breath. All that she knew was the blinding white pain. Then, as suddenly as it began, it was over and all her senses came alive once more.

It was no wonder she'd been so easy to find without the ring. All of the free-floating magic in Hong Kong was flowing toward her. Her reserves had been drained in the last few minutes of fighting and that emptiness was a vacuum demanding to be filled. She wasn't trying to draw power to herself, yet here it came. Her eyes opened and the starlight came flooding in. She was alive, and that meant she had won.

"What an impressive specimen you are."

Sully had only the time it took to turn her head before Blavatski's spell rolled over her in a wave. This time the old witch wasn't trying to send her off to a gentle rest, she had learned her lesson the first time around. This spell set like amber, pinning her in place, suffocating the flows of magic around her.

The woman had shed her fur coat at some point over the course of the evening and her wrinkled skin was on display above the plunging neckline of the sequined black dress that she wore. Her sunglasses too had vanished, although Sully was willing to admit that she might have broken them when she had punched the hag. Blavatski's eyes were milky with cataracts, yet she stared right into Sully's own without difficulty.

The white-fire curse that Sully had thrown at her earlier, designed to consume all of her magic as fuel, had clearly faltered at some point during the fight with the Lemurians. If she could have opened her mouth, Sully would have asked how that had happened.

"My patrons are reasonable. Atlanteans recognize what the Lemurians did not. There is a boundless potential in you, Cambion. The demon would have been simpler, cleaner. You will take research to divest of your full power. Some effort. But for me, this will be a pleasure."

With arthritic slowness, Blavatski crouched down beside Sully's head, joints crackling like bubble-wrap. "It is my hope that you enjoyed your life before, because now it is done. There will be nothing but pain for you. No hope. No rescue. You will know nothing else, as I learn every part of you, inside and out. Body and soul."

Sully was straining against the spell that bound her, but this set her into a fresh frenzy of stilted motion. From the outside, it must have appeared that she was barely shaking, but inside she was throwing herself against the restraint with all of her might. She was depleted after all of the fighting. Exhausted after what felt like a week of running. The oblivion that Blavatski planned to inflict on her would be easier than carrying on.

Sully bit the edge of her tongue with the last convulsion and blood began pooling in her mouth. The rich penny taste was so familiar and as it began to trickle down her throat and choke her, she wondered how many times she'd been here on the edge of death. She couldn't remember any more.

Her convulsions grew more and more erratic as she drowned, but it wasn't until darkness had encroached on all sides and blood was spraying from her nostrils that Blavatski finally realized that something was wrong. "Oh no. You shall not escape me so easily."

She leaned in closer, and loosened the spell's grip on Sully's face. That was all it took. Sully spat the mouthful of blood up into the old woman's face. Blind or not, blood in the eyes still stung like hell. Blavatski's concentration was barely interrupted, but still in the midst of unraveling the complex knot of her binding spell, the moment it bought Sully was all that it took. Spellfire poured out of every pore on her body and set the curse alight.

It cost her more than it should have to break free like that; inefficient, yes, but effective. With the structure of the spell broken, it was no trouble at all to swallow the magic down.

Blavatski had her hands up and a smear of blood across her cheekbones by the time Sully had rolled to her feet, back-stepping out of punching range over the uneven ground and the half-molten chunks of dragon. Nice to see that they were both ready to go down fighting. Sully grinned, blood trickling down her chin. "You know, I felt sorry for Le Plongeon. He got suckered into his deal with the Outsiders. But you? I'm going to enjoy kicking the shit out of you."

Spells were coiling around Blavatski's fingers, shapes that Sully had never seen or even dreamed of. "To the last, he was a fool. He offered his patrons more than he had to give, and he paid the price."

They both cast at the same time, the spellforms Sully had been tracing behind her back and the ones Blavatski held in the palm of her hands both snapping into alignment in the same moment. Blavatski launched another binding curse and Sully summoned a whip of flame that lanced out and intercepted it head on. As it completed its orbit around her, the spell tried to detonate and catch her in the blast, but it was no use. It was too late. She had already sent it back at Blavatski.

The crone flicked a shield into place halfway between them, then discarded it when her own curse enveloped it and started to crush its life away. As they flicked evocations back and forth, there was an almost playful rhythm to the attacks. A lance of flame here. A bolt of lightning there. Each of them strained to turn the other's spells aside and keep her own attacks coming. Parry and riposte, over and over.

Blavatski's spells grew denser and more complex the longer that they went on. Sully's deflections soon became head-on interceptions, and within the span of seconds her own curses were subsumed in the need for an endless barrage of fresh shields.

At first Sully thought that the old woman was casting impossibly fast, but then she came to realize that the magic of Atlantis wasn't in any petty trick like that. Every one of Blavatski's spells led seamlessly into the next. The discarded traces of the last spellform caught alight as it met the next one being cast. She wasn't throwing a hundred spells at Sully. She was casting one grand spell in a hundred smaller parts.

If that grand spell went off, Sully had no illusions about her chances of survival. She needed to fight back. She needed to stop Blavatski before it was too late.

The next icicle that Blavatski flung at Sully found its mark, slamming through her stomach to jut out her back. The razor-winged butterflies that followed after shredded her thigh and set femoral blood squirting out onto the shattered boardwalk. Curse after curse rained down on her, not one of them enough to kill or incapacitate her, but each enough to weaken her, enough to keep her off-balance so that the next one could strike home, too. The conjured winds roared in her ears. The crackling of lightning and flame danced around her as spell after spell hammered home.

Through it all, her fingers were moving, her bloody lips speaking, her spellfire flowing out all around her in the shape of one great spell of her own. When Sully fell to her knees, Blavatski's unrelenting assault stopped as quickly as it had begun. She crept closer, curses held half cast in her hands, and she stared up at Sully's spell in puzzlement. "What were you trying to do?"

Sully couldn't answer her because the last of her breath had gone into the spell and now her lungs were filled with something sharp and squirming. The old woman's lips were moving as she read the spell-forms, her brow furrowed. "A barrier spell? Protecting the bloodless from us? Chivalry turned to a fool's errand."

Another drifting rune caught her eye and Blavatski turned to follow it. "No, a portal spell? What is this?"

Within Sully's chest, the last of Blavatski's curse was consumed in flame and she could breathe once more. She didn't waste her words on answering the crone. She spent it on one final incantation.

The barrier snapped into place around the two of them, a great pearlescent sphere that obscured the whole world from sight. Now it was Blavatski's turn to fall. She collapsed like a heap of empty clothes amidst the sundered boards and ice.

One by one, Sully countered the witch's spells, forcing what she could out of her body and absorbing the rest to fuel her healing. Her own magic had been exhausted by this last desperate maneuver, the final gamble in a long line of them that had led inexorably to this moment.

Hand over stump, she crawled through the rubble until she reached Blavatski. The old woman lay drooling, expression vacant, mind gone. With the barrier around them, Atlantis could no longer reach into Blavatski's mind, and without Atlantis filling the gaps, Blavatski was as hollowed out as Sully had been when she came home from the war.

She had been a great woman once, the kind that might inspire a young witch to greatness, but now she was either a tool for the old powers or a vegetable. Sully couldn't let her go on being either one.

She wrapped her hand around the old woman's leathery neck, thick makeup flaking away at her touch, and she squeezed as hard as she could, leaning all of her weight down on that fragile stretched skin.

If she was sobbing as she choked the life out of the old woman, nobody could see her through the barrier and when she collapsed in utter exhaustion with her fingers still cramped shut on Blavatski's throat, nobody would find out until long after the barrier fell.

AUGUST 6, 2013

Marie's apartment. It might have been a new place on the other side of the world, but her style was unmistakable. Pastel colors, old southern glamour, posters advertising musicals, drapes and dried flowers. Underneath it all, that smell that Sully could still remember after all these years, the honeyed scent of her sweat and skin beneath the floral dresses and floral perfumes.

Marie's bed. There were many worse places to wake up and Sully had woken up in most of them. The situation would have been greatly improved if Marie had been in the bed with her, of course, but she'd settle for the small comforts now. They could work up to the bigger ones. She closed her eyes to let her other senses roll out over the building and found that they were missing. A brush of her thumb let her know the Cold Iron was firmly back in place. Marie was all right. Despite all the chaos and fighting, she had survived and she'd put the ring back on Sully's finger.

Sully turned her head carefully, making sure that it was going to stay attached despite all the sensations to the contrary. She was smiling despite the pains. Marie was all right. Songling was sitting by her bedside, all of his blank-faced attention focused on her.

Sully groaned. "Not the vamp I was hoping to wake up to."

"You must forgive me for this intrusion, Miss Marie has gone out on some errands and I assumed that you would want to be appraised of the situation when you awoke." He was sun-scarred, but only slightly. The older vamps seemed to have the sunrise hardwired into their internal clock. He was quick on his feet and he knew the city like the back of his hand, so it was hardly surprising that he'd survived the brief daybreak. Sully had vaguely hoped he might have died fighting the Fae so she wouldn't have to have this conversation, but her luck only stretched so far.

She smiled anyway. "Nothing like a friendly face."

"The Mongol invasion was successfully repelled with little cost to life. The wards of the city have been reinforced and it seems that the Mongol conscript army took it as an ill omen when the sun turned dark."

Sully chuckled. "I aim to please."

"I must beg your forgiveness. I was dubious of your abilities before. I assumed that your legend had been aggrandized. I shall not make the mistake of underestimating you again." He actually gave her a little bow. It made her very uncomfortable.

"Yeah, don't, uh . . . don't do that."

He settled into his straight-backed pose as if the bow had never happened, then pressed on. "With regret, I must inform you that the death toll of last night was catastrophic. Between the Outsiders and Manhattan, it seems that a solid ten percent of the population expired."

"I don't want it." Sully turned away, staring at the "Khan and I" poster on the far wall like it was her first time seeing it.

Songling cocked his head. "I beg your pardon?"

"The guilt you're trying to hand me. I don't want it. I didn't put your city in the crosshairs and I did everything I could to keep people safe." She took a deep breath. "You people decided to host this party. You don't get to put any of those deaths on me."

"With all of the power at your disposal—"

She cut him off dead. "I could have killed ten times as many trying to fight my way through all the shit that was flung at me. There are always going to be could-haves and should-haves and I don't want any of them, either. That is how you end up going down the same road that all those empires did, rewriting history to suit yourself, again and again. There is no going back to how things were. There is no changing the past anymore. There is only here and now."

"All those deaths, and you regret nothing?"

She turned to meet his placid stare. It was like trying to stare down a pond. "My regrets are my business, not yours."

That almost earned her the hint of an expression. "You are an infuriating woman, Miss Sullivan."

"I've been called worse by better." She shrugged her shoulders, uncomfortably aware that she was naked under the sheets. The silence dragged on for a long moment, but it turned out Sully had more patience than she'd ever been given credit for. Songling spoke first. "I came here to thank you."

"You're doing a piss-poor job of it," she snorted. That earned her another long silence. Another languid stare that could have meant anything.

Eventually, his curiosity won out. "The sun, will it come back?"

This was safer territory. "Not as long as the city stands. You got a two-for-one there: that spell reinforces the wards, and the dark makes the whole place pretty unappealing to anybody with a pulse and ideas of expansion."

"The thought had occurred to me also."

She couldn't match the deadpan tone of a dead man, but she came close. "You're welcome."

Songling took another moment to compose himself, then he spoke. "Though there are many in the city who view the destruction that you wrought on us as a debt that can never be repaid, it is my feeling that you have already repaid it."

Sully grinned up at him. "That's more like it."

"Infuriating." That was definitely irritation, that was a win.

Her grin grew even wider. "You'll learn to love me."

"I hope that is not so." He gave another awkward half-bow. "However, I will extend to you my welcome if you choose to remain in Hong Kong, my welcome and my protection."

Sully glanced to the door. "Me and Marie will need to talk about that."

"Of course. Rest and heal well, Miss Sullivan."

"Same to you."

To say that the room was quiet after he left would have been an outright lie. This was still Hong Kong and there were still a thousand voices outside, arguing and braying, screaming and selling. This city had never slept before she changed things up and now the vamps had no sun driving them inside. Sully settled back on the pillows to enjoy it for a while, the song of the city warbling on and on. She closed her eyes to really enjoy the racket, but the sounds grew quieter and quieter until she could hear nothing at all.

AUGUST 7, 2019

Sully blinked awake again at Marie's touch. She was lying on the other side of the bed on top of the covers, which was disappointing, but there was some promise in the purr of, "Good morning, Darlin'."

"Is it morning?" Sully turned her face toward the cool hand cupped to her cheek.

Marie was smiling, Sully could hear it in her voice. "Who can tell anymore?"

The main lights were off and only the dancing neon outside the window illuminated the room. Marie looked like she was in one piece, but Sully didn't trust her eyes. She ran her fingers over Marie's face, through her hair, down her neck. She was as perfect as she'd ever been. "The sun missed you?"

"It's missing everybody these days. That was a neat trick, Darlin'." Marie's hands were moving too. Tracing over the places where old scars should have been, the places where Sully was smooth now, where she'd always been rough.

Sully tried the old quip again. "I aim to please."

"Darlin', you ain't never tried to please nobody but yourself and me. And I reckon pleasing me is more luck than anything else." She might have looked like a country girl, but Marie's laugh had always been surprisingly deep. Smokey.

Sully's hand drifted lower, smoothing Marie's dress down over her hip. "I'm feeling pretty lucky right about now."

"Iona Sullivan, what kind of girl do you think I am?"

Sully leaned in for a kiss. "My kind of girl?"

"Oh no, I ain't giving it up that easy." Marie giggled and shoved her back. "We've got some things to talk about first."

"The uh . . . the Cambion thing?" Sully braced herself.

The noise that came out of Marie was entirely undignified. She only looked like a sleek vampy femme fatale. "What, you thought seeing you all pumped up on magic was going to scare me? You think I'm surprised you ate a demon? Darlin', it's you. If you weren't doing weird, impossible shit every day, I'd be worried. That ain't what I'm talking about at all."

"Then what are you talking about?"

Marie pushed her back against the pillows and straddled Sully's stomach, pinning her down. "That shitty little ring you gave me, that ain't going to do at all. Cold Iron? No, thank you. I'm expecting a diamond, at least."

Sully was smiling so hard that tears started to gather at the corners of her eyes. "I'm sure I can come up with something."

"You'd better, and it better be fast. I don't want no long engagement." Marie leaned in closer.

Sully was straining up to meet her halfway, but Marie still wouldn't close the distance. "Can we even get married in Hong Kong?"

"If we couldn't, you'd just bully everybody into it anyway."

"You ain't wrong."

When they kissed, it didn't make the world rock on its axis. It was too soft for that, too familiar. They kissed like they'd go on doing it forever. They were in no hurry.

Somewhere in the gentle brush of lips and gentle touches, Sully ended up on top of Marie, the covers still tangled between them. As the air conditioner sputtered to life, it shot a chill over her back and she sat up, startled.

Marie dragged her back down onto the bed until they were lying face to face, side by side. "So, we're staying here, then?"

"I can't think of anywhere better in the world." Sully sighed. "Can you?"

"You know I'd follow you anywhere."

"But you'd rather stay here?"

Marie shrugged. "It seems . . . right?"

"Okay, then."

They kissed again, and time stopped meaning much. One kiss led to the next. Sully wrestled herself free of the sheets that imprisoned her. Marie divested herself of her dress. They could have taken a day or an hour or a year and neither would have noticed or minded. There was enough time in the world for the two of them to be together.

Eventually they stopped moving, lying curled around one another under the sheet as the groaning air conditioner lost its battle against the heat and humidity. Sully's fingers were coiled in the curls of Marie's hair, just behind her ear, and she couldn't find the will to untangle them.

Marie's voice was soft as a sigh. "What are you going to do with yourself?"

"I don't know. Find a job? The usual things people do."

"You ain't people. You're you." Marie giggled. "First time I look away, you'll be up to your neck in trouble."

"Guess I'd better find a way to make trouble pay the rent."

OCTOBER 31, 2019

They say that Hong Kong is a city the same way that a well is a bath—that somebody could get drowning-deep in a moment in a city with no laws beyond the ones that the gangsters and smugglers hand down—but these days there is a rumor spreading around that if some kid has got a sad story and a little bit of money, there is a new woman in town who might be willing to help out. Just a hand reaching down to lift them up before they sink to the bottom of the well.

Down by the docks there is a little alley that nobody could ever find without somebody to steer them, a place that would be pitch black without the blinking blue neon crow plastered halfway up its wall. Through a door that is never closed there is a rickety set of stairs leading up past abandoned accountants' offices and massage parlors of dubious medicinal benefit. At the very top of the building, so high that the rain rattled the light fixtures, was something between an office and an apartment, with a door marked with gold leaf: M. K. Sullivan. Private Investigator.

Sully looked up from her newspaper when the door creaked open, eyes tracing up and down what should have been her latest client. The dame had legs for days, a dress so tight it could turn a priest to sin, and hair like brushed cotton all arranged in loose ringlets to draw attention to the cupid's bow of deeply red lipstick. Anybody could see all of that, but it took a detective's eye to spot the details. The tell-tale pallor of a vampire combined with the rings on her finger and the satisfied smile marking her as a newlywed. Not a common match anywhere else in town, but in this office, it went beyond common. Sully could set her watch by Marie's daily visit. And she needed a watch now that she charged by the hour.

Out of all the chargeable hours of the eternal night, Sully set aside this one each day for a bad coffee and a good conversation. Sometimes Marie had an audition, sometimes her customers had fed her stories that she passed along; either way it was the highlight of every one of Sully's days.

They kissed before they parted, every day, like clockwork, and each kiss was just as sweet as the first had been, strolling on Park Slope all those years ago.

After that, office hours kicked in; with a seemingly countless parade of gangsters, hookers and lost souls passing through the door. Almost as many were tossed right back out again. Sully didn't discriminate between the living and the undead or the good and the bad, but she could smell a liar from a million miles away. Honesty was her price as much as the stipend she often forgot to charge her clients.

Beyond the city walls, war raged on everywhere that an eye could be turned. The empires in their dying throes were intent on burning all that they had built and the rising powers chewing on their borders bayed as they watched the carnage. Sully and Mol Kalath would have found good reasons to throw themselves into the fray, but in combination their worst natures had been tempered.

Whatever Sully felt she owed the world was paid up. She didn't need to be a martyr. She didn't need to save the world. She just needed to live, at least for a little while.

She lit a cigar, put her feet up on the desk, and waited for her own personal delivery of chaos to come knocking. When a rap on the door sounded, she couldn't hide her grin.

ABOUT THE AUTHOR

G.D. Penman is the author of more books than you can shake a reasonably-sized stick at, including series like Witch of Empire, Savage Dominion, Deepest Dungeon and The Last King.

Before finally realizing that the career advisor lied to them about making a living as an author, G.D. Penman worked as an editor, tabletop game designer, and literally every awful demeaning job that you can think of in-between.

Nowadays they can mostly be found writing fantasy novels and smoking a pipe in the sunshine.

They live in Dundee, Scotland with their partner, children, dog and cats. Just . . . so many cats.

DID YOU ENJOY THIS BOOK?

If so, word-of-mouth recommendations and online reviews are critical to the success of any book, so we hope you'll tell your friends about it and consider leaving a review at your favorite bookseller's or library's website.

Visit us at www.meerkatpress.com for our full catalog.

Meerkat Press
Asheville